Summerfield

Summerfield

Dianne H. Lundy

Gratuity
Direct Number: 2134389957
(888) 290-0987
9350 Wilshire Blvd, Suite 203,
Beverly Hills, CA 90212

Published by Gratuity: 10/03/2024

ISBN: 978-1-965386-08-8(sc)
ISBN: 978-1-965386-09-5(e)

Contents

This book is dedicated to my mother, Dolores G. Hollis

She was the guiding force and inspiration in my life, and she made me what I am today. She taught me to live by Christian principles, to enjoy the beauty in the world around me, to appreciate music and art, to show compassion for all of God's creatures, to do my best at any project I might undertake, and to always be brave when facing adversity. It was through her nurturing that I developed a love for reading and writing that has been with me since my early childhood days. Without her influence, this book would not have been written.

Dolores G. Hollis, 1913-2000

A Mother's Love

A mother's love embraces us
From early dawn 'til twilight's dusk.
A spark that grows within the womb,
It follows us from birth to tomb.
At babe's first cry the flame ignites,
Then reaches up to unknown heights
To light the torch that guides our way
Along life's journey day by day.
Her tender smile and loving kiss
Are long remembered, often missed,
As we give thanks to God above
For sending us a mother's love.

Written by Dianne H. Lundy
In Memory of Dolores G. Hollis

Part I

Introduction

Summerfield

Summerfield, a small quiet college town where nothing out of the ordinary ever happens – or so it seems. Like a hidden jewel, it is nestled among hills and lakes with a river running nearby. It offers a variety of activities for its citizens as they go about their everyday lives, and anything not found in Summerfield is usually available just across the river in their larger sister city, Brooksville. The population is constantly changing as many visitors pass through the town. Some stay, but others move on, seeking their fortunes elsewhere.

Those who choose to stay often find themselves involved in situations that they did not anticipate. Such is the case of four women, all unrelated, who happen to end up in Summerfield. Each woman has her own unique story, yet they are somehow all looking for the same things – a satisfying career, a sense of accomplishment, and stability in their love life. These are their stories.

Part II

"Class Dismissed"

Elaine's Story

Class Dismissed

The phone jangled loudly as it rang on Detective Tony Villard's desk. He looked up irritably from the seemingly unending pile of papers that lay on his desk where he had been sorting through them methodically. The blinking light on the in-house phone showed him that the call was coming from the police captain's office.

What now? he wondered. He had been working for the Brooksville police department for just a little over a month after he had transferred from his job in another state. Most of his work had been done inside the walls of the department, with little contact with the outside world. He was ready to get back to the normal duties of a detective and start investigating some older cases, the job he had been assigned to do.

He picked up the phone, hoping that he was about to get off desk duty and back into action.

"Hello, Villard here," he said as he spoke into the phone.

"Detective Villard, I need you to come to my office immediately," came the reply, his captain's voice reverberating through the phone's headpiece.

"Yes, sir, I'll be right there," Tony replied as he rose from his desk. He hung up the phone and put his coat back on, knowing that a coat and tie were the standard dress for a detective when working in the office.

He made his way down the hall, greeting people who sat at their respective desks as he passed by. It hadn't taken him long to make friends with his fellow police officers.

He reached the captain's door and paused to knock sharply before hearing the captain's terse command to enter. He walked into the room and was surprised to see several other detectives sitting there. His curiosity was growing stronger with each new event. First, the phone call and now additional detectives who probably knew more than he did regarding what the captain was about to tell him.

"Tony, I know you have been carping about having so much desk duty since you arrived in Brooksville. I've got some news for you. That's about to end."

"Oh? Sounds good. Tell me more," Tony responded.

"I understand that you attended college before becoming a detective and that you have an interest in Shakespeare."

"Yes, you might say that" Tony replied hesitantly. "I earned a degree in English literature before deciding that teaching was not for me. I tried student teaching, but I just couldn't stand being cooped up in a classroom all day. I want to be out on the streets, helping to solve crimes."

He could hear the snickers from the other detectives as he spoke.

"Shakespeare? Who would have dreamed that you liked such a dull subject," Carl Krenshaw drolled as he spoke.

"Yeah, how many lines can you quote?" asked Charles Tatum.

"Ever kiss Juliette?" Ron Nolan added.

Tony clenched his teeth, forcing himself to endure the teasing. However, his face began to turn redder with each quip.

"Enough with the smart remarks," the captain interrupted their verbal jousting match, much to Tony's relief. "As I said, Tony, you are about to get out of the office, but you may not like your assignment. The Summerfield police department has asked for our help. They need an undercover cop, someone who won't be recognized by anybody in their town. You fit the bill because you just came here, and you haven't been on any outside duties, so there is little chance of your being recognized as a cop. Are you up for the assignment?"

"Yes, I'll take anything to get out of the desk chair," Tony told him.

"Okay, here's the deal. There are some Summerfield students who need to be investigated without them knowing about it. The best way to do that is to have someone work at the school they attend. There should be a reason for a new person to come into the school, so I need you to pose as a student teacher in the English department. Since you're well-versed in Shakespeare, that should be right up your alley. They're about to begin a study of 'Romeo and Juliet' in the senior class."

Tony took a step backwards. If that had been a chair behind him, he would have collapsed into it. He couldn't have been more surprised if the captain had invited him along on a weekend fishing trip.

"So, that's my main qualification, I'm a Shakespeare fan?" he asked.

"Well, you do have a few more things going for you," the captain informed him. "You appear young enough to be a student teacher. You're athletic, easy on the eyes, and you have more hair on your head than the rest of us in this room put together."

Tony glanced over towards the other detectives, who were looking somewhat sheepish.

"That could be true," Tony mused, as he stared briefly at the bald, shaven head of Charles Tatum, who was now blushing.

"Aw, Captain, you know we were just joking," Charles protested. "I had hair. I just decided to shave it off."

"Yeah, what was left of it," Ron jumped into the conversation, causing Charles to roll his eyes.

"Tony, you know we'll always have your back," Carl assured him. "We just have to joke around with a new guy sometimes."

"I trust all of you," Tony replied, speaking in a serious tone.

"There's just one more thing," the captain added.

"What else could you possibly saddle me with?" Tony exclaimed.

"You also need to apply for a job to work nights at a local grocery store called D'Amico's. That's where we think the drugs are coming in, most likely through the produce department. So, you will be working on the loading docks at night when the shipments come in."

"How late at night?"

"The store closes at 8:00 p.m., and the shipment comes in at 9:00 p.m. It takes about an hour to unload the crates and store them in the cooler."

"Okay, I'll do it, but I'm going to need an extra cup of coffee just to keep my eyes open in the mornings," Tony told him.

"Good! Now that's settled, here's your weekend homework," the captain informed him as he handed over a large ring binder full of papers. "There's just one more thing we need to discuss. What do you plan to drive?"

"I don't know," Tony spoke thoughtfully as he considered the possibilities. "I can't look like a cop."

"It just so happens that I have just the car for you. It's a second-hand Mazda. Not too fancy, but not too shabby, either. I have the keys here in my desk," the captain told him. "Don't worry. We'll have somebody park your car in the enclosed parking lot here.

"Sounds like I have a full weekend ahead of me. Do you know anything about the teacher I'll be working under?"

"Yes, it's all been arranged. Your supervising teacher will be Miss Elaine Roberts."

Carl let out a low wolf-whistle. "Wow, aren't you the lucky one?"

"What do you mean?" Tony asked.

"You'll see when you get there," Ron chimed in. "Yep, you'll see."

Tony was already rattled enough between the teasing and the unexpected assignment. He was at a loss for words. He turned his attention back to the captain.

"That's it for now," the captain remarked. "Report to the front office of Summerfield High at 7:30 a.m. on Monday morning. Good luck, and I'll be checking with you on a regular basis. Here, use this burner phone for all communications with the police department."

He handed Tony the phone and keys as he spoke, and the other detectives rose, indicating that the meeting had ended. Tony walked out the door clutching the phone, keys, and folder he had been given. He didn't know what lay ahead, but he knew it wasn't going to be easy. He had better start brushing up on "Romeo and Juliet" in addition to whatever other assignments were outlined in the notebook, he decided. He paused at his desk long enough to rake the papers from the top of the desk to a drawer, which he locked. He then walked out of the building and headed to the police lot to find the Mazda that had been assigned to him.

###

Elaine Roberts stifled a sigh as she pulled a note from her teacher's mailbox after signing in on Monday morning. It was from Miss Lydia Kurtz, the school guidance counselor. She was to report to the guidance office immediately upon arriving to school. She stuffed the note into the side pocket of her purse and picked up her teaching materials before she headed out of the teachers' lounge and down the hall.

A summons from Miss Kurtz was rarely a good thing, Elaine reflected, as she walked towards the guidance office. It usually meant an additional student in her class or some extra assignment she needed to do for the school, mostly on her own time.

Miss Kurtz was a force to be reckoned with. She stood barely five feet tall in the high heels that she always wore and weighed about one-hundred pounds if Elaine's guess was right. She was a former graduate of Summerfield High who had returned to serve as the school's guidance counselor. There was little that went on in the school that Miss Kurtz didn't know about, a fact that she prided herself on.

Elaine took a deep breath and then knocked on Miss Kurtz's door. She set her shoulders as she prepared to enter the room.

"Come in," a voice rang out through the thick door.

"Miss Roberts, just the person I need to see," Miss Kurtz stated as Elaine entered the room. "Please be seated. We have a matter to discuss."

Elaine sat down, perching on the edge of the seat in case she needed to make a quick departure. Nobody liked to linger in Miss Kurtz's office.

Miss Kurtz looked Elaine straight in the eye as she began to speak. "I have something to tell you, something that may help you," she said. "You are going to be getting a student teacher starting tomorrow. I'm sure it will be of assistance to you not having to prepare an extra lesson plan."

"A help to me? Why is it that people who don't have student teachers think that supervising teachers have it so easy?" Elaine asked. "We have to consult with them about their lesson plans, supervise them while they're teaching, and grade them on everything they do."

"Nevertheless, the matter has already been settled. The college has an extra student teacher and nowhere to place him, so you were chosen because he is majoring in English literature and your class is about to start studying 'Romeo and Juliette,'" Miss Kurtz replied.

"So I have no say-so in the matter?" Elaine asked, forcing herself not to use a sarcastic tone.

"That is correct," Miss Kurtz responded. "I was informed about it by Principal Johnson. The college contacted him first, as he *is* the head of the school."

"Yes, I know that. I understand the situation. I'll do my best to accommodate him," Elaine agreed reluctantly.

"You will meet with him during your planning period today. Mr. Johnson is showing him around the school as we speak. He'll be observing your classes for several days until he can get his lesson plans prepared. It will give you time to get better acquainted."

"Yes, that would be helpful," Elaine admitted.

"Well, that's about all for now. You'll learn more when you meet him."

"Thank you," Elaine responded as she rose and prepared to leave the office.

She walked back down the hall and headed towards her room, silently seething. *Drat that woman! Can anybody be more annoying? As if I didn't already have enough to do. I just hope this guy, whoever he is, really knows his Shakespeare. I don't have time to teach him and the students, too.*

Tony had reported to the school promptly at 7:30 a.m., as instructed. He had been met by the school secretary, who had escorted him into the principal's office. Principal Morris Johnson was a large, imposing man with a stern manner about him that suggested military training. He had been informed of the situation and had agreed to cooperate with the police department.

"Good morning, Mr. Williams." He greeted Tony with his alias name. "I understand that you'll be working with us as a student teacher. Welcome aboard."

"Thank you, sir," Tony replied, silently reminding himself that he must now remember that his new name was Tony Williams.

"Since you won't be meeting with your supervising teacher until her planning period, why don't I show you around the school?" Principal Johnson suggested.

"I think that would be an excellent idea," Tony agreed. He was slipping into his new role and new name. He had been practicing it enough over the weekend, standing in front of a mirror.

"Let's start with the outside grounds because the students are entering the building," Principal Johnson informed him as he walked towards the door and opened it for Tony to exit.

They walked the entire perimeter of the grounds, with Principal Johnson pointing out the various buildings, the school entrances, the football field, the soccer field, and all the other game arenas. Tony took careful note of everything, snapping some pictures with his phone as they moved about the grounds.

They then headed back inside the building, where they began a tour of the halls, the auditorium, and the gym. Their movements didn't go unnoticed by the teenaged girls, who whispered to one another excitedly as the principal and a handsome new man passed by their doors. Teachers began to take notice, also, and hurried to close the doors as the girls craned their necks to get a better view of the stranger on campus.

Tony was instructed to wait in the teachers' lounge until the bell for second hour class rang, as that was Miss Roberts' planning period. Principal Johnson told him that her room number was sixteen, and it was located on the fourth wing of the school.

After the bell rang, Tony waited for the halls to clear before he walked to Elaine's room. Her door was open, as she had been waiting for him. She looked up from her desk when he appeared in the doorway.

"Come in," she told him, and he entered the room quickly. She stood and looked into the bluest pair of eyes that she had ever seen. They were complemented by a head of wavy, black hair that seemed to have a mind of its own. She stood there, speechless, totally mesmerized by those blue eyes.

She cleared her throat and began to speak. "I'm Elaine Roberts, but you probably already know that. I understand that you are going to be my student teacher for the next nine weeks."

"Yes," he replied. "I'm Tony Williams, and I hope I can do the job justice."

"Nice to meet you, Tony. You'll be teaching my two senior classes a unit on Shakespeare. We will be studying 'Romeo and Juliette.'"

"So I've been told," he said. "Shakespeare is one of my favorites, although some people find his writings a little dull nowadays."

"Well, we will just have to see if you can find a way to make it exciting for the students," she told him. "What I need you to do is to observe my classes for several days and see how things are done. In the meantime, you can work on your lesson plans, which I will have to check before you present them."

"Sounds like a plan to me," he agreed.

###

He spent the next few days observing all of Elaine's classes, paying special attention to the two classes he would be instructing. He was trying to learn the names of all the students in those two classes. Elaine had provided him with seating charts that he could use to help him with the task. *Good thing that police work taught me to be aware of names and how to remember them,* he thought. He just hoped he didn't goof up and call somebody by the wrong name.

Concentrating on the names proved to be the least of his worries. He couldn't help but watch Elaine as she walked about the room with a graceful stride. *Since when did teachers start to look like Greek goddesses?* He wondered.

Her oval face was accented by green eyes, and she had full lips and long, blonde hair, which she usually wore up. However, on some occasions, he noticed, she wore it down, and it swung gracefully over her shoulders whenever she bent down beside a student's desk to help them with a question on their assignment. She was usually dressed in a sensible skirt and blazer, which she had a nervous habit of adjusting whenever she walked back to the front of the room, as if she thought someone might be watching her movements.

He noted that the girls of the classes seemed excited to see a new man in the class, and they often giggled and whispered when they thought nobody was looking. The boys were more standoffish, leading Tony to believe that some of them might view him as a threat to their popularity. He also realized that some of them in the senior class might be the ones involved in the illegal drug activity, making them suspicious of any new personnel on the campus.

As the week drew to a close, Tony wrapped up his observations, completed his first week's lesson plans, and turned them in to Elaine for approval. They scheduled a meeting after school so they would have plenty of uninterrupted time to discuss any changes that needed to be made.

Elaine had time to look over the lesson plans during her planning period, and she was surprised to learn that Tony did actually have a working knowledge of Shakespeare's writings. She made note of a few suggestions to some of the lesson plans, but by and large, they were satisfactory. Maybe the job of being a supervising teacher wouldn't be as hard as she thought, she reasoned.

Tony took over the two senior classes, while Elaine taught the remaining classes. Tony was a little nervous, and it showed. Elaine sat at a table located on one side of the class, grading papers, while observing Tony at the same time. Tony couldn't help but glance in her direction quite a few times. His actions did not go unnoticed by the students, especially the girls in the classes.

Elaine couldn't keep her eyes off Tony, no matter how hard she tried. She pretended not to see him looking her way, but every time he did, he seemed to flub his lines, making quite a few errors in his presentations. The students found his actions amusing.

Tony had mastered learning the names of all the students in the classes, and he began to run background checks on the most likely suspects. He also found himself overwhelmed with paperwork with so many papers to grade. He brought up that subject with Elaine at one of their conferences, but she just teased him about it.

"Now you are beginning to see what teachers have to do," she told him.

"I didn't realize there were so many papers to grade, and I am teaching just two classes," he lamented.

"I've noticed that you look a little bleary-eyed in the mornings," she told him.

"Yes, that's because I also have a night job."

"A night job! What were you thinking? Don't you know that teaching is a full-time, demanding job?" she asked incredulously.

"I know that, but I have a car to pay for. It's not much, but it's all I could afford. A friend of mine found it for me, and I got a good price on it, but it's just partly paid for. So, I have to work part-time at D'Amico's to pay off the rest of the note."

"I see, but you have to be organized. Don't worry. You'll get used to it if you decide to continue teaching," she said. She had doubts that he would actually continue with that profession. Somehow, it just didn't seem to suit him, despite his love of and knowledge about Shakespeare.

Elaine, in the meantime, had developed a comradery with her other classes and had become quite popular with them. She managed to keep discipline in the classes while still making the classes fun for the students. Her previous experience in teaching was paying off.

It was time for the students to begin the actual reading of "Romeo and Juliette" aloud. Tony began assigning the parts to various students, who argued about who was best for each role.

"Mr. Williams, why don't you read the part of Romeo and show us how it's really done?" asked Dora Smith, one of the boldest girls in the class.

"Yeah," chimed in Ricky Chapman, one of the football players. "We guys just can't read all of that romantic stuff right. It's like reading Greek to us."

"To you, maybe," added Dusty Hopkins, the football captain, causing the rest of the class to laugh at him.

"How are you going to learn if I do everything for you?" Tony responded.

"You don't have to read it all. Just do the love scenes," Dora told him.

Elaine was beginning to look a little uncomfortable as the conversation progressed. All she needed to hear was Tony reading the love scenes from "Romeo and Juliette."

Although she was attracted to Tony, she was convinced that finding the right man was not going to be an easy thing for her. She had left her hometown after the relationship with her high school sweetheart didn't work out. Nobody in Summerfield knew her secret. Her heart had been bruised but not broken. She knew that getting involved with a student teacher would not look good on her record.

Tony was also feeling unsettled about the situation. He was supposed to be investigating a drug operation, not falling in love with his supervising teacher. Elaine was one of the most beautiful women he had ever seen. Now he could see what the other detectives had been talking about when Elaine's name came up. Still, he knew he had to put his feelings aside, at least until the case was solved.

###

Finally, the time arrived that the entire senior English classes have been waiting for—the final love scene between Romeo and Juliette. Tony played his part with a little extra flair, his eyes shifting to Elaine as he spoke. She blushed as he recited his lines. His partner in the play did justice to the dying scene, also. The students were pleased that things had gone so well, and their suspicions were confirmed that sparks were igniting between two of their favorite teachers. Elaine was relieved when she was rescued from further embarrassment by the ringing of the bell, signaling that class was over.

It was the last class of the day, and both Tony and Elaine began to gather their materials in preparation for leaving for the day.

"Good job in teaching the entire play," she told Tony as she put the last of her papers in her carrying case.

"Thanks, I enjoyed it more than I thought I would," Tony replied. "Shall I walk you to your car?"

"Thank you for the offer, but I have to stop by the office first. I'll see you tomorrow," she said.

Tony left quickly, leaving Elaine to make her own way out of school. The excuse of stopping by the office had been just a ploy to avoid walking with him. She put her materials in the car trunk and then got into the car, started it, and began her journey home. She glanced into the rearview mirror and noticed that a car seemed to be following her. She had seen it before as she drove about town.

Feeling a little frightened, she made quick work of parking in her driveway, getting the papers from her trunk, and entering her apartment. She looked around, and nothing seemed to be out of place. She then pulled the curtains of the front window back slightly and peered outside. The car that had been following her was parked on the other side of the street. Her nerves were on edge, but she didn't know what to do. There was no proof that the driver had done anything wrong. Maybe it was just a coincidence, she told herself.

She fixed herself a quick meal and decided to take a long, warm bubble bath to relax and put all her worries aside. She lit a few candles and put on some relaxing music while she had a long soak in the tub. Afterwards, she watched TV for a while and then decided to go to bed early. She took one last peek out the front window, and, to her relief, the mysterious car was gone.

Tony had continued with his investigation. He had managed to pry open one of the false bottoms on a produce case of lettuce after realizing that it weighed more than it should. A quick check had shown several bags of what appeared to be heroin stowed underneath the real case. He had carefully replaced the board he had pried loose and waited to see if he could catch somebody in the act of removing the drugs. He didn't have any luck the first night, so he realized that he was going to have to bide his time.

He had taken time off from his night job on Friday nights to attend the school ball games and other activities, taking note of which students had a habit of disappearing suddenly in the middle of the events or when the events ended. His notebook of names was growing fuller every week.

Finally, with both football and basketball over, it was time for intramural sports to begin. Tony volunteered to play on the faculty basketball team against the seniors. He felt that he could hold his own, as he had played basketball in college.

Elaine was drafted to be one of the cheerleaders for the faculty team, partly because she was one of the few teachers still small enough to fit into one of the old cheerleader uniforms. She tried on the one she was given and was thankful that it fit, although she felt rather conspicuous in such a skimpy outfit. One of the cheerleaders loaned her a pair of pompoms.

On the day of the game, Elaine ran out to the sidelines, accompanied by the rest of the female teachers who had volunteered to act as cheerleaders for the faculty team. She was the most graceful and athletic of the crew, having served as a cheerleader in high school. She lined them up and showed them a few moves, which they attempted rather clumsily. Some of them even lost their balance and fell to the floor, much to the amusement of the crowd. Elaine, however, managed to do her jumps and high kicks gracefully, with her long, shapely legs totally revealed in the skimpy outfit.

Those legs didn't escape Tony's attention, nor did they remain unnoticed by some of the teenaged boys in the audience. It was another reason for Tony to keep glancing her way as the game began.

Things didn't go well for the faculty in the first half of the game, with the high school team running circles around the teachers, many of whom were out of condition. Tony kept missing passes every time he looked Elaine's way. When halftime arrived, he realized that the only way his team was going to win was for him to concentrate on the team rather than on Elaine. He started playing like he did in college, scoring several three-point shots, and grabbing quite a few rebounds. The score grew closer and closer until it was down to just a two-point difference. Tony managed to make one last three-point shot just as the final buzzer of the game sounded. Elaine and the other female teachers were elated and cheered loudly as the teams ran off the court.

Tony headed straight for Elaine, who greeted him with a wide grin. "I didn't know you had such talents," she exclaimed.

"I wasn't sure myself since I haven't played in such a long time, but it all came back to me," he commented breathlessly as he stood drenched in sweat, mopping his forehead with one of the team towels.

"The seniors will never live down being beaten by the faculty," she noted. They were already headed to the dressing room with a hangdog look on their faces.

"Oh, they're young. They'll get over it, especially as soon as they start thinking about the girls again," Tony assured her.

"I guess that completes the intramurals for the year. The next big activity is the prom," she told him.

"I hope that doesn't mean more work for me," he sighed as he spoke.

"No, it's voluntary for you, but since I'm a junior sponsor, I have to help supervise the decorations," she said.

"Do they have a theme?" he asked.

"Yes, they voted on it. Their choice was 'Night of Dreams.'"

"Sounds romantic. I hope you can come up with some good ideas for the decorations."

"We have a committee. I think they have a pretty good plan; I hope you can come."

"I'll try my best, although I do work at nights most of the time," he reminded her.

"Yes, I know. I'll just keep my fingers crossed that you make it."

"I'd better go and change. I'll see you Monday."

"Good night. I'm headed home for a long soak. All that jumping will probably make me sore," she told him.

Tony headed to the locker room, and Elaine headed to her car. She looked around for any sign of the car that had been following her, but it wasn't in sight. Feeling relieved, she got into her car and drove home. She approached her apartment carefully, scanning both sides of the street for the unidentified, mysterious car.

She unlocked the door to her apartment and walked in. Something didn't seem right. A few things were out of place, although nothing seemed to be missing. Then she spotted it. A picture that she kept on her bureau from her college days was gone. It was one of her with a group of her best friends. Someone had definitely been in her apartment.

She called the police department to report the break-in, and several detectives arrived almost immediately. She answered their questions as best she could, stating that she had no idea of why someone would break in or why they would take that particular picture. They took a few fingerprints and left, promising to investigate the matter thoroughly. She decided not to mention it to anyone else.

Elaine threw herself into the work of decorating for the prom. It was the last major activity before graduation, and the students were enthused about it. The dance was to be held in the downtown convention center. They had completed the decorations, so all they needed to do was put them up the day of the prom. Elaine took off the entire day, with other teachers covering her classes. The students assigned to decorate showed up at 8:00 a.m., and the work began in earnest.

They covered one wall on the end with dark blue paper with a pale-yellow paper moon in the center. The rest of the space was filled with glittering paper stars. It formed a perfect background for prom pictures. The other end wall was covered with the same paper and matching stars. They hung white balloons from the ceiling to represent more stars. The other two walls were decorated with chains of crepe paper in the school colors of blue and white. A garland of greenery enhanced with white roses was placed around the frame of the entrance door.

A place for the DJ to set up with his music was provided, and a refreshment table for a punch bowl and trays of cookies and sandwiches would be at one corner of the room. Elaine looked around after everything was finished and was satisfied that everyone had done their best.

"Looks great, everyone. Thanks so much for helping," she told them as they left to get ready for the prom.

Elaine hurried home and took a quick shower and then tried to decide what she should wear. She had several garments to pick from, but she had been unable to make up her mind which was more suitable. She finally settled for one of her college formals, an emerald-colored dress that matched her eyes. She put her hair up and highlighted it with a rhinestone clip. A pair of high-heeled sandals, some rhinestone drop earrings, and a small silver clutch bag completed her outfit. She took one last glance in the mirror and approved of what she saw. She looked good, and she knew it.

She walked into the gym and was greeted by Principal Johnson, whose bushy eyebrows met almost in a frown as he reminded her sternly, "Remember, you are here to chaperone, not just to have a good time."

"Yes, sir. I won't forget," she promised. *As if I could find anybody to dance with, anyhow,* she thought. She wondered if Tony would keep his promise about attending.

The music started, and Elaine began circulating around the sidelines of the dance floor, pausing to speak to the other chaperones, who complemented her on her appearance. Several of the senior boys asked her to dance, but she turned them down, stating that it wouldn't be appropriate for a teacher to dance with her students.

She kept glancing towards the door, looking for Tony, but he was nowhere in sight. She began listening to the music, just to stay entertained, and she found herself slowly swaying to the tunes, her mind drifting back to her high school days when she was the belle of the ball, and her date was Jason McKnight, the football captain. They had dated for several years, and she had thought they would get married. Then Jason left for college and suggested that they might "try dating other people, just to be sure." That was the last she had seen of him until he had returned to town a year later with a new girl on his arm. She sighed, realizing that those days were behind her.

Suddenly, she became aware of a slight commotion at the door as Tony walked in, wearing a tuxedo. He was dressed to the nines, and he had never looked more handsome. He scanned the crowd, apparently looking for someone. Then his eyes met Elaine's and she felt a twinge of happiness that made her tingle all over. Before he could head her way, a group of girls immediately rushed towards him, each one hoping to grab him for a dance. He managed to ward them off and disappeared through another door and down a hall. Elaine felt the tingle draining away, right down through her toes. Trying not to look disappointed, she turned back to watch other couples dancing.

Tony had an ulterior motive for slipping out of the prom. He was about to wrap up his investigation of drug distribution at the school. If his instincts served him right, both drugs and alcohol would be passed around among the students, out of sight of the chaperones. He pulled out the burner phone and walked quietly down the back hall, hoping to catch some of the students passing out drugs. He slipped out the back door after opening it slowly and peeked around a dark corner, careful not to let himself be seen.

A few students were standing in the shadows, and some small bags and pills were definitely exchanging hands. He waited for the right moment when he could get a clear picture in the dim light. He held the phone around the corner and snapped several pictures and then quietly walked away, heading back to the sound of prom music.

###

It was later than he thought, he realized, when he heard the DJ announce that it was time for the "Sweethearts' Dance," the final dance of the evening. Elaine had told him about it during their conversations. Tradition held that a couple was supposed to dance together to Garth Brooks' tune of "The Dance" to seal their pact of love. Any girl who didn't snag a partner for that dance just might wind up single for the rest of her life, according to the legend.

He felt inside his tuxedo coat and tapped lightly to make sure that his surprise for Elaine was still there. He could hear the crinkle of the cellophane that was protecting a rose he had bought for her. He pulled it out of his coat as he approached the hall door heading back into the ballroom and carefully removed the cellophane, discarding it into a trash can that sat by the door as he entered the room again.

Elaine was standing on the sidelines, looking a little sad when she felt a tap on her shoulder. She turned around and was surprised to see Tony. He held out a long-stemmed red rose and said, "May I have this dance?"

Elaine glanced towards Principal Johnson, who was looking their way.

"I'm not sure. I probably shouldn't," she protested.

"Come on, it'll be okay," Tony promised as he stepped forward to take her into his arms.

She took the rose into her left hand as she placed that hand on his shoulder. They began to circle the room as they danced. They passed directly in front of Principal Johnson. Elaine glanced at him quickly under veiled eyelashes. She couldn't believe it! His frown had turned into a smile. *Could it be that he actually approved of her dancing with her student teacher?* She wondered.

"I would never do anything to get you into trouble," Tony whispered into her ear. "I'll explain it all to you later." *Much later,* he thought.

The strains of the music began to die down, and the couples slowed in unison, some kissing at the end.

Tony took Elaine's hand and gave it a brief kiss. Then he was gone as quickly as he had appeared. Elaine was left staring in his direction as he mingled with the crowd.

It's like Cinderella in reverse, she thought. *I found my Prince Charming only to lose him again.* She clutched the rose to her breast and took a deep breath. She had a lot to think about after she got home tonight.

Elaine watched as the students filed out the doors, mostly in couples. She walked over to the side of the ballroom and consulted with the rest of the teachers. They all gathered their purses from the locker that had been provided. The school janitors were supposed to come tomorrow and remove all the decorations. The punch bowl and serving trays belonged to the school, so they gathered them up and loaded them into the home economics teacher's SUV. The parking lot emptied quickly, leaving Elaine to walk to her car alone. She wished that Tony was there to make sure she got home safely.

She had a lot to think about on the way home. She had tried to fight the attraction between her and Tony, but it hadn't worked. She couldn't get those blue eyes out of her mind, and he obviously felt the same attraction to her. Still, she had to think about her job. Tony wouldn't be her student teacher forever, but there was still the age difference between them. He must be twenty-one if he was in his senior year of college, she calculated. That made her about four years older than he was. How would he feel about marrying an older woman?

But she was getting ahead of herself. Yes, Tony was attracted to her, but that didn't mean he wanted to marry her. He probably had a girlfriend, maybe more than one, she reasoned.

She reached her apartment and pulled into the driveway. The street was deserted except for a lone car sitting at the end of the block. She recognized it as the unidentified car that had been following her about town. As a precaution, she took her cell phone out of her purse before she got out of the car. She walked to her door and opened it. When she flipped the light switch on, she was startled to see Jason seated on the couch.

"What are you doing here, and how did you get in?" she demanded to know.

"It was easy. I told your landlord that I was your brother from out of town. All it took to convince him was to show him this picture of you with your friends," he explained as he held out the missing picture.

"So, you were the one who took the picture. How did you get in to nab it? Plus, how did you find me? I didn't tell anybody where I was going when I left my hometown."

"First, you left the kitchen window unlocked. I just climbed in and out through it, although getting over the sink did give me a little trouble."

"I'm glad!" she exclaimed.

"Second, social media. Didn't you know your face is all over Facebook and TikTok?" he asked.

"No, I never used those sites," she told him. "You need to leave. You threw me aside for another girl."

"I've changed. Let me prove it to you," he begged.

"No, it's over between us. We can never be a couple again." She was dialing 9-1-1 as she spoke.

He rose from the couch and quickly approached her, reaching for the phone. She managed to get out a few words before he grabbed it. "Hello, this is Elaine Roberts. I have a prowler in my house…"

That was all she got out before he hung up the phone, which was now firmly in his hands. The sound of sirens could be heard approaching the end of the street.

"Why don't you go now and save yourself a lot of trouble?" she asked.

He backed away, dropping her phone in the process. "I'm sorry. I didn't mean to scare you. I just wanted us to be a couple again."

The door burst open as three policemen entered. "What's going on?" one of them demanded to know.

"I…I have an intruder," Elaine stammered.

"Okay, buddy, up against the wall, hands over your head," one of them instructed.

Jason complied, showing little resistance. One officer patted him down, checking for weapons and then pulled out a pair of handcuffs and secured Jason's hands behind his back.

"We'll be taking him downtown now, ma'am," the officer informed Elaine.

"Could I say just one thing?" Jason asked.

"Okay, but make it brief," the officer replied.

"Elaine, I never meant to hurt you. I just wanted you back. I can see now that I was wrong. You don't have to worry about me. I won't bother you again."

"Thank you for that," Elaine responded.

"Let's go," the officer ordered, as he and the other officers escorted Jason out of the apartment.

Elaine sank down on the couch as soon as the door closed behind them. She believed Jason was telling the truth. He was out of her life forever. She had sworn off men until Tony came along, but he probably wasn't the right man for her either. She had a lot to think about over the weekend.

In the meantime, Tony had been busy over the weekend. He met with the captain and turned in all of the information he had gathered, including the pictures on his phone. They revealed that Dusty, the football captain, and some of the other football players were the ones who had been selling drugs to the other students. Tony really hated that because Dusty had shown great promise as an athlete, enough to get a college scholarship. *Why did kids have to get themselves into such messes?* He wondered.

The only task remaining was to find out who was taking the drugs from the crates in D'Amico's store. That was going to be a little tricky. He suggested that they set up surveillance cameras in the stockroom to see if they could catch anybody opening the false bottoms on the crates. It was done quickly the next day by some technicians dressed as utility workers.

The captain had a monitor in his office, and Tony and the other detectives were given access on their cell phones. Now all they had to do was wait for another produce delivery. Tony and a female cop named Holly waited inside the darkened store on the following Monday night, while the other detectives waited in parked cars spaced inconspicuously along the street that passed the store. They didn't have to wait long.

A delivery truck pulled up, and two workers began to unload the produce. As soon as the truck left, the monitors showed the workers opening the crates and removing the bags of drugs from underneath some crates.

Tony was wearing an earpiece and a miniature microphone for communication purposes. As soon as he saw the drugs had been removed from the cases, he knew it was time to move in.

"Let's go. Move in now." he spoke softly, but clearly into his microphone. He and Holly moved through the double doors and entered the stockroom, guns drawn.

The two workers looked up, startled by their sudden entrance. One of them pulled a gun and aimed it in the direction of Tony and Holly.

"Gun!" Tony shouted. "Take cover!" He and Holly dove behind the tables holding the produce.

The other detectives and several uniformed officers entered from the loading dock, guns drawn. Shots rang out as one of the workers shot in Tony's direction before being hit himself with police fire. His shots ricocheted off the wall. One hit Tony, who heard moans coming from Holly's direction.

"Officer down," Tony shouted, as he crawled towards Holly, who lay in a pool of blood. "Call a bus," he ordered. "Holly, stay with me," he said, as he tried to stop the bleeding. He could see that she was fading fast.

The two workers were collected and handcuffed, with the wounded one carted away on an ambulance, which had arrived quickly. It was too late for Holly, much to Tony's dismay. It was then that he realized he had been hit.

"Hold still," a familiar voice rang out as Tony looked up from the place where he had collapsed. It was Carl Krenshaw. "We're going to get you to the hospital."

That was the last thing Tony remembered until he woke up in a hospital bed, his shoulder bandaged and an IV in his arm. A nurse was peering down at him.

"Ah, you're awake. You lost a lot of blood and took a bullet, but you're going to be okay," she told him. "The doctor will probably release you tomorrow when he makes his rounds."

Tony blinked several times, trying to get his eyes to focus again. "Tomorrow?" he asked.

"Yes, tomorrow. You are here for overnight observation," the nurse stated firmly.

Tony turned his head toward the ceiling, resigned to his predicament.

###

Elaine was sitting on the couch, waiting for the ten o'clock news to come on. Tony had finished his student teaching, but she had been thinking about him all day. She had prepared herself a sandwich, but she had little appetite for food. The sandwich lay in the refrigerator in a plastic bag. She just couldn't bring herself to eat it.

Suddenly, a news flash came on the TV. There had been a shooting at D'Amico's and a drug arrest. Elaine's heart skipped a beat. Tony…all she could think about was Tony when she heard the announcement. She forced herself to listen to the rest of the story, nerves on edge.

One officer had been killed and another person was wounded but in stable condition at the local hospital. What if Tony had been shot, or even worse, killed?

She turned off the TV, grabbed her purse and car keys and headed to the hospital. She thought she had enough excitement, but this was worse than she had ever imagined.

She arrived at the hospital quickly and walked up to the reception desk. She recognized the nurse as the mother of one of her students.

"I just heard on the news that someone had been shot at D'Amico's grocery. Could you tell me who was shot?" she inquired.

"I'm sorry, but we can't give out the names of our patients. However, a police guard has been placed at the door of the injured patient. He is on the third floor if you want to speak to the officer," the nurse replied.

Elaine hurried to the elevator and pushed the up button. Upon entering, she pushed the button for the third floor. It seemed to take forever, but when she arrived on the third floor, she stepped out of the elevator and immediately spied a policeman standing guard in front of one of the rooms.

She walked over to him and began to speak. "My name is Elaine Roberts, and I came to inquire about the patient who has been shot."

"Elaine Roberts, you say. I know who you are. Tony has been mumbling about you all night," the office informed her.

"He has?" Elaine asked incredulously. "Could you be talking about Tony Williams?"

"No, I'm talking about Tony Villard."

"Tony Villard, but I don't understand..." Elaine broke off in mid-sentence.

"Tony will explain everything to you," the officer commented as he opened the door to the hospital room.

Elaine peered into the dimly lit room and recognized Tony lying on the bed. He opened his eyes as she entered.

"Elaine, come in." He spoke softly, his voice a little weak.

"Tony, I thought your name was Tony Williams."

"That was my alias. I'm really Tony Villard, a Brooksville detective."

Elaine sank into a chair at the head of the bed. "I can't believe it. You had me fooled all this time, and the students, too."

"It was part of my job. I was working undercover on a drug investigation. Drugs were being smuggled in through D'Amico's store."

"Not Mr. D'Amico?" she gasped as she spoke.

"No, he was in on the plan. I'm sad to say that some of the Summerfield football players were involved. They were selling the drugs at school. I was there to find out who the dealers were."

"I'm sorry to hear that, but what about you? You're injured."

"Not too injured to do this," Tony replied as he reached up with his good arm and pulled Elaine down for a kiss.

"Tony!" she exclaimed as she pulled back, resisting her impulse to let the kiss linger.

"Elaine, it's okay. I'm not a student teacher anymore. I never was, at least, not in Summerfield."

"Oh, it's so hard to get used to the idea," she explained, shaking her head.

"Well, try harder," he instructed, as he pulled her closer for another kiss. This time, she didn't pull back.

"I have just one thing I want to say to you."

"And just what would that be?"

"Elaine, I love you. I think I loved you from the first moment I walked through your door on that day we met."

"I think the same thing happened to me," she admitted. "I couldn't get those blue eyes of yours out of my head."

"I'm glad you couldn't," he said, as he grasped her hand with his good hand, looking straight into her eyes.

"Elaine, would you marry me?" he asked.

"Yes, yes, I will, just as soon as you get out of the hospital" she replied, as tears filled her eyes.

"I promise to make a very speedy recovery," he replied, as he pulled her close for another kiss.

"You'd better," she teased as she dabbed at her eyes with a tissue she had retrieved from his bedside. "I can't wait much longer to be your wife."

He kissed her again, and they were soon lost in their own world, oblivious to anything about them. They didn't even notice as the door opened just a crack and the guard peeped in. He smiled to himself as he softly shut the door. It looked like having that new detective in their department was going to work out just fine.

###

Part III

"Cats and Dogs"

Jillian's Story

Cats and Dogs

Little Megan O'Reilly peered anxiously at the hole in the line of shrubs edging the right side of the back yard. Her small forehead wrinkled with concern, which was mirrored in her large blue eyes.

"Snowball? Here kitty, kitty," she called softly. *Where had that cat gone?* she wondered.

She knew she wasn't supposed to be outside. Not yet anyhow. Mama had told her to stay in the den and watch her "Sponge Bob Square Pants" DVD. She was doing just that when she had looked out the window and spied a pretty red bird at Mama's new bird feeder. She had opened the door, hoping to get a closer look. That was when it had happened. Snowball, their unpredictable white long-haired Persian cat, had slipped past her and began stalking the bird. When the bird flew away, Snowball had headed towards the shrubs and disappeared. Now she was going to be in trouble if Mama found out before she caught Snowball and brought her back into the house.

The hole wasn't very big, but maybe if she just poked her head through it she could spot Snowball, she decided. Crawling on her hands and knees, she managed to get her head all the way through, and then the rest of her small body. She lost a hair ribbon in the process, making a mess of the ponytail Mama had tied up for her earlier in the morning. Besides that, she left a piece of her shirt behind on one of the sharp twigs and got dirt on both her pants legs. Now Mama was going to be really mad. It was worth the effort, though, because there was Snowball, clear across the other side of the neighbor's yard, chasing a butterfly.

"Snowball, you bad cat. Come here right now," she demanded, stomping her tiny foot as she spoke.

Before either one of them could move, a large, dark shape shot out through the back door of the neighbor's house and headed straight for Snowball. It was a dog! Snowball darted back towards Megan and the hole in the shrubs, while Megan stood transfixed, unable to move. The dog was barking fiercely, its white teeth gleaming in the bright sunlight. Megan opened her mouth and let out a high, piercing scream as the dog bore down upon her.

Jillian O'Reilly hummed softly as she spread the sheets over the bed in the upstairs bedroom and began tucking them in. It had been a long time since she had hummed or even felt the slightest inclination to do so. Here she was in a new town about to start a new life and a new job as a fourth-grade teacher. She had gotten her degree some time ago but had never had a need to use it until now.

She had met her husband, Douglas O'Reilly, when they were both seniors in college. Theirs had been a whirlwind courtship with an engagement by Christmas and a wedding in June, the week after graduation. She had earned a degree in elementary education, while Douglas had majored in biology. He had obtained a job as a pharmaceutical sales representative with a major drug company, making it possible for her to stay home rather than working. It was something she had loved to do – thinking up little exotic dishes to surprise him at night and keeping the house spotlessly clean and charmingly decorated. Their world had seemed complete when their daughter, Megan, was born two years later. It was a picture-perfect family.

That world had come crashing down one night when Jillian answered the door to find two state troopers on her doorstep. Douglas had left several days earlier to attend a conference in Chicago and was due to return home later that night.

"Mrs. O'Reilly? Mrs. Douglas O'Reilly?" one of them had asked when she opened the door.

"Yes, I'm Mrs. O'Reilly. What seems to be the problem, officers?"

"I'm afraid we have some bad news for you, Mrs. O'Reilly," one of the officers replied. "Your husband was killed in an auto accident this evening."

Jillian had swayed and almost fainted from shock. The two officers had escorted her back into the house, helping her onto the couch and providing her with a glass of water. One of them had managed to extract from her the information about who her parents were and had phoned them about the situation. The kind officers had remained until her parents arrived about thirty minutes later.

Jillian had spent the next six months moping around the house, caring little about her appearance or the upkeep of the place. Her once pristine home was beginning to resemble a pig sty, according to her mother.

"You've simply got to snap out of it, Jillian," her mother had told her. "Get counseling. Get whatever you need but think of Megan. She needs you right now."

Jillian had pulled herself up by the bootstraps, determined to make a happy home for Megan and herself. That's what Doug would have wanted. He wouldn't have approved of all the grieving and carrying on.

Their little house held too many memories. She had to get a fresh start and the only way to do that was to move. So, here she was in Summerfield, a small college town in another state. It had almost broken her parents' hearts to see them go, but it was something she had to do. She just had to find out if she could make it on her own.

The new house was a little bigger than she had actually wanted. But the real estate lady had been insistent, and she was sold, once she saw the back yard with the enormous oak tree. It would be an ideal spot for a swing set for Megan. Plus, the tree would attract all sorts of birds, making it a great place for bird watching through the picture window of the den.

It was their first day in the new house and she was hurrying to get the beds made so she could start working on their evening meal. She was determined to have a regular sit-down meal as their first one in that house. She had instructed Megan to watch TV and that should keep her out of trouble for at least an hour, she estimated. Maybe it was about time for her to check up on her daughter. It was awfully quiet downstairs.

"Megan, have you finished watching your 'Sponge Bob' DVD yet?" she called out as she stood by the head of the stairs. "Meggie? Can you hear me?"

There was no answer. *What could that child be up to now?* Surely, she hadn't disobeyed her mother and gone out into the yard before it could be checked out. She walked downstairs to find the TV set on, but there was no sign of Megan and no sign of Snowball, either, for that matter.

She opened the back door and scanned the yard quickly. This was getting serious.

"Megan! It's not nice to hide from Mama. Where are you? Come out right now!" she yelled.

That's when she heard it – the high, piercing scream coming from over the hedge. It was Megan. There was no doubt about it. Her baby was in trouble!

###

Cody Hawthorne was playing with his GI Joe toys when their German Shepherd dog, Duke, began to scratch on the back door.

"What's wrong, Duke? Do you want to go outside?" he asked.

He supposed it would be okay. Maybe Duke had to, well, *go*. Daddy had said it was all right to let Duke out in the back yard only. The front yard was still off-limits, though, for both him and Duke.

He had opened the door just a crack when he spotted the pretty white cat in their yard. It was chasing a butterfly. It looked just like the cat on the cover of his favorite book, the one Mama used to read to him for a bedtime story. Then Daddy had said cats were for girls and what every boy needed was a good dog. The book had been stored on the top shelf of the hall closet, way up and out of his reach.

Before he could close the door, Duke nosed his way through it and was off like a shot. Once he spied a cat, nothing could stop him. Duke charged the cat at full speed, barking furiously as Cody ran behind him shouting, "No, Duke! Stop! Come back!"

###

Before Jillian could move, a streak of white ran past her legs and through the open door. It was Snowball, who had wisely wasted no time in evading the large dog with the loud bark and gleaming teeth. Snowball, apparently unaware of the trouble she was causing, sat down in front of the fireplace and began to clean her coat at a leisurely pace.

Jillian ran out the door and around the house to the front edge of the hedge that separated the two lots. What she saw almost made her blood run cold. There was Megan, frozen in place and screaming at the top of her lungs, with a large and apparently dangerous dog just three feet away from her. The dog kept lunging toward a hole in the shrubs, but it always stopped just short of reaching Megan.

Jillian began to run towards Megan, her feet feeling as if they were filled with lead. Somehow, she had to save her baby! Her heart was pumping so fast she was sure it would burst out of her chest. Would she reach Megan in time?

Then, out of nowhere, a man came running through the back door of the other house.

"Duke, stop. Sit!" he commanded.

Amazingly enough, the dog did just that, sitting on his haunches and panting from his exertion efforts.

"Cody, what's going on?" he demanded to know, addressing a small boy who was standing in the background. "Why did you let Duke outside?"

"I thought he had to *go*, Daddy. Then he started chasing a cat," the boy replied in a low voice. He looked as if he were about to burst into tears at any minute.

Jillian and the unidentified stranger reached Megan at the same time. Jillian snatched her five-year-old daughter up into her arms, hugging her tightly and sobbing with relief.

"I'm so sorry, ma'am. Duke is a perfectly good dog, but he can't resist chasing a cat whenever he sees one. It's a habit I've been trying to break. I want you to know your daughter was never in any real danger. You see, I had this yard equipped with an electronic fence, so Duke won't go past a certain point. Otherwise, he gets a shock from the collar he wears."

"You should be sorry! People should not be allowed to own dogs like that. He was trying to kill my cat!" Jillian declared, as she still clutched Megan tightly to her chest.

"Please allow me to introduce myself," he said. "I'm your neighbor, Jake Hawthorne, and this is my son, Cody."

"I'm Jillian O'Reilly, and this is my daughter, Megan," she replied, although she wasn't feeling very neighborly at the moment.

"Well, Ms. O'Reilly, we didn't get off to a very good start, but I hope Cody and I didn't make too bad of an impression on you. I heard I was getting a new neighbor, but I didn't know it would be so soon."

"It's Mrs. O'Reilly, not Ms.," she corrected him, "and I had to get here before school started. I will be teaching the fourth grade at Summerfield Elementary in just a few days."

"I see. Well, I suggest that you keep your cat inside the house in the future. It would make things a lot easier on all of us," he observed.

"I intend to do that, Mr. Hawthorne. I intend to do just that," she retorted, as she set Megan back down on her feet and began towing her towards the front end of the hedge.

Jillian marched around the hedge, head held high, going at a pace that forced Megan to an almost-running gait.

"Mama, you're going too fast. I can't keep up," Megan protested.

She glared down at her bedraggled daughter. "And just what were you doing outside, Miss? I told you to stay in the den and watch TV."

"I know, Mama, but I was looking at a pretty bird. Then Snowball got out and I was just trying to find her."

"Megan, listen to me very carefully. You are not to go outside anymore without my permission. Is that clear?"

"Yes, Mama."

"And just look at your clothes. You've practically ruined your shirt and your jeans are all dirty. We don't have a lot of money to buy new clothes, so we have to take care of our clothes from now on."

"Yes, Mama."

"Now go upstairs to your room and take off those clothes and put on another shirt and some more pants. Then I want you to put the clothes in the hamper in the upstairs bathroom. Go!" With that remark, Jillian waved Megan upstairs as she sank onto the couch in the den, weak from relief her daughter had escaped serious injury from such a gigantic dog.

Dogs! Ugh, she hated them! And she was afraid of them, too. The world would be a better place without any dogs at all, she had decided a long time ago.

Her fear had started when she was just a small girl. The family had gone to visit her mom's sister, Aunt Edna, and her husband, Uncle Luke. The couple's dog, Elvis, was a very large and friendly golden Labrador retriever. Elvis had a habit of greeting each and every visitor to the place with a wet, sloppy kiss that was usually aimed right at their face. She had been only four at the time and Elvis's display of affection had scared her badly. Ever since then, she had avoided dogs at all costs. Cats were the perfect pets, she had decided. No worrying about them being overly affectionate.

Just my luck, she sighed. *I find what appears to be the perfect house, and I end up next door to a dog owner…and one who is too handsome for his own good, at that.* The fact that her new neighbor looked somewhat like a Greek Adonis had not escaped her notice. How could it, when he ran out the door with no shirt and only his cutoffs on? He obviously worked at keeping in shape with those well-developed biceps and muscular legs, all complemented by a head of neatly trimmed blond hair and blazing blue eyes. The little boy was almost a carbon copy of his dad, so there could be no doubt they were related.

Oh, well. No use dwelling on that subject. Dog owners were

definitely nobody she wanted to associate with, no matter how good-looking they might be! Anyhow, the guy was married, so what was she thinking? She and Megan would just stay in their own yard and forget about the people next door.

###

Jake watched the duo leaving as they swung around the front edge of the hedge. The little girl was obviously Irish with that head of red hair and those enormous blue eyes. She evidently took after her father because the mother sported wavy light brown hair and hazel eyes. And very long legs that fit curvaceously into her jeans.

"Well, I guess she told us," he commented to Cody. "Let's get Duke back inside, and don't let him out again if you see a cat anywhere in sight."

"Okay, Daddy." Cody sniffled as he spoke.

"Oh, son. It's all right. The little girl didn't get hurt, and the cat's okay, too. Just remember, we're trying to train Duke not to chase cats anymore."

He held the door open as Cody and Duke scampered back inside. Then he slowly followed. What was supposed to be an ordinary Saturday afternoon had been anything but. What was going to happen next?

Fate had a funny was of giving things an odd twist, he decided. Finally, he had lucked out and gotten a beautiful neighbor, but she was, of all things, a cat owner. Plus, she was married. Cats! Blast, he couldn't stand the things! What were they good for anyhow? Oh, maybe they could catch a mouse every now and then but give him a good old dog he could take hunting and fishing. Yep, he'd take a dog over a cat any day!

He had to smile, remembering how his love of dogs had started early in his childhood. His dad had surprised him on his fifth birthday with a long-haired collie pup named MacIntosh. He had promptly shortened the name to Mac, and they had grown up together, becoming inseparable companions.

He and his two best friends, Noah Tabor and Justin Marshall, had decided to form their own club called DLO (Dog Lovers Only) with

Mac as their mascot. They had built a tree house in his backyard and put up a sign to mark it off-limits to anyone else. They had also decided girls were yucky, so they added "No Girls Allowed" beneath the title. He considered that old tree house to be one of his best architectural works, despite the crooked corners and the floorboards that didn't quite meet in some places. They had vowed to be friends forever and had sworn an oath to positively and at all costs never ever have anything to do with girls.

That oath had lasted until the seventh grade. Noah was the first to break it. He succumbed to the charms of none other than Natalie Allen, who blinked her big brown eyes at him one day at the bus stop. He was a goner after that, but Justin and Jake just rolled their eyes and stayed true to their oath.

Then came the ninth grade and junior varsity football. Justin fell for a little blonde-headed cheerleader named Emma Cook. That left Jake all alone with just Mac for company. By that time, he had stopped using the tree house, partly because he was too big to fit in it anymore. Nevertheless, it was the principle of the thing, he told himself. Dogs were still better than girls. Plus, they didn't giggle all the time.

By their senior year all three boys had developed into fine young men, with the effects of their football training evident in their muscular physiques. Jake had been voted "Most Handsome Boy" in his class for three years running, but he still refused to date. Somehow, his aloofness made him seem even more desirable to the girls of the class. They were constantly plotting ways to get him to walk them to class. Each girl hoped that maybe, just maybe, she would be the lucky one he finally asked for a date. But Jake just smiled at them as he carried their books and then left them at the doors of their respective classes, much to their disappointment. Then he went home to Mac, who was getting on in years by that time.

Eventually, one day the unthinkable happened. He went home, expecting Mac to greet him at the door, as usual. Instead, he found Mac in the den lying on a rug in front of the sofa. Mac raised his head and wagged his tail weakly when Jake came into the room.

"Mom, come quick. I think there's something wrong with Mac," he yelled.

Together they managed to load Mac into the back of the family sedan and rushed him to the vet. After a brief examination, Jake got the bad news.

"It's his heart, son. I'm afraid it's just given out," the vet told him. "There's really nothing more we can do for him. The kindest thing would be to have him put down."

Jake reluctantly agreed to the procedure after talking it over with his mother. They brought Mac home and buried him in the back yard, close to where the tree house was located. Jake staunchly held back his tears, determined that an eighteen-year-old boy shouldn't cry. He was well on his way to becoming a man on that fateful day.

Several months later after graduation his two friends opted to attend the local college. Noah wanted to be a doctor, while Justin had decided on business and marketing as a major. Jake surprised everybody by announcing he was going to follow in his dad's footsteps and become a police officer. His father, William, had worked his way up in the force while Jake was growing up and had finally attained the rank of captain when he took over as the head of the department.

Jake continued to live with his parents and still showed no real interest in dating or finding a steady girl. Noah and Justin both met their future wives in college and eventually got married, with Jake serving as a groomsman in both weddings.

"Man, you're still thinking about our DLO club, aren't you?" Justin had teased, just before the ceremony.

"Yeah, why don't you give it up? Girls are more fun than dogs," Noah had added.

"Sorry, guys. I guess the right girl just hasn't come along," Jake had replied.

That was before he met Holly Robbins.

He was in his fourth year as a policeman on the force when another group of rookies came in. It was the custom to pair each rookie with a veteran cop for at least six months of patrol duty. As captain, it was his dad's job to decide on the partnerships. Jake sat in on the meeting announcing the most recent assignments.

"And, finally, the last of our new recruits, Holly Robbins, will ride with Jake Hawthorne," his dad said, as guffaws broke out among the ranks. It was well known that Jake avoided contact with females at all costs.

Jake managed to maintain his self-control, although his face turned red, as did that of his new partner, Holly. She didn't understand what all the ruckus was about, but she could feel the bad vibes from Jake coming in her direction.

Jake walked into his dad's office a few minutes later. "Dad, we need to talk."

"I'm listening, son. What's the problem?"

"Why did you pair me with that new female recruit? You know how I feel about girls."

"I'm quite aware of your avoidance of the opposite sex, son. However, this new recruit is something special. I think she can go a long way on the force, and I wanted her to be taught by the best. You, son, are the best young officer on the force. That's why I want you to train her. Put your personal feelings aside and do your job. That's all I'm asking of you."

"Yes, sir." Jake could see arguing was of no use. So, with that remark, he turned on his heels and walked out.

###

Jake spent the next six weeks working closely with Holly, unaware of the bets on the side about how long it would be before they started dating. He was surprised at what an accurate marksman she proved to be on the shooting range.

"My dad used to take me hunting with him when I was growing up," she told him. "I've been using guns ever since I was about twelve years old."

It was just about that time he began to notice how beautiful his new partner really was. Her heart-shaped face was framed with soft blonde hair accented with sparkling green eyes. She stood barely five feet and three inches tall in her uniform, but what she lacked in size, she made up for in spirit.

One night they answered a call to a case of possible animal abuse at a trailer park on the outskirts of town. When they finally got someone to answer the door, they discovered a litter of puppies inside the filthy trailer. The mother of the pups was in sad condition with almost every rib showing.

"We have to notify animal control," he told Holly.

While they waited for the additional help, one of the pups caught his eye. It was the runt of the litter, and it was too weak to even lift its head. It was obvious the pup hadn't been getting much nourishment.

When the animal control officer arrived, he looked over the litter with expertise.

"They're in pretty bad shape, but we'll do what we can to save them," he informed the officers. "I can tell you right now, I don't think that smallest puppy is going to make it. He needs special care, and we just don't have enough staff members to provide it."

"Could I take him?" Holly asked in a soft voice.

Jake stared at her, almost in disbelief. He hadn't known she was a dog lover.

"Well, I don't know," the man replied hesitantly.

"I'll help her. Please, it's the only way the pup will have a chance," Jake pleaded.

"Well, it's against department regulations, but seeing as how you are both police officers, I'm going to make an exception. You'll need to have him checked out by a vet, though, first thing in the morning."

"We'll do it. Thank you so much," Holly had reassured him.

Jake retrieved the emergency blanket from the trunk of their squad car, and they gently wrapped the pup in it. Jake carried him out to the car and deposited him into Holly's arms.

"Poor little tyke. We have to try to save him," Holly cooed as she gently stroked his head.

"Well, the first thing we need is some kind of bottle to feed him with. I guess we had better stop by the Quick Mart and pick up that and some milk. Let me see if I can get my old vet on the phone to see exactly what we need to feed him," Jake said as he headed the cruiser back into town.

Jake and Holly bonded that night as they took turns staying up to feed the pup every two hours. They were in Holly's apartment with the pup safely tucked away in a padded box next to the warm kitchen stove. Jake dozed off on the couch, while Holly slept in her bedroom. They were both so engrossed in saving the pup it didn't occur to them what a strange and awkward situation they were in. Keeping the frail puppy alive was their first priority.

The following morning, Jake dropped Holly and the pup off at the vet's office while he ran home to shave and change clothes. The pup was already looking a bit stronger, so they were hopeful their efforts had not been in vain. The vet examined the pup and reported he had a chance, provided they kept up the feeding schedule and gave him some antibiotics. They would have to wait until he gained a few pounds before giving him his vaccinations.

During the next few weeks they threw all their efforts into caring for the pup, working out a schedule so that at least one of them would be available to feed him on time. That resulted in Jake being at Holly's apartment quite a few times just at mealtime. She couldn't let him go hungry, so she made enough food for two and they consumed it, each secretly cherishing the time they spent together.

"We need to think of a name for the puppy," she announced one day.

"Yes, I guess we can't just keep calling him 'Pup.' What do you suggest?" Jake asked.

They went through a list of names, some funny, and some discarded as being just plain ridiculous. Finally, one night they hit on a name they both liked.

"What about Duke?" Holly inquired.

"Why Duke?" he asked.

"Oh, I don't know. I just think it suits him. He'll be a big dog some day and he deserves a name to go with his potential size."

"Okay. I like it, so Duke it will be," he agreed.

By that time the betting pool had gone through the roof. Then, to no one's surprise, Jake finally asked her out on an official date one night. Oh, it was nothing spectacular, just a movie, one of those romantic comedies women love so much.

That was the beginning of their real courtship, which ended in a storybook wedding with the whole police force attending. Jake and Holly never found out about the bet, which had been won by Officer Bowman, but a new betting pool was started on when the couple would be visited by the stork.

The next few years flew by, with Jake being blissfully happy and almost unable to believe his good fortune in finding such a beautiful wife. Before he knew it, he was the proud father of a son they decided to name Cody. Holly was a wonderful mother and their family seemed almost too good to be true.

It was then tragedy struck one day while he was out of town attending a police convention in the state capitol. He got a call to come back home immediately for an emergency situation, but nobody would tell him what was going on. It wasn't until he arrived back in town he got the devastating news that Holly had been shot and killed in the line of duty. How such a thing could happen in their little peaceful town was hard to comprehend, but she had been the victim of a drug bust gone wrong. The boy who wouldn't cry finally did. He had been inconsolable in his grief. Even now, he could hardly bear to think about it.

That's why he was so surprised he even noticed how attractive his new neighbor was. *Did an unexpected sudden interest in a woman mean he was finally getting over Holly?* he wondered. It was something he would have to give careful thought to, he decided, as he went back to completing his Saturday household chores.

###

Across town in the local real estate office, Mrs. Laura Hawthorne was at her desk, finishing up the details of her most recent sale of an older house to a beautiful newcomer to the town. It had taken all her efforts and her best sales pitch to convince the lady to buy it. Heck, she had even had to eat the closing costs herself, but it just might be worth it, she thought. If her instincts were right, and they usually were, Jillian O'Reilly was the answer to her prayers. This was the woman who was going to pull her son out of his depression.

Oh, she had no doubt sparks would soon be flying between the two families. Jillian had mentioned she owned a cat, and her son was an avowed dog lover. She knew if there was one thing he couldn't abide, it was cats. Jillian had shown her a picture of her little girl, who was just the same age as her grandson, Cody. He had been so lonely ever since his mom had died. It was about time he got a new playmate.

She and her husband, William, had moved out of their house and into a condominium several years ago. They had sold their old home place to Jake and Holly after Cody was born.

"Every little boy needs a yard to play in," she had told Jake, "And think about your dog, too. He can't stay cooped up in an apartment all the time."

So, the moves had been made, much to everyone's satisfaction. It did her heart good to know Jake's old tree house might be put to use again one day.

She knew it wasn't a matter of if, but when, the two new neighbors would meet. The hardest part was done, she told herself. All she needed to do was sit back and let nature take its course.

###

During the next few weeks, Jillian threw herself wholeheartedly into her schoolwork. It was a full-time job, just learning about her students and trying to keep one step ahead of them in her lesson plans. Teaching proved to be much more tedious and time-consuming that she had thought it would be.

Megan and Cody were classmates in kindergarten, she learned on the first day of school when she had bumped into Jake as he was dropping his son off on his way to work. He smiled at her and gave her a friendly greeting, but she responded rather coolly to his "Good morning, Mrs. O'Reilly." *Just see if she ever warmed up to a dog lover*, she vowed.

Then came the first PTA meeting for the purpose of planning the annual fall festival. It was one of the major money-making events for the school. Jillian attended out of necessity, as the presence of all faculty members was expected. She was surprised to see Jake walk through the door. She wasn't the only one who was surprised. Men were usually as scarce as a hen's teeth when it came to PTA meetings, her fellow teacher, Elizabeth Peterman, informed her in a loud whisper.

When it was time to assign committees for the event, Jillian didn't know what to volunteer for. As she was pondering the situation, her train of thought was interrupted by the sound of her principal's voice.

"Mrs. O'Reilly, why don't you and Mr. Hawthorne work together on the dunking booth?"

"Well, I don't know," Jillian replied uncertainly.

"I happen to know Jake has some very fine carpentry skills. I'm sure you'll work well together since you both have children in kindergarten," said the principal, Mrs. Caroline Stewart.

Jillian and Jake both found themselves blushing, but they reluctantly agreed to the assignment. Each of them wondered if they could possibly get along with someone who owned an animal they couldn't abide. They made plans to meet at a later date to discuss the details of their committee assignment.

When the meeting was adjourned, Mrs. Caroline Stewart just smiled to herself. She hadn't been friends with Laura Hawthorne over twenty years for nothing. When Laura had called her for a favor, she had been most happy to oblige. Those two young people belonged together. They just didn't know it yet!

###

The following Saturday, Jillian was awakened by the ringing of the telephone. She had slept past her usual time of arising. Teaching inquisitive fourth graders had completely exhausted her. She peered at the Caller I. D. with one eye closed, wondering who could possibly be calling since she didn't know many of the townspeople.

She groaned when she discovered the caller to be none other than her neighbor Jake Hawthorne. She supposed she had better answer it, as she had promised to work with him on that blasted dunking booth. *Confound it all, did the project have to start so early in the morning?*

"Hello," she said, speaking into the receiver as she tried to stifle a huge yawn.

"Mrs. O'Reilly? I hope I didn't wake you up. This is your neighbor Jake Hawthorne."

"Oh, no, that's quite all right, Mr. Hawthorne," she replied, trying unconvincingly to sound wide awake. "What can I do for you?"

"I wanted to check with you on the dunking booth. We really need to get started on it if we're going to have it finished in time for the festival. I believe we had an appointment to work together today."

"Yes, yes, we did. I remember now," she responded as she sat up in the bed. "There's just one more detail we forgot to work out, though. What about the children? Won't they be in the way if we're sawing and hammering all those boards together?"

Jake chuckled. "I've come up with the perfect solution to that problem. My mother has volunteered to babysit for us. She loves children and they always have a great time at her house. So, if it's okay with you, Megan and Cody can stay with her while we work on the booth."

"Well, if you're sure she won't mind."

"No, she's looking forward to it. Just have Megan dressed and Mom will pick her up at your front door. How soon can she be ready?"

"Give us half an hour and we'll be good to go," Jillian promised.

True to her word, Jillian had Megan dressed and waiting at the door when Mrs. Hawthorne arrived. They had wolfed down a hasty breakfast of cold cereal and milk, Megan's favorite. Megan offered little protest when Jillian informed her that she was to spend the day with Cody. In fact, she seemed almost too eager to go, making Jillian wonder what those two children had been up to when they were together at school.

But she didn't have time to think about that. She splashed water on her face, applied the scantest hint of makeup, and ran a comb through her hair, tying it into a loose ponytail. *After all, a girl still had her pride,* she reasoned, *even if the work might prove to be a hot and sweaty ordeal.* She then donned her oldest pair of jeans and a faded plaid shirt, which she tied into a knot at the waist.

She walked out the front door and over to Jake Hawthorne's house, pausing on the front porch to ring the doorbell. From the inside, she could hear the sound of a dog barking. She had almost forgotten about the dog, which appeared to be the size of a small pony. Almost in a panic, she turned to leave just as the door opened.

"Ah, Mrs. O'Reilly, come in," said Jake. "Since we're going to be working together, shall we get on a first name basis? You can just call me Jake."

"Well, I suppose that would be okay, Jake," she replied as she stepped cautiously into the foyer. "And you can call me Jillian. Did I hear a dog barking?" She looked around nervously, scanning all the doorways for the dreaded dog.

"Oh, that's just Duke. As the old saying goes, his bark is worse than his bite. He's really just a big baby at heart. I'm afraid he was spoiled rotten when he was a puppy."

As Jake was speaking, Duke bounded into the foyer. Apparently overjoyed to see a guest, he headed straight for Jillian. She shrieked as she backed into the door, which Jake had closed behind her.

"Please, get him away from me. I'm afraid of dogs," she pleaded.

"Afraid of dogs! You've got to be kidding! You're talking about man's best friend," Jake exclaimed.

Jillian made no reply, but she stood trembling, with eyes full of unshed tears, a point which did not escape Jake's notice.

"Say, you really are afraid, aren't you?" he said gently. "Just hold on, and I'll shut Duke up in the basement. He won't like it, but he'll be fine." He grabbed Duke by the collar as he spoke and began leading him out of the room. "Come on, boy. Let's get you a bite of food."

Duke seemed to understand there was some sort of reward awaiting him if he followed his master, so he offered little resistance. Next to chasing cats, eating was his favorite pastime.

Jake re-entered the room minutes later to find Jillian still backed against the door. She was still trembling, and all the color had left her face. He could see it was going to take some work to get this woman even halfway accustomed to dogs.

"Okay, Duke's all tucked away safely. You have nothing to worry about," he reassured her. "Let's go into the den, and I'll show you the plans I have sketched out. Then we can get started on the actual work. This is going to take quite a bit of time, so I hope you have several Saturdays free."

"Free Saturdays are no problem for me, but what about your wife? Won't she be upset with you being busy every weekend?" Jillian asked, as she made her way to the sofa and perched nervously on the edge of one of the cushions.

"There is no wife. I'm a widower," he replied.

"I'm sorry to hear that."

"That brings us to another question. What will your husband think about your spending so much time with another man?" he inquired.

"My husband passed away some time ago. He was killed in an auto accident," she said.

"Now it's my turn to say, 'I'm sorry,'" he apologized. "I guess that explains why you moved to another town."

"Yes. Yes, it does. Now what about those plans?" she asked, changing the subject.

Jake proceeded to show her the sketches, which were quite detailed. He had apparently thought of everything.

"I didn't realize you knew so much about carpentry," she exclaimed as she examined the sketches. "Are you sure we'll be able to finish it in time? Perhaps we need to get some other parents involved."

"No, I work better alone, or with just one helper. Too many cooks spoil the stew," he said, quoting an old adage.

A few minutes later, Jillian found herself inside a large workshop that was located in Jake's backyard. It was equipped with every sort of tool imaginable, most of which she couldn't even identify.

"This was my dad's workshop when I was growing up. My interest in carpentry began when I was just eight years old. My two best friends and I built the tree house in that large sycamore over in the corner," he explained.

Jillian eyed the somewhat dilapidated tree house that was partially covered with vines.

"It looks like it has seen better days," she observed.

"Yes, but I have been intending to fix it up for Cody. He's been bugging me about it. I just haven't had time to get around to it yet."

"What's that sign I see hanging on the front? I can't quite make out the lettering from here."

"Oh, it's really nothing. Just some fool idea that we kids had," he replied, sincerely hoping she couldn't make out the "No Girls Allowed."

"Well, we'd better get started on this booth if we're going to be finished on time," he noted, relieved when she turned her attention away from the yard and back to the task at hand.

They spent the next several hours engrossed in the project until they both realized they were getting hungry. Jillian offered to run home and make some sandwiches while Jake searched through his pantry for some chips and colas.

When she re-entered through the kitchen door, triumphantly holding a plate of sandwiches, he remembered sharing those first meals with Holly as they were caring for Duke. He quickly brushed the thoughts from his mind because it hurt too much to even think about those happy times.

Jillian seemed to sense his change of mood but wisely said nothing. She knew what it was like to be lonely, and he had that far-away look in his eyes. *He had to be remembering his wife*, she reasoned.

They continued working through the afternoon, measuring, and sawing boards and labeling them as to their location on the booth. Jake had come up with the perfect plan. They would cut the boards and other parts in the workshop and then assemble it on a trailer he had borrowed and stored in his garage. The finished booth would then be ready to be hauled to the festival, where it would slide off onto the ground.

As the sun began to sink in the west, they both noticed that the hours had passed rather quickly, and they were surprised to see it was nearing suppertime. Not once had the topic of dogs and cats come up in their conversation, but by the end of the day they both knew more about the person they were working with. Each of them was busy digesting the information, although they were reluctant to admit it.

"Well, I guess I had better call Mom to deliver those two kids back home to us," he said. "We've made good progress and you have been a great helper. Let's plan to meet again next Saturday."

"Okay, same time, same place. I'll be here," Jillian half-joked as she spoke.

Jake couldn't help but notice how pretty she was when she smiled. And when she wasn't chewing him out or backed up against a door, half-scared out of her wits. He was beginning to suspect there was a plot afloat to throw them together, spearheaded by his mom, no doubt. But she was a cat owner, and he couldn't abide the creatures. This was going to require some thought on his part, he decided.

Jillian had been trying all afternoon to avoid looking at those muscles rippling beneath his tee shirt as he worked. Plus, the way his eyes lit up when he spoke of Cody signified his great love for the boy. Still, he was the owner of one of the largest dogs she had ever seen. There was no getting around that and she was deathly afraid of dogs, no matter who their owner might be. *Why did life always have to be so complicated?* she wondered?

###

They continued working together on the dunking booth over the next few weeks, feeling they were making excellent progress. It was almost to the point of being finished just in time for the festival.

Jillian was still no more comfortable around Duke than when she had first entered the Hawthorne residence, so he was shut in the basement every time she came over. Jake was hoping to make some progress along those lines, but he realized that such a deep fear could take some time to overcome.

Jillian was continuing to get settled into her new home. She ordered the swing set for Megan. To her surprise, Jake volunteered to help her assemble it. They didn't have any spare time on the weekends due to the dunking booth project, so they worked on the swing set late in the afternoons when they both got off work.

Not wanting to impose on Mrs. Hawthorne for babysitting duties, she insisted on stationing the children in her den to watch TV while she and Jake worked. The sound of the children's laughter was a welcome relief from the almost tomb-like silence she had grown accustomed to following Doug's death. *It was about time for Megan to have fun again,* she decided.

###

The swing set and the dunking booth were both completed just before the fall festival, with barely enough time to test out the mechanics of the booth, using a sack of rocks as a dummy weight. There was much joking between Jake and Jillian as to who would be the one to sit on the chair of the dunking booth.

"There's no way you're getting me into a bikini in front of all those students," she informed him.

"I guess that means it's up to me to serve as the target. Let's just hope it's a warm night because that water is going to be pretty cold," he reluctantly noted.

"Don't worry. I'll have lots of towels handy," she teased. "Maybe most of the men will be really bad throwers."

"I wouldn't count on it. Most of the police force will come just to try and dunk me," he lamented.

"As long as it raises money for the school, it's worth it," she replied.

###

On the night of the festival, Megan excitedly dressed in her costume.

She had decided to be a fairy. Jillian thought her daughter had never looked cuter than she did wearing that little ruffled pink net dress and carrying her shiny "magic wand" with a silver tip.

Jillian had chosen to dress as a witch, wondering how many of her students might think she had chosen an appropriate costume. Megan informed her that she looked plenty scary as she topped off her stringy witch's hair with a pointed black hat.

They were riding with Jake and Cody, so Jillian was rushing around, determined to be on time. The doorbell rang promptly at 6:15 p.m. and she opened it to come face to face with Cody, who was dressed as a pirate. He was apparently relishing the role as he sported an eye patch and waved a fake plastic sword that was rounded at the tip for safety.

"I'm going as a surfer," Jake joked as they climbed into his SUV. "There's no point in my dressing up, as I have to strip down to a bathing suit for the dunking booth."

"Well, you got your wish for a warm night," Jillian observed. "And I brought plenty of towels for you, too."

"Thanks, you're a real pal," he retorted, laughing as he spoke.

True to his prediction, Jake spent a large part of the night in the water, using up all the towels Jillian had managed to scrape together for the event. He was a good sport about it, Jillian noted. She had great fun recruiting potential dunkers and collecting money for the booth. She couldn't help but marvel at his excellent physique. She didn't get many chances to admire males in bathing suits anymore. She might as well enjoy the view, she thought.

Jake was busy doing some admiring of his own. Although her curves were amply covered with the witch's costume, he still had plenty of time to watch her in action as she laughingly waylaid people passing by, enticing them to try just one shot at the target. She was quite a salesperson with her twinkling eyes and musical laughter that reached up all the way to his seat high above the water. It was a much different picture from that first day they met when she had just about eaten him alive as she chewed him out about his dog. *If only she could overcome her fear of Duke, they could have so much fun together,* he pondered.

Their dunking booth proved to be the hit of the night when the money was counted at the end of the festival. It had brought in more cash than any of the other events. Mrs. Caroline Stewart was both excited and pleased at such results. The festival money would go a long way toward buying new playground equipment, she informed them.

Megan and Cody were all giggles on the way home, making Jillian once again wonder what they had been plotting.

"You two certainly are a barrel of laughs tonight," Jake commented.

"Oh, it's probably just all of that extra sugar, plus the excitement. I'm sure they'll be fine in the morning," Jillian observed, sincerely hoping she was right and that it was nothing more. She was thankful the following day was a Saturday morning, and she would be able to catch up on some much-needed rest.

When they arrived back at their two houses shortly afterwards, Jake and Cody insisted on walking the girls to their front door.

"We're gentlemen, you know," Jake teased.

"Yeah, we're gentlemen," Cody echoed.

The two children had become friends during their parents' working sessions as both the swing set and the dunking booth were completed. Cody had been fascinated with Snowball, and he had timidly learned how to pet her as they watched TV in Jillian's den.

Likewise, Megan had become acquainted with Duke when Cody secretly led her to the basement while Jake and Jillian were totally absorbed in their tasks in the workshop.

Although she was scared at first, she soon found Duke to be a friendly dog who appreciated having his ears scratched. She somehow sensed that mentioning her contact with Duke to her mother would result in a severe scolding, so she kept mum about the whole affair.

The children had quickly learned that the fastest way to visit each other's yard was through the hole in the hedge. Cody had joined Megan in playing on her new swing set. The had also traipsed around Cody's backyard, exploring all the nooks and crannies and trying out his tire swing. He had pointed out the old tree house and proudly informed Megan it was now his.

"My daddy is going to fix it up for me," he told her.

"What's it like up there?" she wondered.

"I don't know. I've never been up there, but it would be fun to look at it. Maybe we can climb up there sometime and see," he said.

"I don't think my mama would like that. She's always worried that something will happen to me," she mused.

"Well, if she doesn't know, she won't worry," he observed.

"I guess we could climb up and look and come back down," Megan decided.

"Okay, but we have to do it when our mama and daddy won't see us," said Cody. "I know. Let's climb up there for a picnic. Can you make sandwiches?"

"I can do peanut butter and jelly," she replied.

"Okay, you make them, and I can get some bottles of water from our pantry. We'll go up there after the school party. They'll be tired then, so they won't care if we go outside and play," he said.

True to their plans, the children arose early on the Saturday following the festival. Both parents were still sleeping, tired to the bone from the previous week's busier-than-usual activities. Megan managed to make the sandwiches, as promised, leaving tell-tale signs of her task behind in the kitchen sink. She spotted her mother's red-and-white checked picnic cloth when she opened a cabinet door looking for some plastic sandwich bags. Mama always joked it wasn't a picnic without that cloth, so she tucked it into her backpack along with the sandwiches. Cody located the bottles of water and put them in his backpack along with a bag of chips and a couple of candy bars. Both children were feeling rather proud of themselves, as they managed to sneak out of their houses without making enough noise to rouse their parents.

There was one unforeseen glitch in their plans. Just as Megan opened the door to go outside, Snowball managed to slip past her and darted out towards the birdfeeder. Megan knew she had to try to get the cat back inside, but Snowball refused to cooperate and ran even further into the yard when she was called. Megan chased her all the way to the big oak tree, but Snowball managed to evade her again and scrambled up onto a branch that was out of Megan's reach.

Just about that time, Cody poked his head through the hole in the shrubs.

"What's taking you so long?" he called softly, still aware of the sleeping parents in both households.

"It's Snowball," Megan answered. "She got out and now I can't catch her."

"So why don't you just leave the back door open a little bit and maybe she'll go back into the house?" Cody suggested.

"I guess that might be okay," she agreed.

They searched around the yard for something to prop the door open and found a loose brick lining one of the flowerbeds.

"This might work," said Cody, as he lifted the brick from the border. He carried it to Megan's back door. Together they managed to prop the door open just wide enough for Snowball to fit through whenever she took a notion to come down from the tree.

"Come on. We'd better hurry before our mama and daddy get up," he said.

They scooted through the familiar opening in the hedge and headed for the sycamore that held the old tree house. The wooden strips Jake had nailed to the tree as steps years ago were still in place, although some of them were a little crooked after years of exposure to the weather. Megan eyed them doubtfully.

"I don't know if I can climb that high," she told Cody.

"Oh, it's easy. I'll go first. You can just follow me," he assured her as he adjusted his backpack more securely. "It'll be fun. You'll see. I'll bet we can see over into your yard from up there."

"Okay, if you say so, but you have to go first. What if there are spiders up there? I don't like spiders."

"Oh, don't be such a scaredy-cat. If we see any spiders, I'll stomp on them," he declared, demonstrating his stomping skills, much to Megan's delight.

Megan watched as he slowly climbed up onto the old strips. The tree house was starting to look a lot higher than she had thought it would be. He made it to the top and crawled in through the opening. It was no small task, as vines were now covering most of the outside of the tree house.

"Okay, your turn. Come on, you can do it," he called down to her.

She took a deep breath as she put her foot on the first step. Mama always said it helped to do that when you were scared. If Cody made it to the top, she could, too. She wasn't about to be outdone by any old boy!

Several minutes and a few splinters later, she arrived at the opening, although it had taken quite a bit of coaxing on Cody's part to get her all the way to the top.

"Don't look down," he had wisely instructed, a warning she was glad to heed.

They were almost ecstatic about their accomplishment of making it all the way up into the tree house. They stood at the windows, pushing the vines aside so they could see out.

"I told you we could see your yard," Cody almost crowed. "Look, there's Snowball still in the tree."

"I see her," Megan exclaimed.

"Let's pretend we're pirates, and this is our ship," Cody suggested.

Megan agreed, and they spent quite a bit of time engrossed in that game until they both realized they were getting hungry. Then they spread the picnic cloth and sat down to devour the sandwiches and chips.

"What time is it, I wonder," Megan said as she washed down a sandwich with some of the water supplied by Cody.

"I don't know, but I guess we had better go back down pretty soon," he replied. "That way our mama and daddy won't know we came up here."

"Yeah, they might get pretty mad if they found out," Megan agreed.

"Okay, I'll go down first," Cody volunteered as they picked up the cloth and the remains of the picnic feast.

He stepped out onto the wooden strips and started to make his way down when one of them gave way beneath his feet. He managed to hold on and pulled himself back up into the tree house. Both children stared down at the broken strip as the seriousness of their situation began to dawn on them.

"Now what are we supposed to do?" Megan asked.

"We could try yelling for help," said Cody. "Maybe somebody will hear us."

"Help, help!" They called out for what seemed almost an eternity, but there was no response to their cries. It was just about that time they noticed the wind starting to blow, and the sky was getting darker, too.

"I think it's going to rain," Megan observed.

"It's okay. "We'll be all right, said Cody, as he tried to appear brave. He couldn't let a girl see he was scared.

Both children were startled by a sudden rustling sound beneath them and then Snowball appeared at the edge of the tree house. She jumped in and began to make herself right at home, rubbing against Megan's legs.

"Snowball, you've been a bad cat again. You were supposed to go back into the house." Megan scolded her.

"As long as she's up here, she might as well stay," Cody decided.

The wind picked up speed, shaking the limbs against the roof of the old tree house. Lightning flashed, and the rain started to pelt the sides of the house. The wind whipped the vines back into place, covering the windows. The children cringed back against one of the solid walls, clinging to each other for moral support.

"I'm getting cold," Megan complained.

"Let's use your tablecloth for a cover," Cody suggested.

They pulled it out of Megan's backpack and snuggled under it with Snowball right in the middle. Somehow, the warmth of the cat seemed to comfort them. They were growing tired from all the excitement and from arising so early in the morning. Despite the noise from the storm, both children were soon sound asleep, totally oblivious to the dangers around them.

Jillian was awakened by the sounds of the approaching storm. She was used to Megan arising early on Saturdays to watch the morning cartoons. Megan could help herself to some cold cereal and milk if she got hungry before her mother got up, which was often the case.

Jillian wandered downstairs, expecting to see Megan in the den watching TV. Instead, she found the room dark and the back door propped open. *What in the world was going on now?* she wondered. It was about that time she spotted the dribbles of jelly and peanut butter in the sink. *What would possess Megan to make a sandwich at this time of day?*

She walked to the back door and found it propped partway open with the brick left by the children. This was all too strange. Something was up. She peered outside, sure that Megan would head in as the rain began to pour down. What she saw was an empty yard with no sign of her daughter. Snowball was nowhere to be seen, either, she observed.

Maybe Megan had gone to the Hawthorne's house to play with Cody. There had been a lot of giggling on the way home, she remembered. She had suspected something was afoot then, but she couldn't put her finger on just what it was.

She picked up the phone and dialed Jake's number.

"Hello," Jake answered sleepily.

"Hi, Jake. It's Jillian. I'm trying to find Megan. Is she over at your house?" she inquired, secretly enjoying the fact that she was waking him up this time.

"I don't know. Let me go into the den and check," he replied as he crawled out of bed.

She waited impatiently for several minutes until he came back on the line. "No, she's not here, and I can't find Cody either," he reported, his voice tinged with worry.

"What do you mean you can't find him? They have to be here somewhere," she insisted, her voice rising a notch, betraying her innermost fear that someday her daughter, too, might be lost to her.

"Calm down. We'll find them. Remember, I'm a cop," he reassured her.

By that time, the storm had hit in full force with the rain coming down in heavy sheets. Jake donned his rain gear and braved the elements, searching both yards and calling the children's names over and over. Jillian stood in the doorway, watching as he slipped and slid through her yard. She couldn't even hear what he was saying with the wind blowing so hard.

Minutes later he entered her doorway, water dripping from his hat and rain slicker.

"No luck," he informed her. "But don't worry. I'm about to get the whole police force involved. Those kids have got to be somewhere around here."

Jillian burst into tears. "What if they've run away or were kidnapped? I've already lost my husband. I can't lose Megan, too!" she blubbered as she spoke.

"There, there," he said, patting her shoulder awkwardly. "We'll find them. Just let me use your phone."

Shortly afterwards the whole street was lined with police cars sporting enough red and blue flashing lights to set off a Fourth of July parade. Jake was a favorite among all the department employees, and they weren't about to let anything happen to his son. If those children were anywhere in the vicinity, they would be found!

Duke, who had been locked inside the Hawthorne house, sensed the excitement and began to bark loudly. He scratched frantically at the screen door in an effort to get out.

The noise was almost more than Jillian could bear. Not only was her daughter missing, but she was being bombarded with the sounds of that dreadful dog's howling. *Could nobody shut him up?* she wondered.

"Jake, please. Can't you make that dog stop barking?" she pleaded.

Jake trotted back to his house and opened the screen door. Before he could say a word, Duke burst through the opening and headed straight for the sycamore. He parked himself beneath it and began to howl as if his life depended on it.

"What's gotten into that dog?" Jake exclaimed.

It was just about that time he noticed something was not right about that sycamore. There was definitely something different about the old tree house, but what?

Before he could determine exactly what it was, two heads poked through the vines covering the windows. It was Cody and Megan! They were safe! Relief flooded through his veins.

Jillian, who had followed him, was watching from the front corner of the hedge. She rushed into the yard as soon as she spotted the two children. Laughing and crying at the same time, she flung her arms around Jake's neck, hugging him tightly. He instinctively hugged her back and kissed her, almost without realizing it. She had run outside with no rain gear on and was soaking wet. Her hair was plastered to her head with water dripping from in in rivulets. She didn't seem to care. All she wanted was her baby back safe and sound!

Jake summoned his fellow officers. "Here, they're over here," he shouted.

A crowd soon gathered at the foot of the tree. Jake's extension ladder was fetched from his garage and one of his fellow officers volunteered to climb up and bring the children down.

Jake took off his rain slicker and draped it across Jillian's shoulders. They stood together, Jake gripping her tightly as they awaited their reunion with the two children.

Megan was brought down first and placed into her mother's arms. Cody soon followed.

"Hey, there's a white cat up here," the officer yelled down to the waiting crowd. What do you want me to do about it?"

"Bring her down. She's part of the family," Jake responded, almost unable to believe he had actually said that about a cat.

Snowball was hauled down the ladder and deposited at Jillian's feet. Perhaps it was the trauma of the whole scene, or maybe it was the rain. Whatever the reason, Snowball didn't run away. She crouched by her mistress's feet and appeared to be perfectly content to remain there, despite her bedraggled appearance as her fur quickly became drenched.

Duke was almost beside himself with excitement as the children were rescued. He bestowed kisses on the faces of both Megan and Cody. Snowball was his next target, and she didn't move when he licked her squarely on the nose. He then headed for Jillian and somehow managed to place a wet, sloppy kiss right on her cheek. She didn't even flinch.

"Daddy, are we in trouble?" Cody inquired worriedly.

Jake looked at Jillian for a cue. She had set Megan back on her feet. Megan was standing with Snowball in her arms, and Jillian had her hand on Duke's neck.

"Good dog," she whispered.

Duke was gazing up at Jillian with what was as close to an awestruck look as a dog could muster.

"No, son. I'd say everything is just about right with the world," Jake replied as he rubbed Duke's ears, keeping his eyes on Jillian the whole time. Jillian slowly moved her hand upwards toward Duke's head and Jake grasped it tightly with his own.

"Do you really think we can make it work? You, me, and the animals?" she asked.

"I know we can, baby. I've never been surer of anything in my life," Jake responded.

Before he knew it, she was back in his arms and they were kissing again. Cheers broke out among the crowd. Megan and Cody exchanged high-fives, giggling as they began to dance in front of the couple. Duke excitedly ran in circles around them, barking the entire time.

The only quiet one in the whole place was Snowball, who had taken refuge in the shrubs after being plopped back onto the ground by Megan. She viewed the scene disdainfully with unblinking eyes. She was reserving judgment about her new family and the gigantic dog until later. Much later.

###

Part IV

"Mr. Perfect"

Luci's Story

Mr. Perfect

Luci Carlito sat behind the steering wheel and glared across the seat through the passenger-side window as she viewed the ramrod-straight figure of a man walking briskly away from her taxicab. Sparks almost shot from her dark brown eyes as she felt an angry flush creep slowly up her neck and into her cheeks, adding even more color to her deeply tanned olive complexion.

"Wait for me and keep the air conditioning running," he had told her. "I like my ride cool whenever I'm paying the bill."

"Keep the air conditioning running," she mimicked into the mirror as she resisted the urge to stick her tongue out at him. *Who does he think he is, anyhow? Doesn't he know running an engine costs money?* She made it a point to never run the air conditioner unless a fare was actually in the cab. The business was operating on a shoestring as it was.

She studied the departing figure now entering a six-story building. *Does the man ever get a wrinkle in his clothes? Mr. Perfect, that's who he is. Never late, never wrinkled, never nervous. I'll bet he never even gets a five o'clock shadow.* She squinched her eyes tightly, trying to picture even the faintest hint of such a shadow in the cleft of that perfectly chiseled chin. Against her will, the rest of the face floated into the picture – piercing blue eyes set in a strong, square face that was topped with a head of curly black hair. *Oh, botheration! Why do I always have to get stuck with him as fare?*

She absentmindedly tucked a strand of her brunette hair back under the cap she wore whenever she was driving one of her father's cabs – an attempt to disguise the fact that she was a female. Life was so much easier for men, she had decided. No use inviting trouble by revealing her curvaceous figure to anyone who happened to hail her cab. Baggy clothes and a ball cap with her long hair pinned underneath seemed to solve the problem.

She talked as little as possible to her passengers, usually just responding with only a curt nod. The fare was posted automatically on the meter, so she didn't even have to tell them how much it was. She just held out her hand across the back of the seat, and the money was usually deposited in it, hopefully with a "Keep the change" as a courtesy tip. So far, her plan seemed to be working.

###

Jeremy Clark grinned to himself as he walked away from the taxi. He had gotten her goat, and he knew it. Yes, she was trying to pass herself off as a man, but there was no way a man could ever have such ridiculously long lashes and such gorgeously full lips that begged to be kissed. Oh, he would let her continue her little charade – at least for the time being.

He had watched her struggle to load his bags into the taxi yesterday when she had picked him up from the airport. It had taken all his self-control to resist helping her lift them into the trunk. Something about the set of that beautiful jaw sent forth a message that she was a force not to be reckoned with. That's what made teasing her so much fun.

His erect posture and impeccable grooming were carryovers from the years he had spent as a pilot in the U. S. Air Force. He had planned on making it a lifetime career, but a bout with malaria had left him with unpredictable attacks of chills and fever. Flying a plane with those symptoms was definitely an unsafe undertaking, so he had opted for an honorable discharge and vowed to seek his fortune elsewhere.

The perfect opportunity arose when his father had decided to step down as the CEO of Futures Unlimited, an investment company the family owned, leaving the door open for Jeremy to assume that position. He had a natural knack for picking just the right projects, and a few college courses in business, marketing, and economics had given him the background he needed to assume full control of the company. No business was too big or too small for consideration. The main qualification was he had to have faith in the project's ability to make a profit.

Traveling had become a way of life for him, and this small, somewhat sleepy town had beckoned to him like a lighthouse beam on a foggy night. It was the suburb of a much larger city, and people were beginning to move here to escape the problems of city life. It was the perfect time to cash in on some financial opportunities, and that was just what he intended to do. He saw no use in owning a car, as he usually flew from one destination to another. Taking a taxi was the most convenient way to get around. Besides, the drivers knew their way about, saving him much-needed time. It wasn't until he came to the little town of Summerfield that he hit the jackpot of taxicab drivers when he hailed cab number two of the On Your Way Taxi Company with Luci at the wheel. After that, he always requested cab number two whenever he phoned for a taxi.

###

Luci was definitely not in the happiest time of her life. She had been enrolled in her senior year at the local college and was planning to become a lawyer. She was to be the first person in her family to obtain a college degree. That had all changed when she received an urgent phone call one night from her sister-in-law, Terri.

Her brother, Anthony, had fallen from a ladder and broken his leg while remodeling the house he and Terri had bought. That meant he could not drive cab number two of her papa's taxicab fleet. Owning his own cab company had always been one of Papa D'armon's dreams. He had driven cabs owned by other people for years, and it was time for a fifty-year-old man to be his own boss, he told the family. Two cabs didn't provide much of an income, but it was a start. They needed every fare they could get, and without Anthony to drive the second cab, the business would go under.

There had never been a question in Luci's mind of what she had to do. She couldn't let Papa down. Not Papa, who had sacrificed so much to put her through college. She wouldn't lose the credits she had already earned, and there was always next year. Never mind that she wouldn't be there to graduate with all of her friends. The family had always stuck together through both happy times and hardships. She wasn't about to leave them hanging!

So, here she sat in cab number two, waiting for a fare who positively irritated her to no end. Oh, it wasn't that he was impolite. Just the opposite – he was Mr. Manners personified. Maybe that was what she found so annoying about him. Or maybe it was just his good looks. It was so unfair for someone to be so polite, good-looking, and obviously rich while she sat in the cab day after day in her baggy clothes and ball cap. *When will it all end?* she wondered. *And how would it all end?*

The one bright spot of the day for the entire family was gathering at the dinner table for their traditional Italian meals. Her mother, Rosa, was an excellent cook, having learned all the recipes firsthand from her own mother. Mama Rosa was a born optimist who believed that any problem was better solved on a full stomach, preferably one filled with Italian food.

There was never a lack of pasta topped with Mama special sauce from their own family recipe. The all loved her meatballs, chicken Marsala, lasagna, ravioli, veal Parmesan, and baked four-cheese manicotti. She always made her own bread every day, as it quickly disappeared as soon as the breadbasket hit the table. She didn't make desserts very often, but when she did, they were delicious. Nothing could compare to her Italian crème cake, another old secret family recipe.

Luci's mouth was almost watering, just thinking about the food that would be waiting at the end of her shift. She certainly hoped Mr. Perfect wouldn't take too long in his meeting. She was ready for this day to end!

To her relief, he exited the building in less than an hour and got back into the cab with instructions to drive him to his hotel. She didn't have to ask which one, as there was only one in their small town.

When they arrived at the hotel, she held her hand over the back of the seat, as usual, to collect the fare. He slowly placed the bills into her hand. Then he surprised her with a question that caught her totally off guard.

"Thanks for the ride, Miss. By the way, what's your name so I'll know what to call you the next time I catch your cab."

"It's not 'Miss,'" she snapped. "You can just call me Lu. Do you think I would dress like this if I were a girl?"

"Sorry, *Lu*. My mistake," he said, emphasizing her name. "Actually, if you *were* a girl, I could picture you in one of those sexy little dancing dresses that women like to wear, preferably a red one. Yes, I think a little red dress would suit you just fine – if you were a girl, that is."

With that remark, he exited the cab and closed the door firmly behind him.

He knows! Drat it all, he knows I'm a female. Can any one person possibly be more annoying? What else is going to go wrong to spoil my day? Thank goodness, it's almost over, as he was my last fare. Now it's home to Mama and her wonderful cooking. I'm going to leave all my problems right here in this cab when I park it tonight, she decided.

Luci entered the house, greeted by the usual delicious smells of Mama's cooking. She could barely hear the drone of the family's chatter as she walked down the hall to change out of her manly disguise. It was always a relief to look like a girl again.

Sometime later, thoroughly refreshed from a quick shower and a change of clothes, she joined the rest of the family as they were seated around the dining table. Anthony and Terri had joined them tonight. Anthony sat with his broken leg propped up on one of the dining chairs.

"Hey, sis. Join the party," he said.

"Yeah, some party," grumbled Papa.

Everyone had a hangdog look somewhat akin to losing their best friend. Even Mama's spaghetti and meatballs sitting in the middle of the table didn't seem to cheer them up.

"What's the problem? I'm starving," Luci announced, as she reached for the breadbasket.

"You may soon be starving in a different way," Anthony told her.

"What do you mean? What's going on?" she inquired anxiously, as she paused with the breadbasket in mid-air.

"We just got the report back for the last quarter's earnings, and it's not good," Papa said sadly.

"Yes, we're losing money," Anthony added.

"What do you mean 'losing'? I thought our business was picking up. I know I've certainly been running the roads delivering fares all over town," Luci commented.

"You may have more fares, but the price of gasoline has gone up," Terri explained.

"Yes, and that means less profits for us. We have been barely getting by as is. I really wanted to own my own business, but I don't see how we can keep it going at this rate," said Papa. "Besides that, if anything happens to one of the cabs, it will be the end for us."

"Well, I know one thing. Problems cannot be solved on an empty stomach. Eat, eat, and then we think," exclaimed Mama, who could not bear to see her food go to waste.

With that remark, the family dug into the food, but only half-heartedly. Sometime later, with the table cleared and the dishes washed, a family meeting began in earnest.

"All right, I am the head of this family, but I cannot make a decision about the taxi company alone. It is our family business, so I need help from all of you in deciding what to do," Papa told them.

"We have to figure out a way to cut back on expenses," said Anthony.

"Well, let's see. We could increase the fares," Luci suggested.

"That won't work. Our competition won't raise their fares and we would just lose our customers," Papa observed.

"What about cutting our salaries?" asked Luci.

"We can't afford to do that," Terri protested. "There's something we haven't told you, but I guess this is the time. Anthony and I are going to have a baby, so we need all the money we can get."

"A baby! I'm going to be a grandmama," Mama exclaimed. "Did you hear that, Papa? We're going to be grandparents."

"Yes, yes, I heard, and I'm so proud. But we cannot get off the subject now. We still haven't decided what to do," said Papa.

"We need more efficient cabs," Anthony commented. "That would save on the gasoline bills."

"Yes, but the bank won't loan me any more money for that. The business just isn't profitable enough," Papa told them dejectedly.

"Then we'll just have to get more customers. Don't worry, Papa. We'll make it somehow. Anthony and I won't let you down," Luci stated determinedly.

With that remark, the family meeting ended. Anthony and Terri took their leave, and the other three family members adjourned to their rooms to try to get some sleep. It promised to be a restless night with the faltering taxi business on all their minds.

Jeremy had gone back to his room after being dropped off at the hotel. There was a dining room in the hotel, but he was getting tired of eating the same fare every time he came to town.

"Are there any other restaurants in this town?" he asked the desk clerk when he walked to the desk to check his messages.

"Well, there's McDonald's and Wendy's. We also have a Domino's pizza place," the clerk responded.

"What about a regular restaurant with family-type meals? Isn't there any place like that in this town?" Jeremy inquired.

"No, we used to have one, but this is a college town. Most of the kids prefer fast food, so it closed when the cook moved out of town and the owner couldn't find another one. I think the building is up for sale now," the clerk replied.

"Well, somebody should open a restaurant soon because this town is growing. You know, I think I've changed my mind about dinner. Just have a club sandwich and a glass of iced tea delivered to my room. I've got some business I need to take care of," he told the clerk.

He hurried back to his room and got out his laptop computer. *Okay, think real estate, Jeremy,* he instructed himself. *If that restaurant is for sale, it should be listed somewhere in the real estate ads for this town. You don't own any restaurants yet, but it's about time you started.*

The search proved successful, and he located the ad rather quickly. He vowed to call the owner the first thing in the morning. And even better, he would be sure to request cab number two for a ride to look over the place. Yes, this trip was going to be both profitable and interesting. He would sleep well tonight.

The Carlitos were up at dawn, as usual. They had all tossed and turned throughout the night, each with their own special worries about the company's lack of profits. Luci was feeling groggy and somewhat irritable due to the lack of sleep. Driving a taxi was becoming less and less appealing to her with each passing day.

Their breakfast was interrupted with a loud ringing of the telephone, as the calls from their office were forwarded to their house until they reported for work.

"I'll get it, Papa. Finish your breakfast. I'm not really hungry, anyhow," Lucy said as she jumped up to answer the phone.

"Hello. Yes, I understand. I'll be there shortly," she said as the family listened in on the one-sided conversation.

"Okay, Papa. Gotta go. That was a fare from the hotel. Mama, hand me one of those cinnamon rolls you just took out of the oven and a cup of coffee to go. I'll grab a bite while I'm driving," she told them.

"You eat like a bird. Pretty soon you'll be skinny like one, too," Mama protested as she handed over the food.

Luci exited through the back door and got into her cab that was parked in their driveway. It was easier to pick up early fares when they took the cabs home, something they had been doing ever since Papa started the business.

Now who could be requesting a cab at this time of the morning? There's hardly anything open for another hour. And from the hotel, too. I certainly hope it's not my favorite person, Mr. Perfect. That's exactly how I DON'T want to start my day, she pondered.

Within minutes she was pulling up in front of the hotel. To her dismay, there stood none other than Mr. Perfect. *Well, I see that luck is not going to be with me today.*

"Where to?" she asked as he entered the cab.

"Take me to the corner of Fifth Street and Elm," he instructed.

"Fifth and Elm. That's where an old restaurant is located, but it's not open now," she told him, talking more than usual to her fare.

"I know, but it's okay. I'm meeting the owner there. I might be interested in buying it if I can find a good cook," he replied.

Five minutes later she drove into the parking lot of the restaurant and brought the cab to a stop.

"Do I have to say it?" he inquired as he opened the cab door to exit. "Wait for me and…"

"…keep the air conditioning going." Luci finished the sentence for him.

This time he was gone longer than an hour, but he exited the restaurant wearing a smile.

"It's a done deal, Lu," he told her, as he re-entered the cab. "I'm now the proud owner of a family restaurant. Know where I can find a good cook?"

"I know lots of good cooks, but that doesn't mean they want to work in a restaurant," she replied, deciding it was no use to pretend with him any longer. Maybe a man who appreciated good food wasn't that bad.

"Now that I'm going to be an entrepreneur in this town, it's about time I took in the sights. How about driving me around town to some of the most interesting places?" he inquired.

"Fine. I grew up here, so I think I know just about everything there is to know about Summerfield," she replied.

They spent the next half-hour touring the town, with Luci pointing out the schools, several churches, the library, the courthouse, and the main cemetery. Just as they were about to head back to the hotel from the cemetery, the cab's engine began to sputter. Luci barely managed to pull over to the side of the road before it died completely.

"I'm so sorry," she exclaimed. "Our cabs are old, and I'm afraid they're down to their last spark plug. Let me radio the office for another cab to come and pick you up. Looks like this one will have to be towed."

She made the necessary call, and Papa arrived within minutes with a worried look on his face.

"It's bad, Papa. I can't even get the engine to turn over. We'll need a tow truck to get it back to the garage," she told him.

"Anthony is minding the office until his leg mends. Radio him and tell him to send a tow truck, and I will deliver Mr...."

"Clark, Jeremy Clark, sir."

"I will deliver Mr. Clark to his destination. You wait here and ride back in the tow truck."

"Not meaning to interfere, sir, but are sure it's safe to leave Lu here all alone?" Jeremy inquired.

"Oh, it's perfectly safe. We have a very low crime rate in this town. Besides, Bart, the tow truck driver, practically lived at our house while he was growing up. He'll be glad for a chance to catch up on what's been happening in our family," Papa said.

###

Luci viewed the back of the departing cab with disdain. It was not that she minded waiting for a tow truck, but did they have to call Bart, of all people? Bart and Anthony had been practically inseparable while they were growing up. He was even the best man in Anthony and Terri's wedding. She had grown to love him like a brother, but Bart had other ideas. He was positive she was the one and only woman for him, and he teasingly reminded her of it every chance he got. She didn't know how much longer she could keep stalling without deeply hurting him, something she was reluctant to do.

Bart arrived quickly, expertly backing the tow truck in front of the cab. He hopped out and hit the switch to lower the tow truck's bed for loading the cab.

"Hello, Sunshine. How's my beautiful girl today?" he inquired cheerfully.

"I'm not your girl, Bart. I have to keep telling you that," she reminded him.

"I know, but I have to keep trying. Give me a couple of minutes and we'll be ready to tow this baby home."

The ride home was filled with endless chatter, as Bart inquired about all the family members and wanted all the details about each one. He was delighted to hear Anthony and Terri were going to be parents.

"Wow, that means I'm almost an uncle," he exclaimed.

The conversation took a more serious tone as the pulled up to the garage where the Carlitos' taxi service was stationed.

"Luci, we really need to talk," he said.

"Not now, Bart. I can't talk about anything now. Papa may lose the taxi business if we can't get this cab fixed," she told him as she stepped out of the tow truck. Somehow, Mr. Perfect's face had floated back into her head on the way home. It was an image she couldn't seem to shake, no matter how hard she tried.

Jeremy's ride back to the motel had proven both interesting and informative. It had started with a question from Papa.

"Tell me something Mr. Clark. Why did you call my daughter Lu when her name is Luci?"

"Well, sir, that's what she told me to call her. I could see she is trying to pass herself off as a man, so I just went along with it."

"Oh, she's not a man. She's very much a girl, my Luci. I tried to tell her about that disguise, but she just keeps on wearing those baggy clothes. She's very headstrong, my Luci."

"Yes, sir. I gathered that."

"Well, it doesn't really matter now. I do not think she will have to do that much longer. I already told the family we cannot afford to get the cabs fixed if one of them goes out, so this may be the end of our company."

"Surely, you could get a loan, sir. Have you talked to a bank?"

"Yes. I talked to them, and they say no more loans. I have to pay back the loans I already took out when we started the company. My Luci was going to college. She wants to be a lawyer, but she came home to try to help us out. Now we have nothing, and she will not be able to return to college. It is bad. The whole family is very sad. Tell me something, though, Mr. Clark. Why were you visiting the cemetery when you are a stranger in town?"

"It's very simple, actually. I'm an investor for my father's company, and Luci was giving me a tour of the town. I just bought the restaurant on the corner of Fifth and Elm. I've been eating at the hotel every time I come to town, and I decided what this town needs is a different kind of menu to choose from. I plan to renovate the place before opening it. Then I have to find a great cook. I hope to offer quite a few jobs to people who want to work there."

"Well, I tell you what I'm going to do, Mr. Clark. Since you have been so patient and listened to my story, I'm going to invite you to dinner at my house tonight, if you like Italian food, that is."

"It's my favorite, sir."

"Good, then we're all set. I will send Luci in this cab to pick you up at seven o'clock tonight. You may be her last fare."

Luci flipped through the clothes in her closet, discarding one after the other as unsuitable. Papa's announcement that there would be a guest for dinner had been totally unexpected. She and Anthony had been inclined to invite friends over constantly while they were growing up, but Papa rarely asked anyone outside the family to dine with them. It was not as though there was a lack of food. Mama's table was always bountifully filled. Papa just preferred to have the evening meal with his family – their together time, he called it.

Finding out the guest was to be none other than Mr. Perfect was almost more than she could bear. She would be civil to him, she resolved. After all, the man was investing in their community, and he appreciated good food – two counts in his favor.

Suddenly she spotted it – the little red dress she had bought to wear on her birthday last year. It was the one that had sent Bart into a tizzy when she walked into their living room before they headed out to celebrate. Little red dancing dress, indeed. She would show him!

Thirty minutes later and dressed to the nines, she exited her room and headed for the back door towards Papa's cab.

Anthony and Terri had already arrived for their second dinner in a row with the family.

"Hey, sis. Be careful you don't fall and break an ankle in those heels you're wearing," teased Anthony. "Whatever happened to your disguise anyhow?"

"Disguises are good only when they fool people, Anthony. Tonight the real me is being revealed," she retorted.

She climbed into Papa's cab, praying it would start. She was rewarded when the engine turned over and began to pick up speed as she revved up the motor.

"Thanks, old girl," she whispered. "At least we still have you."

Minutes later she was, once again, pulling up in front of the hotel. There he was, standing in the front entrance, dressed in yet another perfectly tailored business suit. *Chalk another one up for Mr. Perfect,* she reflected.

"Hello, Lu. Thanks so much for coming tonight to drive me over to your house for dinner. Since this is not a regular fare, do you mind if I ride in the front seat with you?" he inquired.

"I suppose not. And you don't have to call me Lu. My name is Luci," she replied.

"And you can call me Jeremy," he said, thinking he was at least making progress with this beautiful, somewhat prickly girl.

The dinner went off without a hitch, with the family cleaning their plates and going back for seconds. Mama had gone all out and even baked her Italian crème cake for the occasion. Jeremy proved to be a master orator, and he kept them laughing at his descriptions of his adventures in the Air Force.

"Mrs. Carlito, I can't tell you when I've enjoyed a meal so much," he said. "Italian food is my favorite, and I never pass up a chance to eat it whenever I can."

"Thank you, Mr. Clark. I enjoy cooking," she told him.

"You know, this gives me an idea. I think I will go with an Italian theme for my new restaurant. What would you think about selling me your recipes? I'll pay you top dollar for them," he said.

"I don't know. Those recipes have been in my family for generations," replied Mama doubtfully.

"That makes them even more valuable. What would you say to the sum of $120,000?"

The family sat in stunned silence, almost unable to contemplate such an amount. Mama looked as if she were about to faint. Papa was grinning like the Cheshire cat. Terri and Anthony were gripping hands so tightly their knuckles were turning white. Only Luci appeared to be unmoved by the offer.

What's he up to now? she wondered.

"What? That's not enough? I can give you more," he exclaimed. "I simply must have those recipes."

Papa found his voice first. "The price is fair, Mr. Clark, very fair. But it's up to Mama. They are her recipes, not ours. So, what do you say, Mama?"

"I say I will do it. Yes, I will sell you the recipes," Mama replied. "But they're not really my recipes. I learned them from my own mama, Lena, when I was growing up, and I passed them on to Luci."

"That gives me another idea. It's the perfect name for my new restaurant. We'll call it Rosa Lena's," Jeremy declared.

"I'll have my lawyer draw up the contract the first thing tomorrow morning, he promised, as handshakes were exchanged all around. "Now I have one more request to make before I leave. I really feel like celebrating. Luci, would you do me the honor of accompanying me across the river to Brooksville tonight to go dancing? I see you found the little red dress."

"Very well, Mr. Clark…Jeremy. I'll go out with you. But how do you propose to get there, seeing as how you have no vehicle of your own?"

"I will drive you in the remaining cab," Papa interjected. "After tonight we will be able to buy two new cabs that get better gas mileage. I feel like celebrating, too!"

"Luci, grab your coat and purse and we'll be off," Jeremy instructed.

Twenty minutes later, Papa dropped them off at the Circle of Light Club, a nightspot well known for its music and dancing. Its atmosphere was almost like a throwback to the dancing and supper clubs of earlier eras.

Jeremy secured a table and ordered drinks. Then came the moment Luci had been half-dreading and half-anticipating. The band started playing one of her favorite tunes.

"Shall we?" Jeremy inquired, holding out his hand as she rose from her chair.

She slipped easily into his arms, as if she were meant to be in that very spot. They moved together flawlessly across the floor, their bodies acting as if in one accord. Luci could feel herself growing somewhat breathless, not from the exertion, but from the closeness of that near-perfect male body. Just when she thought she could no longer stand it, someone tapped Jeremy on the shoulder.

"Mind if I cut in?" The remark came from none other than Bart.

Jeremy reluctantly surrendered Luci to her new partner.

"Bart, what's the big idea, and what are you doing here?" Luci almost stammered as he swung her back out onto the dance floor.

"Oh, I just felt a little depressed, and I thought this place might cheer me up. We had a lot of good times here, remember?" he replied.

Before Luci could speak, he continued. "No, don't say anything. I can see I've lost you. He's the one, isn't he?"

"Maybe." Now she was feeling thoroughly confused. *Could Mr.*

Perfect be the one and only man in her life? Could someone so irritating be the one she was meant to live with day in and day out?

The song ended and Bart escorted her back to the table where Jeremy sat waiting. He and Bart exchanged glances that spoke volumes. It was apparent they had reached an understanding regarding Luci. Bart quickly disappeared into the crowd, leaving Luci and Jeremy all to themselves.

"You know, Luci, I'm going to need somebody to train my restaurant workers on how to prepare those Italian recipes. The job is yours if you want it. You could make enough money to go back to college," said Jeremy, as he helped her into her chair.

"How did you know about my schooling?" she inquired.

"Oh, you papa is a very talkative man, especially when it comes to his family."

"Why are you being so nice to me?" she demanded to know.

"Let's just say I've never met another taxicab driver like you, Miss Luci Carlito. Oh, I know you didn't like me at first. Do you think you could learn to like me even a little bit now?"

Luci felt a smile tugging at the corners of her mouth. "Well, I suppose I could try."

"Now, that didn't hurt too much, did it? What say we try another dance?"

She slipped back into his arms, and they glided across the floor, passing a table where Bart sat, looking rather dejected.

"Do you think I should tell Bart I have a younger sister?" he inquired laughingly.

"If she's anything like you, I think Bart would be most pleased to meet her," Luci replied.

Jeremy looked down at the beautiful girl in his arms, and somehow, he knew that by the end of the night those lips wouldn't beg to be kissed any longer. She was going to be *his* girl and that was all there was to it. He simply wasn't going to take no for an answer, he vowed.

Luci ventured a look up into his eyes. *Just what is he thinking?* she wondered. *Just how perfect is Mr. Perfect?* She had though him positively exasperating, but after his display of generosity towards her family, maybe there was more to him than met the eye. He was obviously *very* rich, quite handsome, and had proven himself to be utterly charming, much to her surprise. It was too soon to make up her mind just yet. She would have to see more of him, and working in the restaurant would give her a chance to do that.

They had worked their way across the dance floor and ended up back in front of their table when the song ended. Jeremy silently pulled out a chair and helped her to a seat. He sat down across from her and waited for her to speak.

"I've made up my mind about your job offer," she told him as she sat with her hands folded on the tabletop.

He remained silent, his face a completely unreadable mask. He had learned during his business dealings it was best not to let your feelings show before the deal was made.

"I've decided to take you up on it. I know how to make all of Mama's recipes. I've been cooking ever since I could hold a spoon and stir. I can give you six months of my time. After that I need to get back to college before I forget everything I've learned," she continued.

Jeremy smiled and she noticed the smile was reflected in his eyes. Funny, but she hadn't realized that the blue in his eyes was intensified with specks of even darker blue. *How was that even possible?* she wondered. Either you had blue eyes or you didn't.

"Great," he replied. "I'll have my lawyer draw up another contract just for you, specifying your salary and your job description."

He ventured as far as covering her hands with his when he spoke. She didn't draw away, and that was a good sign. He didn't want to rush things. Not with this girl. He had learned his lesson about that with previous girlfriends, but they were all in the past and not one of them could hold a candle to Luci. It wasn't just her outer beauty that attracted him. She had a beautiful spirit, and that was what he loved the most about her. He had sensed it the first time she had picked him up in one of her father's cabs. Ever since then he hadn't been able to get her out of his mind. Now it had come down to this. He had a narrow window of opportunity to win her over, and he wasn't about to blow it.

Things were coming to a close at the club as the band began to play their signature tune, a sign that their performance for the night was over. People began filing out, leaving Luci to wonder just how she and Jeremy were going to get home, as Papa had dropped them off and then left.

Jeremy pulled out his cell phone, punched in a few numbers, and began speaking as Luci sat in stunned silence.

He was calling her father's competitive cab company, she had soon realized. So much for him being Mr. Perfect! How could he do that to her family?

"What are you doing?" she almost hissed as he ended the call.

"Patience, my girl. Patience. I want some time alone with you, and I wouldn't feel right sitting in the back of your father's cab," he explained. "Or had you rather have us ride home in the back of Bart's tow truck?" he added jokingly.

She smiled wryly. "No, I don't think that would go over well with Bart," she admitted.

He helped her on with her coat and they joined the tail end of the crowd that was making its way out into the night air. She shivered slightly as a gust of cool air hit them squarely in the face.

Jeremy held his hand protectively behind her in the small of her back, wishing he could wrap his arm completely around her. They spotted the cab at the same time, a white vehicle with a red-and-white checked top and the words "Summerfield Taxi Company" printed on its sides in what Luci considered garish lettering.

She had to restrain herself from wrinkling her nose in disgust as Jeremy raised his free hand to hail the cab. If Papa ever found out she had ridden in *this* cab his feelings would be deeply hurt. Hopefully, he and Mama would be gone to bed by the time she and Jeremy arrived at her home.

The cab drew up to the curb and Jeremy opened the door for her and waited for her to climb in before he followed suit.

The cab driver spoke immediately. He had recognized Luci as the daughter of his competitor.

"Well, well, Miss Carlito. What's the matter? Did those old rattletrap cabs of your father's finally bite the dust?" he asked sarcastically.

Luci opened her mouth to reply, but before she could say anything, Jeremy took control of the situation.

"Quiet, driver! When we want your opinion, we'll ask for it. Since you seem to know Miss Carlito, I assume you know her home address. Take us there, and be quick about it," he instructed.

Luci flashed him a grateful smile and he winked at her. Things weren't going as smoothly as he had hoped, but he managed to slip his arm around her as the cab pulled out of the parking lot. He had twenty minutes and then she would be gone. *What could he accomplish in twenty minutes?* he wondered.

She didn't pull away from him, and that was encouraging. Why did Italians have to be so emotional? It was like riding a roller coaster, only worse. At least with a roller coaster you could see the curves and hills that were coming up. With Luci, he couldn't tell what her next reaction might be. One minute she was hot and the next minute she was freezing him out. Well, one thing was for sure. If he did manage to win her over, life with her would never be boring.

What could they talk about? He had to say something, but he'd best not mention anything about the recent business transaction, seeing as how they were riding in the back of a competitor's cab. He cleared his throat.

"That's quite a moon out tonight," he said.

"Umm," she murmured, almost under her breath as she snuggled a little closer.

Oh, boy, that was lame, he lamented. Here he was, an international businessman, sitting beside the girl of his dreams, and he couldn't even think of anything to say to her. Maybe calling this cab company hadn't been such a good idea, after all.

"Luci," he began again.

She turned her head slightly to look at him, tilting her face upwards to meet his eyes. That movement brought those kissable lips into view. It was more than he could stand.

"Luci," he repeated as he bent his head and began kissing her, softly at first, and then more intensely.

They both realized simultaneously that she was kissing him back.

She drew away, almost shocked at her reaction. Then she came to her senses and realized where they were. If word of this got out, it would be all over town tomorrow. She would never live it down! Just about that time, the cab pulled up in front of her house.

"Wait here, driver," Jeremy instructed as he got out of the cab and helped Luci to her feet.

They walked to the door, fully aware of the front porch light that was shining brightly over the entranceway.

"Well, I guess this is goodnight. I'll call you tomorrow and we'll decide how to proceed with our plans," he told her.

"Okay, I'll be waiting," she said.

He bent down again in hopes of giving her one more kiss, but she eluded him and slipped through the door, which she had just unlocked.

He smiled as the door closed sharply and the porch light went out. He was making progress, but how much? He walked back to the cab and climbed in, giving the driver instructions to take him back to his hotel.

He pulled out his wallet and withdrew the money to pay the fare as the cab stopped in front of the hotel. He noticed a silly grin plastered on the driver's face, so he drew out an additional one-hundred-dollar bill and handed it to him, speaking very slowly.

"Driver, everything that happened in the cab tonight will remain confidential. You will not say one word to anybody. I expect Miss Carlito's reputation to remain totally sterling. Is that clear?"

"My lips are sealed," the driver replied as his hand closed around the crisp bill.

###

Luci leaned against the door after closing it and heaved a sigh of relief. She heard the taxi pull away from the curb and start back down the street, hopefully with Mr. Perfect riding safely inside. This whole night had been too much for her. *How could a person's life be turned upside down in a few short hours by just one man?* Her whole family seemed to be enthralled with the guy. Papa had invited him to dinner after giving him just one cab ride. That wasn't like Papa at all!

Evidently, he trusted the man because he and Mama had both gone to bed, not even waiting up for her or calling her on her cell phone to see if she needed a ride home. Suddenly the whole situation struck her as amusing. She began to laugh, trying desperately to stifle the sound behind her hands. She managed to sober up long enough to head for the stairs, but she couldn't resist making a few swift dance swirls around the floor on her way, humming the tune "I Could Have Dance All Night" and then stopping abruptly just as she reached the foot of the stairs.

A few more nights like this and I'll be ready to play Eliza Doolittle, she thought as she stifled a yawn. Like Eliza, she was worn out and she was going to bed. She planned to sleep in tomorrow because Papa was going downtown to check on ordering his two new cabs. At least that was what he had indicated during the cab ride to Brooksville. Hopefully, by the time the new cabs arrived, Anthony's leg would be healed and he would be able to take over again as Papa's second cab driver. If she never had to sit behind the wheel of a cab again, it would be too soon for her! The restaurant job was sounding better and better. If she played her cards right, she should able to save up enough money to go back to college, as Mr. Perfect had suggested. One way or another, she was going to get her degree. That much she knew!

Her plans for sleeping in were foiled by Mama's insistent knocking on her bedroom door at 8:00 a.m.

"Luci, are you awake?" Mama called out softly as she opened the door.

"No, Mama, not really. What is it?" Luci inquired sleepily.

"Mr. Clark is on the phone. He said he doesn't have your cell phone number. He wants to meet with you to discuss the plans for renovating the restaurant. He doesn't have a lot of time, either, because he has to leave town this afternoon for another appointment."

"Okay, I suppose I can talk to him," Luci replied as she groped for the extension phone near the head of her bed.

"Hello," she spoke into the phone, trying to sound like she was halfway awake and in a good mood.

"Luci, Jeremy here. Hope I didn't wake you. We need to meet to figure out what renovations need to be made to the restaurant."

"Actually, I was still asleep, but I suppose we can get together. Where do you want to meet?"

With that remark, Jeremy had to fight to get the image of her lounging in bed, possibly in the briefest of nighties, out of his head. *Remember, Jeremy, business comes first today,* he reminded himself.

"I'm still at the hotel. Why don't you pick me up in one of your father's cabs and we'll drive over the restaurant," he told her.

"I'm not sure if I can do that," she replied. "Papa has gone to one of the car dealerships to place an order for the new cabs. I'm not sure if he took our last cab or went in his old truck. Let me check and I will call you back."

"Okay, great. Do you have my cell phone number?" he asked.

"Yes, it's on our Caller I. D" she informed him.

Well, so much for sleeping in. I suppose I can catch up on my sleep after Mr. Perfect leaves town. Guess I will have to stop referring to him as Mr. Perfect before I slip up and actually call him by that name. You know his name now, silly, so call him Jeremy, she instructed herself.

She threw on her bathrobe and hurried downstairs to the kitchen where Mama was cleaning up after cooking breakfast for herself and Papa.

"Mama, did Papa take the cab this morning or is he driving his truck?" she inquired.

"Oh, he took the cab. He wants to see how much of a trade-in he can get for it," Mama told her. "Do you want some breakfast?" she asked, ever mindful of her family's eating habits.

"No, thanks, Mama. I think I will just stick with coffee this morning. I don't have time to eat now," Luci replied.

She tripped lightly back up the stairs and picked up the phone in her bedroom. *Why was she in such a good mood?* she wondered. Checking the number on the Caller I. D., she punched in the redial on the phone and waited for Jeremy to answer.

"Hello," he said, answering after the first ring.

"Jeremy, it looks like we're out of luck. Papa took the cab and all we have left is his old truck. It doesn't start half the time, so I don't want to take a chance on driving it," she told him.

"Okay, tell you what. *I'll* take care of the transportation. You just get dressed and I'll pick you up ... oh and be sure to dress casually ... jeans and a tee shirt will be fine."

"All right. See you in a few," she agreed.

Jeans and a tee shirt! What can he be up to now? she wondered. *It's not like I was planning to dress for the prom, anyhow.* She poked through her closet and selected what she considered the most suitable outfit and practically threw the clothes on. After brushing her hair, she headed back to the kitchen, hoping she would have enough time to grab that cup of coffee before he arrived.

Jeremy ran his fingers through his hair after hanging up the phone. Sometimes his ego could get him into a pickle. When would he ever learn? Well, he promised the lady transportation, and transportation she would have! Obviously, he couldn't appear as a knight in shining armor astride his trusty steed, but maybe he could come up with some kind of ride. After all, he did have other business interests in this town and that was why he had come here in the first place.

He checked the list of numbers programmed into his cell phone and found the one he was looking for. After working his way through several receptionists, he was finally connected to the person he needed to talk to. He briefly explained the situation to the manager of the business and was assured that his needs would be taken care of. He didn't even need to bother calling a cab, as they would be sending someone to pick him up.

Now just one problem remained – finding some casual clothes for himself. He always wore business suits to his meetings, so he rarely carried anything as casual as jeans and tee shirts. Another call to a local clothing store solved that problem, and the manager promised to send the clothes right over to his hotel room.

Less than thirty minutes later he found himself in a Harley Davidson showroom. He had invested in the company and this particular business was one that he owned stock in. The receptionists who had been so cool to him over the phone practically fell all over themselves when he walked in. He thought he heard the words "nice butt" as he walked down the hall to the manager's office.

Almost before he knew it, he was standing in the parking lot, the proud owner of a brand-new motorcycle. It hadn't taken him very long to make up his mind which one he wanted because he had ridden them quite frequently in his younger days and even possessed an operator's license. He just hadn't had time to spend on that hobby since taking over as the CEO of his dad's company. It would feel good to be back on the road with the wind in his face again. It would feel even better to have Luci sitting behind him as they breezed down the road. He hoped he could get her onto the bike without too much trouble. One could never *tell* what Luci would do.

Luci was just finishing her cup of coffee when she swore she could hear a motorcycle pulling up in their driveway. She didn't know who owned such a contraption, so who could it possibly be? Then it dawned on her. *Oh, no! I know he didn't!* she thought as she rushed to the front window and peered out. She spotted Jeremy getting off the motorcycle and heading up the front walk, helmet in hand. She almost didn't recognize him without his business suit.

She jumped nervously as the doorbell rang. She had never wished so badly that she had a sister to talk things over with, but she was on her own. She was surprised to feel her heart starting to beat a little faster. She hoped her face wasn't flushed because she was starting to feel rather warm.

She took a deep breath and opened the door, forcing herself to smile casually.

"Jeremy," was all she could muster, but it seemed to satisfy him.

"M'lady, your chariot awaits," he said as he moved his arm in a sweeping motion, pointing towards the Harley.

She could control herself no longer. She burst out laughing. "Jeremy, what have you done?" she demanded to know.

"I said I would provide transportation, and here it is," he announced. "Don't tell me you're scared to ride one of these things!"

"No...I...suppose...not," she replied, her voice tinged with uncertainty.

"Well, come on, girl! Time's a wasting. I have to leave this afternoon," he said as they trekked down the sidewalk and approached the motorcycle. He handed her a second helmet that had been fastened to the back of the bike.

After securing their helmets, he climbed onto the bike and she followed suit, placing her arms around his waist.

"Don't worry, Luci. I would never let anything happen to you," he told her as he prepared to start the bike and head down the road.

He didn't have to tell her that. Somehow, she knew. She just knew she would always be safe with this man.

A short time later they roared into the parking lot of the old restaurant. Luci was feeling exhilarated, partly from the ride, but also from sitting so close behind Jeremy. She didn't know when she had felt so carefree and lightheaded. It made her almost want to shout.

The owner of the restaurant was waiting for them. He hadn't turned the keys over to Jeremy yet, as the sale papers hadn't been finalized. Jeremy assured him that the final details would soon be worked out and that he anticipated no problems would be forthcoming. All they wanted to do today was get a feel for the place and make some sort of list for what remodeling would need to be done.

Fortunately, Jeremy's reputation had preceded him, and the owner had no problems in providing them with a set of keys so they could come and go as they pleased. After exchanging a few pleasantries, he left and they had the entire restaurant to themselves. Jeremy had already contacted the power company and arranged to have the electricity turned on earlier that morning, so they weren't in the dark.

Luci found herself alone with him with no distractions such as driving or dancing. It was a bit disconcerting at first, but she soon felt at ease as they toured the restaurant and began discussing the actual changes they wanted to make.

Since the restaurant was to have an Italian menu, Jeremy wanted it to feature a real Italian atmosphere, complete with red-and-white checked tablecloths, a Terrazzo floor, softly lit candles, an Italian flag, and a wishing well in one corner. They would have Italian music playing through the speakers. There was also enough space on one side of the building to have a fountain and a small rock garden, complete with outdoor dining tables topped with umbrellas.

It would be almost like a scene out of the movie "The Godfather," she thought. But unlike the movie, nobody was going to die in this restaurant unless it was from sheer happiness after eating her cooking. She just hoped she could train the workers to prepare the dishes authentically as she had been taught to make them.

They spent several hours discussing the plans and making lists of what needed to be done. Luci learned she was expected to oversee most of the remodeling process, as Jeremy had to travel overseas for several weeks on business. He promised to check in with her daily to make sure everything was going smoothly.

"Are you sure you trust me to supervise the remodeling job?" she asked anxiously.

"If I can't trust you, then who can I trust?" he responded. "You're a full-blooded Italian. You know what this place needs, and I believe you have good taste. Just follow your instincts and you can't go wrong."

Follow her instincts? That was exactly what she was trying not to do! Her instincts had already gotten her into this deal and now she had to see it through. Her instincts were telling her to watch her step with this man, but now she was tied to him for at least six months. She had given her word on that, and she always kept her word.

They decided they had accomplished about everything they could regarding the remodeling process, so Jeremy dropped Luci off at her house. He assured her he would take care of all the details about opening accounts for her to order the necessary supplies. She knew a reliable contractor who could take care of the construction and carpentry work that would be needed. He left after promising again to call her every day to see how the work was progressing.

She watched him pull out of the driveway, waving as he rode out of sight. Suddenly, she felt empty inside, like she was losing her best friend. *Good grief, how had the man managed to get such a hold on her in such a short time?* Oh, he had been riding in her cab for quite some time, but she had just gotten to know him over the past two days. How was she going to feel after working with him for six months?

Luci soon found herself swamped with work. Not only did she have to oversee the remodeling process at the restaurant, but she also had to decide on how to best equip the kitchen to handle producing the Italian recipes in bulk. For that job, she decided it would be best to consult Mama Rosa. After all, it was her recipes that would be featured in the restaurant's cuisine.

Bringing Mama in on the project proved to be a brilliant idea, and one which Jeremy approved wholeheartedly. She couldn't remember when she had seen her mother so excited about anything. Mama forgot herself and even began speaking in Italian as she toured the kitchen. Luci and Anthony spoke very little Italian, as Papa had wanted them to be proficient in English, so much of Mama's jabbering was lost on her. But she got the main gist of the speeches and was so glad to see Mama so happy again.

As promised, Jeremy and Luci conferred daily by phone, and he made several trips back to Summerfield to check on the progress of his pet project. On many afternoons, they could be found seated at a table in the middle of the restaurant with their heads close together as they pored over the remodeling blueprints, menus, recipes, and ideas for advertising. In fact, Jeremy spent so much time in Summerfield his father began to worry. It wasn't like his son to spend so much time on one project, especially when they had so many other irons in the fire with their international ties. He began to question the wisdom of such actions.

"Jeremy, why are you so wrapped up in this restaurant business? It's just small change. Shouldn't you be paying more attention to projects that will bring in ten times that amount of income?" he inquired.

"Dad, you handed the reins of the company over to me and I haven't let you down yet. You will just have to trust me on this one. If it turns out as well as I expect, we may soon be expanding and opening other restaurants. Who knows? I may even decide to bottle our own spaghetti sauce like Paul Newman did with his salad dressing."

They both got a good laugh out of that last remark, but his dad still wasn't buying it. He had a sneaking suspicion that there was more to the story than met the eye. He hadn't seen Jeremy this interested in anything since elementary school when he had helped him build his entry for the soapbox derby. More than likely, there was some girl involved. It wouldn't be the first time and probably not the last. With his good looks and the family's money, it wouldn't be hard for his son to become a playboy. That was the thing he most dreaded. What if Jeremy took up with some air-headed girl who was just after his fortune?

Wilson Clark wisely held his tongue. He knew better than to try offering Jeremy advice on his love life. Jeremy had been content with mostly playing the field so far, although there had been one or two girls he almost got serious about. The girls Jeremy had brought home had always been beautiful and charming, but there had always been something missing. Somehow, they all seemed to be shallow and lacking in real character. That wasn't the kind of girl he wanted for a daughter-in-law. No, he hoped his son would fall in love with a girl who had her feet set firmly to the ground – someone who could be a genuine helpmate for him in marriage.

After three months, the remodeling of the restaurant was nearly complete. The were ready to start interviewing people for the positions in their staff. Although Jeremy trusted Luci's capabilities for handling the job, he elected to come back to town to assist in the interviews. He realized his time with Luci was growing short.

Luci, too, had been secretly counting down the days on the calendar. She had promised Jeremy six months and half of that time had already passed. She was dreading the day when the time would be up and she would probably never see him again. She vowed to make the most of the time they had left.

Hearing that he was coming back to town for the job interviews gave her spirits a boost. True, they had spent a lot of time together with the remodeling project, but there had always been other people to consult amid a constantly bustling atmosphere. The job interviews would be on a one-on-one basis with just them and the applicant, giving them plenty of time to talk between sessions.

They needed everybody from dishwashers to cooks to hostesses and even cashiers, so they placed an ad in the local newspaper. The TV station in Brooksville had caught wind of their opening and even featured a segment about it on one of their newscasts. People were always looking for work, plus it was a college town, so they were confident they wouldn't have any trouble filling the positions.

The thing that concerned Luci the most was finding the right person to hire as a cook. Obviously, they couldn't afford a real chef since the restaurant was just opening and hadn't yet turned a profit. What she needed was someone with cooking experience who was willing to learn how to prepare authentic Italian foods.

The interviews went rather smoothly and they quickly filled every position except the one they needed most – the cook. It was about that time that a shabbily dressed man walked through the door. He approached Luci and Jeremy slowly, ballcap in hand.

His clothes had definitely seen better days and he obviously did not possess an iron, but at least he was clean.

"I heard you were looking for a cook for this restaurant," he said.

"Yes, we are, but..." Jeremy began to speak, but was interrupted by Luci.

"Jeremy, wait a minute. Let him speak," she said.

"Sir, I've been cooking nigh onto fifteen years now, but I lost my job about a year ago. My wife left me and took the kids and I've been down on my luck ever since. I guarantee you I can cook anything you want me to, with or without a recipe."

Jeremy wasn't buying it. "If you're such a good cook, why haven't you found work before now? Cooks can always find work.

"To be perfectly honest with you, sir, I had a little drinking problem. That was what got me fired. Then after my wife left, things just got worse. I couldn't pay my mortgage and I ended up on the street. The Salvation Army took me in and gave me a job cooking in their kitchen and then I saw the error of my ways and sobered up. But they don't pay much and I can't really get back on my feet until I get a real job. I promise you, I can do it. Just give me a chance and I can cook anything, anyway, anytime you want."

Jeremy and Luci looked at one another doubtfully.

"I don't know. This restaurant is very important to me. If we don't get the right cook, the whole thing will fall apart," Jeremy explained.

Luci intervened once more. "Jeremy, let's give him a chance. He's the only one we've seen today who even claims to know how to cook. I would be willing to work with him."

She looked over at the man, meeting him eye-to-eye. He didn't flinch or drop his gaze. She tapped her pen on the desk as she thought quickly.

"What's your name?" she asked.

"James Lovett," he replied.

"Well, James, you've got a job. We'll give it to you on a trial basis, provided you stay sober."

"And she definitely not kidding about the sober part," Jeremy added.

"You've got yourself a deal," James exclaimed as he shook hands with both of them.

They watched him as he walked out the door, closing it behind him.

"I hope we didn't make a mistake," Jeremy told Luci.

"You said you trusted my instincts, and my instincts told me to hire this man. I think he's a diamond in the rough if he can cook as well as he claims. I just hope my cooking skills aren't too rusty. I've been working on this restaurant so long I haven't cooked in months."

"What else do your instincts tell you, Luci?" he inquired, looking deeply into her eyes as he leaned towards her, resting his arm across the back of her chair.

"Maybe…that meeting you was the best thing that ever happened to me," she said softly.

He bent down and kissed her soundly and was relieved when she kissed him back. He drew away and saw a lone tear running down her cheek.

"Luci, why are you crying?" he asked.

She just shook her head. "I have to go," she said as she hurriedly arose, grabbed her purse, and headed out the door.

He sat silently as he watched her walk away. He was totally bemused, confused, and whatever other adjective could be applied to the situation. He had almost won her over and then she'd gone cold on him again. Women! Had there ever been a man alive who understood them?

Luci, on the other hand, knew exactly why she was crying and walking away. She had fallen for the guy! Despite her best intentions, she had let her guard down and she had fallen for Mr. Perfect. That was the problem – he was way out of her league. There was no way a man so obviously rich was going to stay with a girl from her humble background. Oh, she might amuse him for a little while, but then he would be off hunting a new conquest. Even worse, the restaurant project was drawing to a close and after that, she would never see him again.

Well, she was going to see it through to the end. She had a cook to train tomorrow, so she had better go home and get a good night's sleep. Tomorrow would be a long day.

###

Luci met James at the restaurant at 8:00 a.m., as promised, bringing along copies of her family recipes. They sat and discussed the recipes and talked about various cooking techniques for two hours. The pantry and freezer had not yet been stocked, so Luci decided it was time to take James on a shopping trip to find out how much he really knew about food.

They had to drive to Brooksville in Papa's old cab, as the grocery stores in Summerfield did not stock many of the items her recipes called for. Brooksville had a restaurant supply store and a Sam's Club. She figured they could solve that problem by ordering what they needed and having it delivered to the restaurant, once they were open.

To her surprise, she found James to be quite knowledgeable about the cuts of meat, fresh produce, pasta, and herbs and spices. Maybe this training job wasn't going to be as hard as she had thought. They filled two shopping carts as they made their way up and down each and every aisle of the store. Luci found James to be quite personable in his humble sort of way. As they reached the checkout lane, she dug in her purse for the credit card Jeremy had provided for business purposes. She was glad because the bill turned out to be quite sizeable. She just hoped the food would turn out to be as good as Mama's home cooking.

They arrived back at the restaurant well past lunchtime. Luci was starting to feel a little hungry and she figured James probably didn't have enough money to buy himself any food. They had bought enough supplies to make sandwiches, as they planned on working through mealtime. She came up with what she considered to be a clever solution to the problem.

"Why don't I show you how to make a real man's sandwich, Italian style?" she asked.

"No, let *me* show you one of my sandwich specialties," James told her.

"You've got yourself a deal," she agreed as she sat down at one of the tables and waited to see just what he might have in mind.

Minutes later he brought in two plates and a serving platter containing a huge sub sandwich. He sat them on the table with a flourish.

"No cheating now. Wait until I get back with something for us to drink," he instructed.

He came back into the dining room carrying two glasses of ice and two cans of soft drinks.

"Prepare yourself for a treat," he announced as he took a knife and cut the sub sandwich in half, placing each half on a separate plate.

Luci bit into what was one of the most delicious combinations of flavors she had ever tasted in a sandwich. She chewed it slowly as he watched, anxiously awaiting her approval.

"James, I don't know how you did it, but this sandwich is great! If your cooking is anything like this, you'll have a job here for a long, long time!" she exclaimed.

"Glad you like it," he said as he bit hungrily into his own half of the sandwich.

The cooking lessons began in earnest the next day and continued over the next two weeks. James picked up Italian cooking techniques rather quickly and showed Luci some of his own specialties, to boot. Luci soon realized that it was going to take more than one person cooking to be able to handle all the food orders. James would be the main cook, but he needed some assistants. As much as she liked to cook, she wasn't about to spend all her time in the kitchen once the restaurant opened.

James provided a possible solution to the problem. Some of his friends who were staying at the Salvation Army shelter were also looking for work. Several of them, he felt, were capable of learning enough to help out in the kitchen. Others might be willing to fill in as busboys or any other odd jobs that might be called for.

She had best call Jeremy, she decided. This was one decision she wasn't about to make by herself. Jeremy wasn't too keen on the idea when she finally go to speak with him after he got out of a business meeting.

"I don't know, Luci. I would have to actually meet with the people just to see exactly what type of characters we would be dealing with. Tell you what — see if you can round them up day after tomorrow and I'll fly into town and interview them myself," he told her.

What was the girl thinking? he wondered. She had a soft heart, no doubt, even though she didn't always show it. That was just one more thing he loved about her. Anyhow, this trip into town would give him another chance to see her, even if it was just briefly.

Luci hung up the phone and gave James the good news. His friends had a chance of getting a job, provided Jeremy approved of them. They were to report to the restaurant in two days. She would let him know exactly what time later.

Then she surprised him with another announcement.

"You know, James, so far we have been trying out our recipes on the rest of the hired help and the construction workers. I think it's about time we served up some meals to some real judges of Italian food. Jeremy will be in town overnight and my parents haven't tasted your cooking yet. Why don't we have a little private dinner party to let them sample some of our dishes?"

"That would be just fine with me, Miss Luci," James replied.

Luci sat down and immediately began planning the menu. She and James conferred about her choices, and he agreed that she had made some excellent selections.

They checked on their supplies to make sure everything they needed was on hand. Luci was a bit nervous about preparing a whole meal for so many people. She had done it at home with no problems, but this was a commercial setting and all of the equipment was brand new. She just hoped nothing could go wrong.

She issued invitations to all her family members, and they readily accepted. They were eager to see what Luci had been up to for the past few months. She had checked and double-checked with Mama Rosa about the recipes, and Mama had put her stamp of approval on the remodeled kitchen. They all knew that Luci was an excellent cook, but could she pull it off when she was cooking for such a large crowd? The only way to answer that question was for her to make a trial run, and they didn't mind at all if they were to be used as the guinea pigs. If there was one thing the entire family enjoyed, it was eating, especially eating good food.

Should she warn Jeremy in advance or spring it on him when he came to town for the interview? She pondered the situation. He didn't seem like the type of person who liked surprises, so she decided it would be best to call him and let him know about the party.

She reluctantly dialed his cell phone number, wondering why she suddenly dreaded talking to him.

He answered on the first ring, as usual. "Luci, this is a surprise! What's going on in Summerfield now?" he inquired.

I just wanted to let you know that James and I are going to have a party for my family so they can sample our cooking. I was hoping you would be able to come, too, when you're in town for the interviews," she told him.

"Of course, I'll be there. I wouldn't miss it," he assured her.

"Great! Well, I guess I'll see you when you get here then," she said, racking her brain for something else to say to prolong the conversation. Nothing came to mind.

"Have your father's new cabs arrived yet?" he asked.

"Yes, they came in last week."

"I'll need a ride from the airport when I get into town."

"I'm sure Papa will be happy to pick you up, free of charge, of course," she told him laughingly.

It did him good to hear the laughter back in her voice again. Somehow, she had sounded sad when she called, and that wasn't like Luci at all. *What was bothering her?* he wondered.

###

Luci and James found themselves swamped with trying to get everything prepared for their first party. She fussed over the table settings, while he worried about the food. Could they pull it off? The only way to find out was to actually go through with it. That much they knew. If they planned on running a restaurant filled with customers, they had better get their practice in while they could.

They busied themselves with getting the food started early on the morning of the party. Luci trusted James to carry on without her while she sat in on the interviews with Jeremy. After all, she would be the one working with the people, so she had to put her stamp of approval on them before they were hired.

Jeremy blew into the restaurant in his usual "Mr. Perfect" mode, wearing a business suit and tie. He settled himself into one of the chairs, placing his briefcase on the table as he waited for Luci to come into the dining room.

She peeked through the window at the top of one of the kitchen's swinging doors and spotted him sitting there.

"James, I have to get out of here for now. Jeremy is waiting for the applicants to show up for the job interviews," she announced, shedding her apron as she spoke.

She walked into the dining room and headed for the table where Jeremy sat, unaware that she had a spot of flour on the tip of her nose.

"Luci, how are you doing?" Jeremy inquired as she approached.

"I'm doing just great, Jeremy," she answered almost breathlessly. "James and I are working on preparing the food for tonight, so I hope these interviews don't take too long. I need to get back to the kitchen as soon as possible."

"Well, there's just one little detail you might want to take care of before the applicants arrive," he told her.

"What's that?" she asked curiously, wondering what she could have forgotten now.

"Employers shouldn't look like bakers," he replied as he pulled a handkerchief from his pocket and gently wiped the flour off her nose. "You had a smudge," he explained in response to her puzzled look.

"Oh, dear, thanks for telling me," she said.

Just about that time the job applicants began filing in, approaching the table timidly. The had already heard more than enough about Luci to recognize her. That put them somewhat at ease, but they were still apprehensive about the elegantly dressed man who was sitting with her.

"You must be James's friends!" Luci exclaimed. "Please, come in and we will be happy to talk to you one at a time. Who wants to be first?"

The bravest of the bunch volunteered to go first while the others remained in the background, finding seats at one of the empty tables.

They all needed work, so they desperately hoped they would be hired. It was the first chance they had for a regular job in quite some time.

Jeremy conducted the interviews skillfully, with Luci adding her part when needed. Between the two of them they decided that all the applicants were suitable and could begin their training tomorrow.

Luci had been antsy during the whole process. She couldn't wait to get back to the kitchen and start working on the food again. Jeremy sensed that her attention wasn't totally focused on the interviews, but he tactfully refrained from commenting on it.

She silently breathed a sigh of relief when the last applicant walked out the front door.

"Jeremy, I have to get back to the kitchen now," she informed him.

"May I see what's going on back there?" he inquired.

"No, silly. You have to wait until tonight. It's going to be a total surprise, but, trust me, it will be worth it!" she teased.

"Okay, then I'll see you tonight," he said.

"Oh…go ride your motorcycle…or do something!" she exclaimed as she jumped up and headed for the kitchen.

Jeremy shook his head as he watched her whisk through the kitchen doors. Foiled again! She wasn't getting away from him that easily. One way or another, they were going to have it out, he decided. He would bide his time for now.

The dinner that night turned out to be a smashing success. Mama, along with the rest of the family, heartily approved of the Italian dishes. They ran a skeleton crew, including the hostess, waiters and waitresses, busboys, and dishwashers just to give them some practice and, hopefully, to iron out any problems that might occur. Everyone was in a jovial mood, especially Luci and James. They had done it! Every dish had turned out just right! It was all they had hoped for and more.

All that remained was for Luci and James to train the newly hired workers. They estimated it could be done in a week and then the restaurant would be ready for the grand opening. It was something they were all looking forward to, especially Luci. It meant she was nearing the end of her agreement with Jeremy to work in the restaurant business and she could get back to working on her law degree. The only problem was that she would most likely never see him again. *Maybe it was for the best,* she reasoned. That's what she got for falling for a rich guy who was totally out of her class. Even if he loved her back, his family would most likely disapprove of the relationship and then there would be heartaches, no matter what.

###

The new hires turned out to be quick learners. They were all serious about working and keeping their jobs, so both Luci and James were pleased with their progress. Luci had managed to fill in the remaining jobs with college students, as Jeremy had suggested. She reported the same to Jeremy, and they decided it was time to schedule the grand opening of the restaurant. The phone had been practically ringing off the hook with inquiries about when it would open.

They opted for a "soft opening" featuring just the lunch menu for a week to be followed by the grand opening on a Saturday night with free champagne and live violin music. Luci contacted the television station in Brooksville to see if they could cover the story, and the station happily obliged, agreeing to send out a reporter and a camera crew.

Luci didn't know who was more excited – her, her family, or the hired help. It was the culmination of many months and long hours of work. Now it was all about to come to a head. The only downside was that she was almost through working with Jeremy. It was going to be hard to say goodbye to him and all the staff she had grown so fond of.

Luci had planned to set up a special table for her family, Jeremy, and herself. Then she received a surprise phone call from Jeremy informing her that his entire family would also be attending. She quickly readjusted her plans to include seating for the extra guests, wondering just how it was all going to play out. How would her grassroots family get along with people who dealt with international businesses? It should prove to be an interesting night, to say the least.

###

Jeremy had been totally floored following a conversation with his father. Wilson Clark had been keeping abreast of the restaurant situation and its progress, partly due to Jeremy's enthusiasm about the project. Jeremy couldn't help but share reports of the remodeling process with his parents, mostly at the dinner table on the rare occasions when he was home. He let Luci's name slip out once or twice during the process. His father remained his usual stoic self, but he could see his mother's ears prick up underneath her hairdo. He knew it was a mistake, but it was too late. He couldn't take back what he had said, nor did he want to. He wasn't ashamed of his feelings for Luci and he was still determined to win her over.

What he didn't plan on was having his whole family accompany him to the grand opening of the restaurant. *No, make that his and Luci's restaurant.* That's why his father's announcement at the dinner table had come as a total surprise.

"Son, I believe I would like to come with you and take a look at this restaurant you have been talking about for almost six months now. Why don't you call this Luci of yours and have her reserve a table for me and your mother?" Wilson asked.

"Sure, Dad, I'd be glad for you to come. Just keep in mind it's a small town and there's only one hotel."

"Wilson, what a lovely idea," his mother, Maude, exclaimed. "What should I wear?"

"Mom, whatever you choose, you'll be beautiful. I have just one request. Please leave your fur coat and diamonds at home. Remember, it's an Italian restaurant, not the Ritz."

"Jeremy, what kind of snob do you think I am?" she inquired, her feelings obviously hurt.

"I'm sorry, Mom. I didn't mean it the way it sounded. It's just that you are so used to wearing those things you take them for granted. Just be your usual charming self, and I'm sure everyone will love you."

"Hey, what about me?" inquired his younger sister, Judith, who had been sitting at the table, taking it all in. She, too, had noticed Jeremy's comments about Luci and stowed them away in the back of her mind, wondering if her brother had finally fallen in love. He certainly spent enough time on the phone with the girl. It would be interesting to finally put a face with the name.

"Sis, of course you are coming, too! I wouldn't let you miss it," Jeremy informed her.

Judith smiled mischievously. "And will we all get to meet this mysterious Luci you keep talking about?" she asked.

Jeremy looked rather uncomfortable, but he rose to the challenge. "She's the manager of the restaurant, so, yes, you will all get to meet her and see her in action."

The look exchanged by his parents was not lost on him, but he chose to ignore it. He had every confidence in Luci. The question was not would his family like Luci, but rather what would she think of them? Luci could hold her own with anybody. Of that he was certain.

###

The night of the grand opening was upon them almost before they could turn around. Luci and James had been totally engrossed in making sure that all the details were ironed out. The help had been trained and fitted for uniforms. Luci had confirmed the date with the TV station and the musicians. All the table settings and decorations were in place. Even the weather promised to cooperate. All in all, it promised to be a perfect night. She just hoped nothing would go wrong.

Luci had made a last-minute adjustment in the seating arrangement when she learned that Judith would be attending. She included Bart in the seating plan, reasoning that he was practically family. Although she had never met Judith, she had every confidence that Bart's attention would be totally focused on the new girl instead of her. Things had never been the same between them since that night she and Jeremy ran into him when they went out dancing. Ever since then he had been almost cool to her whenever their paths had crossed.

It was just as well, she reasoned. Being with Jeremy had spoiled her for any other man. She didn't know why it had taken her so long to realize it but being with Jeremy made her totally happy. She was sad only when she thought about how they were worlds apart in social status. Now she could no longer be content with being just a small-town girl. No, she would get her law degree and move on to a bigger city, no matter what happened between her and Jeremy. That was the only thing to do.

Papa D'Armon and his entire family arrived in one of his new cabs. He had elected to take the night off in honor of his daughter's special event. He was almost beaming as he walked in, along with Mama Rosa, Anthony, and an obviously pregnant Terri. Luci hurried over and escorted them to the family dining table, giving instructions to the hostess to seat Bart there, also. She was on pins and needles in anticipation of meeting Jeremy's family for the first time. She was too nervous to sit, so she rotated between the kitchen and the dining room, watching the entranceway anxiously.

She didn't have to wait very long. Jeremy had arranged for a limousine to drive him and his family to the restaurant. This was his big night and he intended to enjoy it. As they exited the limousine and headed for the restaurant, everyone waiting to get inside craned their necks, wondering who the handsome stranger was and why he had chosen to attend this event in their small town. A ripple swept through the crowd as he walked by. The mystery deepened for them as he was quickly admitted, skipping the line entirely. Obviously, he must be someone of importance, but who could he be?

Luci spotted him as soon as he walked through the door. Her heart beat a little faster when their eyes met across the room. She wove her was through the crowd, determined to escort him to the table herself. She would be cordial without letting her feelings show, she resolved.

Jeremy couldn't help but smile as he watched Luci making her way across the crowded room. His family realized who she was almost as soon as they saw her.

"Is that Luci? Brother of mine, you didn't tell us she was so gorgeous," whispered Judith.

Before he could respond, Luci reached them, prepared to escort them to the especially reserved table. The crowd was coming in so fast there was no time for introductions.

"Follow me," she instructed, almost shouting above the din that suddenly surrounded them.

They walked behind her towards the table she indicated. They were silent, but their minds were racing with unspoken questions. Here they all were, finally face to face with the girl their son and brother had been talking about for so many months. Just seeing her in person filled in a lot of blanks. Jeremy was obviously in love with the girl. The big question facing them was where would it go from here? Was Jeremy finally ready to give up playing the field and settle for just one girl?

The family paused as they reached the table, waiting for introductions. Jeremy did the honors since he knew the names of everybody involved. He then pulled out a chair for his sister, and his father performed the same courtesy for Mrs. Clark. After a flurry of settling in their seats, everyone looked expectantly at Luci and Jeremy, wondering what was in store for the rest of the evening.

"Let me get you some menus," Luci announced, waving to one of the hostesses who arrived with the menus and distributed them around the table.

"So many things to choose from. I had no idea your restaurant was offering such a wide variety of food," mused Mr. Clark.

"May I make a suggestion?" asked Luci.

"Yes, please do," exclaimed Mrs. Clark.

"Why don't you all go with the Italian standby of spaghetti and meatballs in Mama Rosa's special sauce?" Luci responded, as Mama blushed from sheer pride and happiness.

"That's a good idea," Jeremy interjected. "All our food is delicious, but you can't go wrong with spaghetti and meatballs."

He signaled a waitress and placed the order for the entire party, requesting garden salads, the entrée, bread, and wine. Feeling rather pleased with himself, he added one more thing to the list.

"Let's start this celebration with some of our best champagne," he told them, indicating to the waitress that she should bring it to the table immediately.

The champagne arrived and drinks were poured for everyone at the table except for Terri, who was limiting herself to sparkling cider due to her pregnancy. Jeremy, always the gentleman, had remembered to request it for her.

Papa D'Armon rose and cleared his throat, preparing to offer a toast.

"To Luci and Jeremy and the success of their new restaurant," he said, raising his glass.

"Here, here," the entire party chimed in as they clicked their glasses together and began sampling the champagne.

Luci sipped hers slowly watching Jeremy through her lashes, wondering what was on his mind.

Jeremy couldn't take his eyes off her. God, she was beautiful! That low-cut black dress of hers with the spaghetti straps was enough to drive a man insane. He felt the hard outline of the box in his pocket pressing against his thigh. He had brought a diamond engagement ring with him tonight and he intended to propose to Luci when the time was right. He just needed to get her alone somehow.

Both families began to loosen up as the meal was served. Papa D'Armon and Mr. Clark found a common bond in their interest of sports. Mama Rosa and Mrs. Clark began exchanging cooking tips on French and Italian foods. Bard, obviously mesmerized with Judith, kept her in stitches as he related some of his experiences in the tow truck business. That left Jeremy and Luci to their own devices.

He saw his chance to get her alone when the dessert menu arrived.

"Luci, let's skip dessert and go out onto the patio and try out some of the music. As long as we're paying for it, we might as well enjoy it," he suggested, hoping she wouldn't refuse. He mentally crossed his fingers. *She had to go with him. She just had to!*

Luci hesitated. "I don't know, Jeremy. I don't want to be rude and leave our guests."

"Go, go," Mama Rosa insisted.

"Yes, you young people go ahead and enjoy yourselves," added Mrs. Clark.

"Well, I suppose I could go for a little while," Luci conceded, rising from her chair as Jeremy assisted her.

They walked out onto the patio into what proved to be the perfect setting for a romantic evening. The soft glow from the candles set on the tables was enhanced by the moonlight streaming in from a full moon that hung low in the night sky. The air was cool, with a breeze that blew softly, ruffling the streamers that had been erected for the grand opening. Even the stars seemed to cooperate, each vying to outshine the other. The violinists were moving slowly between the tables as they circulated among the guests. A few couples were dancing in the open space at one end of the patio, taking advantage of the music.

Jeremy held out his hand as they approached the dance floor and Luci slipped into his arms just as three violinists began playing a Strauss waltz. They moved across the floor wordlessly, keeping time to the music, each lost in their own thoughts.

Luci was torn between her love for him and the thought that she would probably never see him again after tonight. Their project had come to a successful end. She had done her part. Now there was no need for her to stick around any longer. James had progressed a long way in his training and he should be able to manage the restaurant. It was time for her to go back to school and complete her law degree. That was the goal she had been working towards. Seeing Jeremy's family had reminded her of just how far apart their two worlds were. She had known he was rich, but now she realized that he and his family also had class. She came from a poor, working family. There was simply no way she would fit into his world, she thought.

Jeremy held her close, breathing in the scent of her cologne. He would recognize it anywhere. Holding Luci in his arms felt so right, but he could feel her tense up. *What was going through her mind?* he wondered. Just getting her alone had been a hard enough task. Getting her to accept his proposal would be a monumental one. *Would she, could she say yes?*

The music stopped momentarily and people began heading back towards their tables. Jeremy steered Luci in the direction of a bench at one end of the patio, isolated from the crowd and the noise.

"Luci, there is something I need to ask you," he said, working up his nerve as he spoke.

She looked at him, her eyes filled with uncertainty, although in her heart she knew what was coming.

"Yes, Jeremy, what is it?"

"Luci, I love you." He paused. There, it was out. He had finally said it. After all these months, he had finally revealed his true feelings for her. Drumming up his courage, he continued.

"Will you marry me?" he asked.

She looked him straight in the eye, her own eyes filling with tears as she began to answer. "Jeremy, we come from two different worlds. It wouldn't work," she spoke softly.

"We'll make it work. Please, Luci. I know you must love me. Just say 'yes,'" he pleaded.

"I'll have to think about it. Please give me some time. I'll give you my answer tomorrow," she responded as she hurriedly arose and headed back into the restaurant, trying her best to keep from bursting into tears.

He watched her go. Let her go. He could still feel the ring box in his pocket, weighing him down like an albatross. Was there nothing more he could say to persuade her to accept his proposal? He would rattle his brain tonight, trying to come up with a plan.

Luci hurried back into the restaurant and headed straight for the ladies' restroom. Mama Rosa and Mrs. Clark spotted her at the same time. They exchanged glances. Everyone else at the table was too engrossed in a conversation to notice.

"I must go to her," Mama exclaimed.

"No, Mrs. Carlito," began Mrs. Clark when she was interrupted.

"Rosa, please call me Rosa," Mama insisted.

"Rosa, let me go. I think I know what is bothering Luci," said Mrs. Clark.

She arose from the table and excused herself on the pretense of going to powder her nose. She entered the restroom and found Luci standing in front of one of the lavatories, blotting her eyes with a paper towel.

Luci looked up, surprised to see Jeremy's mother standing beside her.

"Mrs. Clark," she exclaimed, unable to get anything more out.

"Luci, my dear, why are you crying?" Mrs. Clark ask, speaking gently.

"I...can't...say," Luci replied hesitantly.

"It's about Jeremy, isn't it? Did he propose to you?"

"Yes, but how did you know?" Luci inquired incredulously.

"There isn't much about my boy that I don't know. Besides, he showed me the ring."

"Ring? He bought me a ring?" Luci asked, sniffling slightly, her voice quavering as she spoke.

"A beautiful ring. But I am so sorry I spoiled his surprise. Please don't tell him I told you about it," said Mrs. Clark.

"I can't marry him. We're worlds apart. There is no way I could fit into his world," Luci insisted.

"My dear girl, is that what is bothering you? We haven't always had money. When Jeremy and Judith were growing up, we were just like any other ordinary family. We lived in a small house and Mr. Clark worked very hard at his job. He just got lucky and got promoted until he worked his way up to being the president of the company Then he decided to venture out on his own and opened a small business. The business took off and he reinvested our money. What you see today is the result of many years of work and sacrifice. Deep down, we are just regular people like you and your family. Please don't judge my son by his monetary worth! There is more to Jeremy than meets the eye. If you love him, you will realize that."

"I told him I would give him an answer tomorrow. With the opening of the restaurant and everything else that is going on tonight, I cannot think straight. It's all too much for me!" exclaimed Luci.

"Then dry your tears and come back to the table. Jeremy will wait for your answer. Don't let this ruin the evening. Tonight belongs to you and Jeremy. You have both worked so hard on this project. You need to see it through."

Mrs. Clark's calm demeanor seemed to rub off on Luci, who suddenly felt like a great weight that had been pressing on her heart had been lifted.

"You're right. Just give me a minute to compose myself," Luci decided, blotting her eyes as she spoke. She glanced into the mirror, thankful for waterproof mascara. At least she didn't have streaks running down her face.

"I'll go first. It will look better if we don't return to the table together," Mrs. Clark stated firmly, opening the restroom door as she spoke.

Luci paused for a moment, almost unable to comprehend what had transpired thus far in so short a time. She took a deep breath and headed out of the restroom and back to the family table.

Jeremy had reappeared and was seated by the time Mrs. Clark reached the table. Mama Rosa looked at her questioningly and she managed to nod indiscreetly to reassure Luci's mother that everything was all right.

Jeremy was unusually quiet, his jubilant and bubbly mood seeming to have fallen by the wayside. Luci arrived at the table with eyes that were dry, but still bearing the telltale signs of a recent crying jag. The rest of the family suddenly became aware that they had apparently missed out on some sort of dramatic event, but they were too polite to question the couple. Nevertheless, the party mood was spoiled for the rest of the evening, so everyone decided to call it a night.

Papa D'Armon herded his family out to his cab, while Jeremy summoned the limo driver on his cell phone. The rest of the Clark family, along with Bart, headed outside, leaving Jeremy and Luci behind to sort things out between them.

"Luci, will I see you tomorrow?" Jeremy asked anxiously, holding her hand as he spoke.

Luci hesitated, drew a deep breath, and then forced herself to look him in the eyes once more. "Yes, I will give you my answer then," she promised, withdrawing her hand as she spoke.

Realizing he would get no other response until morning, he turned and walked out the door, resisting the urge to end all the controversy by grabbing her and kissing her soundly.

This time the tables were turned as she watched him leave. She had some serious thinking to do, but she couldn't let her mind wander in that direction until she had wrapped up all the details for the night's closing of the restaurant.

James had been watching the scene play out. Even though he couldn't hear the conversation, he could read body language and he didn't like what he saw. Although Luci was his supervisor, he had become her sounding board as she tried to sort out her feelings for Jeremy.

"Miss Luci, I can handle the closing tonight. It's been a long day for you. Why don't you go on home with your family and try to get some rest?" he suggested as he approached her. She was still glued to the spot where she and Jeremy had stood.

"No, James, it is my responsibility and I have to see it through," she responded, shaking her head as she spoke.

"Miss Luci, you won't be any good to anybody if you wear yourself to a frazzle. Trust me. I know what I'm doing. I'm used to hard work. Just go and leave the closing to me."

Luci wavered. "Well, maybe just this once…"

"That's the spirit. Take the breaks when you can. That's what I always say."

"Well, goodnight then. I'll see you tomorrow," she finally agreed.

The following morning Luci was up and out of the house before the rest of the family was even stirring. She couldn't bear to face any questions from them until things were settled between her and Jeremy, once and for all.

She headed for the restaurant, which had become her safe haven. She hadn't slept a wink all night. The proof was evident in the dark circles beneath her eyes. Even her concealer couldn't hide them. She had managed to coax her hair into a halfway decent "do," but her brain felt like a rat's nest. She still didn't have the answer to Jeremy's proposal. She realized that she loved him, but could a marriage between two so very different people really work? Evidently his mother was on her side, but what about the rest of his family? Her family was already crazy about Jeremy. That was for sure and for certain. They would welcome him into the family with open arms, should she say yes.

She arrived at the restaurant and parked her car in the usual place near the back door of the kitchen. The only other vehicle belonged to James, who always arrived early. She had to smile as she looked at the somewhat battered truck that James had managed to procure after saving his salary for a few months. It wasn't much to look at, but it was his pride and joy, a symbol of his newfound freedom and independence.

She walked in, maneuvered her way through the kitchen and headed to one of the corner tables in the main dining room. James spotted her immediately and walked over with a cup of coffee.

"Looks like somebody had a rough night," he commented as he placed the steaming cup of brew in front of her. It was just what she needed. Hot, black, and strong. Something to help clear her brain.

James walked away without another word. He had become her friend and confidant in the past few months as they had worked together. She had told him things that she could not and would not tell her own family. He knew all about the situation between her and Jeremy. He was a man of few words and James had the kind of wisdom that came with common sense. That was why she trusted him to keep her secret and why she had confided to him about Jeremy.

She had taken only a few sips of the coffee when Jeremy walked through the front door and headed straight for her table. He slid into a chair across from her, facing her with troubled eyes. He looked a bit disheveled, unlike his usual Mr. Perfect mode. It was obvious to Luci that he, too, had spent a restless night.

Before either of them could speak, James reappeared with another cup of coffee, almost shoving it in front of Jeremy.

"You both look like hell warmed over," he observed. "I'm going to the kitchen to fix you something to eat."

He walked away, mumbling something about people not knowing their own minds.

"How did you know where to find me?" she asked.

"I called your home and Mama Rosa said you had left. I know you have poured your heart and soul into this place. Where else would you be?" he explained.

"You know me too well," she said.

"Exactly how well do I know you, Luci? You walked away before we finished our conversation last night. Things haven't changed for me. I still love you."

He dug into his pocket and produced a jeweler's box. He flipped the box open, revealing a diamond ring in one of the most beautiful settings Luci had ever seen. Holding onto the box, he rose from his seat and moved around to her side of the table, dropping on one knee and taking hold of Luci's left hand.

"Luci Carlito, will you marry me? I promise you that we can work through whatever is troubling you. I repeat, I love you and I want to be with you from now on."

Luci sat speechless, staring at the ring as it sparkled in the light. Then she found her voice. "Jeremy, I love you, too, but what about getting my law degree? That has been my dream ever since I was in high school. I can't just let it fall by the wayside."

"I promise you that I will never interfere with that dream or any other dreams you may have. Don't you see – things will be so much easier for you if we are married. You will never have to worry about money again. You can get your law degree, your doctorate degree, or any other degree you would like."

"But what about your family? Would they approve of me as your wife?" she asked worriedly.

"My family loves you. They told me so this morning when I put them on a plane headed for home."

"Then I guess I'm out of excuses. Yes, I'll marry you!" she exclaimed as Jeremy slipped the ring out of the box and onto her finger. He rose and took both her hands in his as she stood to face him. She slipped her arms around his neck as he bent to kiss her, not once, but twice.

"The second kiss was for making me wait so long for your answer," he joked.

A chorus of cheers rang out from the early kitchen staff, who had been watching the drama as it unfolded. James had kept them all at bay after they arrived, but he couldn't stop them from peeking through a crack between the kitchen doors.

"Wait a minute. You put your parents on a plane. You don't own a car. Just exactly how did you get here, Jeremy Clark? Did you come in one of Papa's cabs?"

He grinned. "How do you think I got here?"

"You didn't…not the motorcycle again."

"Yep, guilty as charged. Let's go for a ride. I need some fresh air."

He tugged at her hand and began leading her towards the door when James appeared, holding two heaping plates of scrambled eggs, toast, and bacon.

"Hey, what about breakfast?" James called after them as they headed out the door.

"We'll be back. Put it in the warmer," Jeremy replied.

"You heard him. Put it in the warmer," he instructed his staff as he bit into a piece of the crisp bacon, smiling as he spoke.

Outside the restaurant, Jeremy and Luci strapped on their helmets in preparation for their ride. He climbed on first and Luci quickly followed his lead.

"Do you like the ring?" he inquired.

"I love it. It's perfect. You're perfect. Everything's perfect," she informed him gleefully.

"That's what I've been trying to tell you all along," he shouted as he prepared to start the motorcycle. "We make the perfect couple."

Luci wrapped her arms around his waist as the motorcycle sprang to life, roaring loudly in response to Jeremy's touch.

"That we do," she agreed, tightening her hold and smiling as she spoke softly. "That we do!"

###

Part V

An Angel and a Swan

"Mac's" Story

An Angel and a Swan

"Hey, Mac, want to go and shoot some hoops? The boys are waiting for us over at the gym."

Kelly "Mac" McGregor frowned at the interruption as she peered over the frames of the tortoise-shell eyeglasses which had slid almost down to the tip of her nose – the same nose that had been crammed into her Advanced Chemistry book for the past two hours.

The dorm door had almost burst open as her roommate, Ashley Gordon, rushed in, breathless, as usual. Not waiting for an answer, she headed for her side of the room, shucking off clothes as she walked.

"Have you seen my blue shorts? I can't seem to find them anywhere," she complained as she pawed through the drawers on her side of the built-in dressing center.

After observing that her roommate was still perched on her bed, leaning against the wall with her book open on her lap, Ashley demanded an explanation for the lack of response.

"Well, why are you just sitting there? Don't you want to go?"

"Oh, Ash, you know I'm no good at sports. Besides, I have a big exam coming up in that chem class and I can't afford to make a bad grade," Mac protested.

"Oh, pooh with that class. You know you're the smartest student in it. Why do you always worry so much? Relax and have a little fun! Besides, as I said, the *boys* are waiting for us."

The boys to whom Ashley was referring were Bud Bishop and

Mark Guillory, longtime friends of the two roommates. The four of them were practically inseparable, having hung out together since their grade school days.

"Well, maybe I could go for just a little while. I've stared at this chemistry book so long everything's going all blurry. Just let me find something to wear," Mac finally conceded.

She walked over to her closet and pulled out a pair of sweat pants and a matching tee shirt and shed her bathrobe and slippers in preparation for donning the selected outfit.

"What! You're not wearing shorts? You'll burn up in those long pants!" Ashley exclaimed as she shimmied into her own shorts, which she had just located under her bed. She topped off the outfit with a sleeveless tee shirt.

"Ash, you should know by now that I don't like wearing shorts in public," Mac explained patiently.

She had always been self-conscious about her figure and was even more so now that she was attending college with so many gorgeous and apparently rich girls on campus. After graduating from a high school where uniforms were the required apparel, she was amazed at the array of beautiful and unique clothes her college peers seemed to possess. Girls were constantly borrowing each other's clothes, but there was no way she could squeeze even one of her legs into Ashley's size zero outfits, and she wasn't about to humiliate herself by even trying to fit into someone else's clothes.

The college was a private school and most of the students came from the upper crust of society. A few, like Mac, had been admitted on scholarships based on their high school grades and ACT scores, but they were definitely in the minority. She could have gone to a state university, but she had envisioned becoming a doctor, and this school had one of the best pre-med programs in the state. That, along with the chance to room with her best friend, had sealed the deal as far as she was concerned. When she found out Bud and Mark would be joining them, she was elated.

"Well, I just hope there aren't too many spectators in the gym today. I hate being in front of an audience," Mac grumbled as she finished dressing and bent down to tie her shoes. "Besides, I'm better at softball than I am at basketball. You know I positively suck on the basketball court."

"Oh, who cares? We're just trying to have some fun. Loosen up, girl," Ashley chided as they headed for the door.

"Easy for you to say," Mac muttered under her breath as she pulled the door closed behind her.

Minutes later they entered the gym, with Ashley gliding in and Mac bringing up the rear, huffing and puffing as she tried to keep up with her slender roommate. They spotted the boys, who were already out on the basketball court practicing at the free throw line.

"What took you girls so long? We were about to give up on you," Mark declared.

"It took a little persuading to get Mac's nose out of a book," Ashley explained.

"We've lined up a few people for a half-court game. Let's get started," Mark announced as he began waving some of their friends to come over from the far goal.

"Game? I thought we were just going to shoot some hoops," Mac protested.

"What? You want to play HORSE? You must think we're back in elementary school," Mark teased as he bounced the ball skillfully at his feet, switching from one hand to the other without even looking down.

Mac blushed and looked over at Bud, who just shrugged his shoulders and rolled his eyes. He wasn't any more athletic than she was, but at least he wasn't overweight, she thought despondently. There appeared to be no way out of the situation. She'd have to play. She just hoped she didn't make too big a fool out of herself.

They chose sides and the game began in earnest. Ashley and Mark ended up on the same team, leaving Mac and Bud to play opposite them. Mac wasn't too surprised at the choices. After all, Ashley and Mark were the athletes in their little group, while she and Bud were the scholars. Like Mac, Bud was attending on a scholarship. He planned to become a CPA and hoped to establish his own accounting firm someday.

Despite the lopsided teaming the score remained close because their other friends who filled out the roster made up for Mac and Bud's lack of skills. Mac managed to avoid actually handling the ball most of the time, much to her relief. All she wanted to do was get through the game and get back to her dorm room.

Suddenly, out of nowhere, someone threw the ball hard at her, hitting her squarely in the chest. She managed to hold onto it, although she almost lost her breath from the impact.

Mark rushed over to guard her, coming so close she caught the odor of his sweat mixed with the cologne he always wore. His muscles rippled beneath his tee shirt as he waved his arms in front of her to fend off any attempted pass. She became even more breathless as her heart began to beat a little faster just from being so close to such a perfect male body.

"Mackie, Mackie, Mackie can't throw the ball," he taunted as she stood frozen in place.

She stepped back with her right leg and raised her arms in preparation for ridding herself of the ball when suddenly her left foot and Mark's feet somehow became entangled, causing both of them to crash to the floor. She was at the bottom of the heap, with Mark landing solidly on top of her. Her suspicions that he possessed a rock-hard body were confirmed. She swore she could feel every muscle in his body before he managed to push himself up and roll off her.

Ashley and Bud rushed over immediately.

"Mac, are you okay?" Ashley inquired anxiously.

Before she could reply, Mark began to chew her out. "Blast it, Mac, do you always have to be such a klutz?" he shouted as he came up holding onto his left knee.

"Shut up, Mark," Bud exclaimed as he extended his arms to assist Mac in her attempts to get up off the gym floor. "It was as much your fault as hers. You shouldn't have been standing so close."

By then Mac could feel the eyes of everyone in the whole gym upon her. It was all she could do to keep from bursting into tears. She didn't know when she had been so humiliated.

"I think I sprained my ankle," she lied. "I'd better go back to the dorm and put some ice on it."

"I'll go with you," Ashley volunteered. "It's about time for supper anyhow. I suppose we've played enough basketball for today."

"Okay, I guess we'll see you girls later," said Mark, who was still favoring his left leg, offering no apology for his outburst.

"Bye, Mac. I hope your ankle gets better," Bud added.

The boys walked off the court and watched as the girls slowly exited the gym.

"Drat that Mac! She's always goofing up," Mark exclaimed as he grabbed a towel to dry his face.

"Don't talk about her that way," Bud admonished him.

"Hey, it's Mac we're talking about. What's come over you? Wait a minute…you like her, don't you? That's it. You really *like* her."

Bud's ears turned bright red as the color slowly seeped into the rest of his face.

"What? No…I…it's just that we've been friends like…*forever*."

"I have to admit, she has quite a brain. If only she would do something about that figure of hers, she wouldn't be half-bad to look at."

"Looks aren't everything, Mark. Brains can get you a lot further in life than looks," Bud retorted, grabbing his own towel and dabbing his face vigorously.

"Maybe so, but can you blame me for going for a looker like Ashley?"

"No, not at all. I like Ashley, too. She's a wonderful girl, but she's not the only girl in the world, you know!"

"And just how would you know that? I haven't seen you on any hot dates lately."

"Maybe I haven't wanted to go on a *hot* date. Not all guys are like you, Mark. Not all guys have girls falling at their feet, panting away, willing to do your bidding at every beck and call," Bud was practically shouting, his face turning redder as he spoke.

"Hold on. I've never cheated on Ashley," Mark yelled back, throwing down his towel in the process."

"I know that, but girls still fall for you, all the same. They can't help themselves, just like you can't help the way you look. Even Superman would be jealous."

"That's it. That's your problem. We have to do something about your looks. We have to change you from a beanpole into a muscleman. I know all about that. I'm a kinesiology major, remember?" Mark's demeanor suddenly changed.

"I don't know, Mark. Some things are just hopeless," Bud replied as he shrugged his shoulders and shook his head. He balled up his towel in preparation for dumping it into the used towel bin.

"Hey, little buddy, have you ever known me to lose? We'll work this thing out together. I'm going to come up with a plan designed especially for you. Follow it and you'll be a totally different man by the time spring rolls around." Mark was smiling as he reached down and scooped his towel off the floor.

"Pretty sure of yourself, aren't you?" Bud responded, the corners of his mouth turning up slightly in a half-crooked grin.

"Time will tell, my man. Time will tell. Say, I'm starved. Let's get cleaned up and head for the cafeteria."

The boys simultaneously tossed their towels into the dirty towel bin as the headed for the exit. Each was lost in his own thoughts – thoughts about two totally different girls.

###

The girls headed back to the dorm with Mac faking a limp along the way.

"Are you sure you're okay?" asked Ashley.

"I'll be fine. I just need to rest for a while," Mac assured her.

Back at the dorm they managed to scrape together a makeshift icepack using some ice cubes from their small dorm refrigerator and a Ziploc sandwich bag. Mac sat on her bed, propping her back against the wall and holding the icepack on her "injured" ankle. She hated lying to her roommate, but there was no way she was going back out on campus tonight. Ashley changed clothes and left, promising to bring her a sandwich from the Subway deli located in the gym foyer. Mac had lost her appetite after the disastrous gym expedition, but she had to eat something, she told herself. She knew Ashley wouldn't let her down.

It was totally remarkable that two people who were such opposites could ever be such good friends, she reflected. It had all started the first day in kindergarten. She and Ashley had been seatmates assigned to the same table. They had become instant pals. She thought Ashley was the prettiest little girl she had ever seen with her flawless skin, sky blue eyes, and golden hair that floated about her face almost like a halo.

She, on the other hand, could barely coax her kinky red hair into a band in order to keep it out of her eyes. Her skin was freckled and the more she stayed in the sun, the more freckled it became. Plus, her eyes, much to her disappointment, were brown rather than blue. To make matters even worse, she was diagnosed with myopia and had started wearing eyeglasses even before she entered kindergarten. But looks didn't seem to matter to the two little girls.

They soon began arranging play dates and took turns visiting each other. At Ashley's house they played dress up, using her mother's real pearls, along with her fancy discarded clothes and shoes. They had tea time with Ashley's tea set that consisted of miniature cups and plates made of real China. A maid brought them dainty sandwiches and fancy cookies that had been made by their cook.

Things were more relaxed at Mac's house, where they often played in the backyard with the family dog or took turns on the tire swing that hung from a rope tied to a huge oak tree. Inside the house they were often found in the kitchen, where they helped Mac's mom make brownies or cookies and got to lick the spoons afterwards. It didn't seem to matter to either girl that they were obviously from two different levels of society.

Mac first began to get an inkling of how differently she was treated by her teachers and peers when they participated in the school's annual Christmas pageant in the second grade. Ashley lived up to her middle name of Ashley Angel Gordon and was chosen to be the angel in their class play. She even got to wear a halo. Mac, on the other hand, ended up being the rear end of a donkey, which was not a pleasant task, by any means.

Then there had been the dance lessons. Ashley was a talented dancer and was always chosen to be one of the featured solo acts at the dance recitals. Mac, already self-conscious about being slightly chubby, was relegated to performing a line tap dance dressed as a milkmaid while carrying a milking stool and a bucket full of confetti. The milkmaids had been instructed to toss the confetti out into the audience at the end of the performance. She got her revenge by tossing hers squarely at a woman in the third row who was wearing an over-sized hat.

As if that weren't bad enough, the following year Ashley got to wear shorts, a tuxedo jacket, and a top hat for a duet tap dance with a *boy* while Mac was assigned to perform in a group ballet dressed in a full-length turquoise dress made with layers and layers of net material. The instructor stuck her in the middle of the stage since she was the tallest (and in her eyes, the largest) member of the group. She was even more embarrassed when she learned the title of the dance was "Dance of the Naked Sea."

Two years of dancing was about all Mac could stand, but Ashley went on to excel in both modern dance and gymnastics. Both accomplishments came in handy when she tried out for cheerleader for the seventh grade and was elected by an overwhelming majority. She eventually worked her way up to head cheerleader in the tenth grade and held that position throughout the rest of her high school years.

Mac delved into music as an alternative and ended up playing the French horn in the school band. She never made first chair, but she was good enough to be in the varsity marching band, and that meant she got to attend all the school's football games free. She and Ashley didn't get to ride the same bus to the games, but they always touched base at halftime and usually spent the night together after each game, alternating between their houses.

Their friendship with the boys had begun in elementary school. Bud and Mark lived in the same neighborhood as Mac, so they often walked to school together. Mark, always the tease, was the one who came up with the nickname for Mac, proclaiming it suited her better than Kelly. The name stuck, and soon everyone except her parents began calling her Mac. Her mother insisted on using her given name, declaring, "Kelly

Colleen McGregor is what I named you, and you will always be Kelly to me." Her dad agreed, partly to keep peace in the family, but also because she had been named after her two grandmothers.

It was only natural that the four friends should hang out together during summer vacation when Ashley was visiting Mac. Although it may have seemed strange to some people that Ashley was allowed to visit someone in a neighborhood that was obviously beneath her family's means, her mother didn't seem to mind after she met Mrs. McGregor at a PTA meeting and the two women hit it off immediately. After that, Ashley was allowed to visit the McGregor household, with her mother's blessing, whenever she chose.

During the summer following the sixth grade when they suddenly found that their bodies had begun to develop bumps in places they had never had bumps before and they were also all knees and elbows, the girls took a brief respite from their association with the boys. Ashley's bumps soon developed into curves that were most attractive while Mac just…well, developed.

They returned to school entering the seventh grade and discovered that the boys they had been playmates with had begun their transformation into young manhood. Mac thought Mark was the handsomest boy she had ever seen and it wasn't long before she developed a major crush on him. He tried out for the football team and was soon too absorbed in sports to notice girls – except for the cheerleaders, Ashley, being the main focus of his attraction. It was only natural that they paired off, leaving Bud and Mac to fend for themselves where the opposite sex was concerned. Oh, she and Bud were friends, but the spark just wasn't there, she decided. They were both bookworms, and bookworms didn't usually attract the opposite sex. The arrangement continued throughout high school, right up until the time Mark became the captain of the football team during his senior year.

Ashley starred in the senior play and was also elected homecoming queen. She could have had any boy she wanted, but she stuck with Mark, despite the fact that he was becoming more and more stuck on himself.

In addition to her band activities, Mac joined the science club, while Bud became a member of the Future Business Leaders of America and was eventually elected president of that organization. Slowly, but surely, the four friends were beginning to shape their futures. They all knew they wanted to go to college, but they had little idea they would all end up attending the same one.

Yet, here they were, three years later, she pondered. Together, but so far apart. She still thought Mark was the handsomest boy…no make that *man*…she had ever seen. Somehow, she never seemed to be able to quite get his image out of her mind – blue eyes, blond hair, and a deeply tanned complexion from so many days spent in the sun practicing football. He and Ashley were like a pair of matching bookends. She would give anything if he would even show the slightest interest in her, but he was too wrapped up in Ashley to even notice another girl, despite the fact that they were continually throwing themselves at him, he now being the captain of the college football team.

Well, her disastrous visit to the gym tonight had tied it, she decided. Things simply could not continue the way they were. She had been laughed at and embarrassed by her looks for the last time. She simply had to do something about losing weight and improving herself, but what? She had to come up with a plan, and fast.

Her thoughts were interrupted as Ashley bounced back into the room with the promised sub sandwich, along with a cola and some chips.

"I thought you might be hungry by now," she said as she plopped the food down onto Mac's desk. "How's your ankle?"

"It's better, and I am hungry. Thanks so much for bringing the food," Mac told her.

"Mark's waiting for me at the library, so I have to go. He has a big test coming up in English and I promised to tutor him. Oh, he said to tell you that he's very sorry about yelling at you, but he was worried about hurting his knee. He may not be able to play in the game Saturday night," Ashley informed her.

"I suppose it would have been too much to expect him to apologize in person," Mac commented sarcastically.

"Oh, I know he's conceited sometimes, but he has a good heart. You just have to look hard to find it." Ashley sighed as she spoke. After gathering her books she headed out the door, leaving Mac to, once again, ponder her situation.

I wonder how many calories are in the sandwich, she thought as she glanced at the napkin Ashley had brought to go with the meal. Subway was known for posting nutritional information about it menu, but she was surprised to find it listed in detail on her napkin. She had never really paid attention to either calories or nutrients in food. She just ate what she liked, and she did enjoy eating!

"Wow, I didn't know just a sandwich could have so many calories," she complained out loud with no one but herself to hear. *Maybe I'd better check out the chips and cola, too,* she contemplated as she began to examine their labels. *Well, at least the chips are baked and the cola is diet,* she reflected. She knew Ashley was concerned about her being overweight, but Ashley would never hurt her feelings. The chips and cola were just gentle reminders.

She finished off the food and tossed the wrappers into the wastebasket, saving the napkin for future reference.

Maybe I could be like that guy on TV who advertises for Subway. He lost gobs of weight by eating just their sandwiches for lunch and supper. She had to laugh out loud at that one! Her parents had already paid for a meal ticket, and she was on a shoestring budget. No, she would just have to learn how to select better meals from the cafeteria food, she resolved.

Well, she might as well get comfortable if she was going to spend the rest of the night in her dorm room as she had done so many times before. A quick shower and changing into her pajamas should mellow her mood, she decided. She walked into the bathroom that separated the two rooms in the suite. Peeking through the bathroom door on the far side, she found that her suitemates were not in. Like Ashley, they were most likely out on campus somewhere with their boyfriends.

Just how much of a job do I have ahead of me if I want to transform myself from an ugly duckling into a swan? she wondered. Stripping down to her underwear, she took a good hard look at the reflection in the bathroom mirror. She was not pleased with what she saw. A roll of fat hung over the waist of her panties, and she was practically popping out of her bra. Getting it fastened had become a major chore she had to face every morning. Gathering up her courage, she turned around and viewed herself from behind. *Good grief, my butt looks big enough to set up a picnic on.* She almost moaned. But there was one consolation. *At least I don't have cellulite. Not yet anyhow. So, that's one point in my favor.*

Did she dare go even one step further and step on the scales? Well, if she was going to start this weight-loss program, she had to do it. She simply had to know how much she weighed.

She pulled the bathroom scales out of the corner and stepped on them squarely, dreading reading the results. The light on the electronic panel flickered and then stopped as a number appeared. Two hundred pounds. She couldn't believe it. *Could it be possible she had eaten her way so far up the scales?* She stepped off and then stepped back on. Again, the same reading appeared. There was no doubt about it. She actually weighed two hundred pounds.

She wanted to die, just die and get it over with. She almost hyperventilated as she leaned against the lavatory. Then she took a deep breath, turned on the faucet, and splashed some cold water on her face. She felt better after that and decided taking a shower might actually help her to relax.

Moments later she stood under the steady stream of hot water that spewed forth from the shower head, leaving a telltale wisp of steam that floated over the top of the shower door. She watched as the lathered-up soap slowly washed off her body and headed down the drain, wishing it was that easy to get rid of those unwanted pounds she had accumulated. She felt like crying, but vowed she wouldn't. No, never again would she apologize to anybody for her appearance!

Emerging from the shower, she quickly dried herself off and put on her pajamas and robe. She had been formulating a plan ever since she went into the bathroom and now it was time to take action.

There was bound to be plenty of information on the internet about weight loss. All she had to do was find the right website. She sat down at her desk, opened her laptop and began typing in the information she was looking for.

One thing she knew for sure. She wasn't taking any kind of weight-loss pills or supplements. There was no telling what kind of effect they might have on a person's health. Besides that, she had heard most of them were expensive, and there was that budget problem again. No, what she needed was help with learning how to select the right kinds of foods.

After a few minutes of searching she came upon what she was looking for. It was a virtual weight-loss website. Anybody could join, and they all remained anonymous. All she had to do was make up a screen name and type in a few other bits of information and she would be accepted in the group. It seemed almost too good to be true. She knew there were a lot of scam artists operating on the internet, so she needed to check it out before joining. A few more clicks on the keyboard proved it to be a safe and secure website.

Well, what can I call myself? she wondered. Obviously, nobody was using their real name with members such as "Sweet Pea," "Lotus Blossom," and "Lonely Girl." *I'm the ugly duckling, but I definitely don't want to use that as my screen name.* After sifting through numerous names listed on another website, she finally settled on "Patience," rationalizing that was what it was going to take to accomplish her goal.

Summoning up all her courage, she typed in the required information and registered on the website. As she began to read the information posted by other members, she was amazed by some of their stories. None of them had it easy, it seemed. There were a lot of people in the world who had encountered problems due to their weight. The world could be a cruel place for overweight people, she decided. At least she had friends. Some of the website members were lonely souls who were reaching out to others in the same predicament. She wasn't quite ready to reveal everything about herself to them yet. Maybe later, but for now she would be content just reading their bios.

Well, no time to dwell on that now. What she needed to find was some kind of help in choosing the right foods. There were so many diet plans to choose from Which diet was the right one for her? Should she go with the Richard Simmons Diet, the Atkins Diet, or the Mediterranean Diet? Then there was Sugar Busters, Weight Watchers, the T-Factor Diet, or the Keto Diet. It was too much for her to absorb in one sitting. One thing became clear to her – following any of those diets while eating in the cafeteria would be almost impossible. What she needed to do was come up with her own tailor-made plan, perhaps combining dieting tips from each of the other plans.

She sighed. *Well, so much for my favorites. No more doughnuts and coffee for breakfast. Forget those hamburgers and French fries for lunch. Even worse, no more Wendy's Frosties or Sonic Blasts. And don't even mention Oreos or Chips Ahoy. Ditto for Cheetos and Fritos Scoops with jalapeno cheese dip.* She was going to have to change her entire way of eating. She knew she could do it mentally, but what would her stomach think about suddenly being introduced to a new way of eating? There was only one way to find out and that was to try it. So, that's what she would do, starting first thing tomorrow morning.

Putting it all in a nutshell, there were three different no-no's according to most of the diet plans. She had to avoid saturated fats, sugar, and salt. What she needed to eat was plenty of fruits and green vegetables, protein and lean meats, whole grains, and complex carbohydrates. The cafeteria offered a variety of foods, so she was confident she would be able to find those items every day.

One thing was certain. She would have to tell Ashley about her plan. Otherwise, her roommate would think she had totally lost her mind, a junk food junkie gone berserk. But Ashley would have to be sworn to secrecy. She couldn't and wouldn't have the entire campus in on the plan. What she ate was her business and nobody else's. Ashley would notice the change in her eating habits, but Ashley could be trusted to keep her secret.

She yawned as she turned off the computer. It had been a long and hard day. What she needed was some rest, and her bed looked awfully inviting. Ashley was still out with Mark. She would come running in just before curfew. Mac knew that from previous occasions. She was used to her roommate bumping around in the dark, trying not to disturb her when she was already in bed. Sometimes it was almost comical whenever Ashley stubbed her toe and tried to stifle a surprised yelp of pain. That's what came from having a boyfriend who wanted you to spend every spare minute with him, something Mac had never experienced. Not yet anyhow.

She slipped out of her bathrobe and slippers, checked the alarm clock, and switched off the light just before sliding into bed. Her brain was still going about ninety miles an hour, practically reeling from all the information she had absorbed during the past couple of hours. What she needed now was sleep. Tomorrow she was going into her battle mode and she needed every bit of her strength.

After what seemed like only moments later, Mac awakened to the insistent shrilling of her alarm clock. She groaned as she picked it up, resisting the urge to throw it against the wall. It was 6:30 a.m., and through the bathroom door she could hear the sound of water running in the shower. Turning on her lamp, she observed Ashley's empty bed with clothes strewn around it. Undoubtedly, her roommate was already up and awake, ready to face the world in her usual cheerful manner. Mac had never been an early riser, but now that she was turning over a new leaf, she supposed that she would get dressed and head to the cafeteria to see what sort of food she could scrape up to begin her new regime. She rolled out of bed and headed for the closet. She turned on the closet light and prodded through her clothes, looking for something suitable to wear. She finally settled on her favorite pair of jeans and a loose-fitting shirt, reasoning it might help to camouflage her figure.

Ashley emerged from the bathroom, looking every bit like her middle name, wrapped in a white terrycloth robe, blonde hair flying around her head in its usual halo façade. As she paused in the doorway, light streamed past her into the darkened room. Mac wouldn't have been surprised if real angels swooped down at that moment and lifted her roommate up to the heavens.

The spell was broken when Ashley spoke. "Mac, whatever are you doing up so early? And why is it so dark in here? Good grief, roomie, shed some light on the subject!"

She walked over to the nearest light switch and flipped it on. Suddenly, the room seemed almost too bright. Mac nearly cringed as she blinked her eyes, trying to adjust to the change in lighting.

"I thought I would start a new routine. Breakfast in the cafeteria," Mac announced as she awaited Ashley's response.

"Breakfast…in the cafeteria. What's up, Mac? It's not like you at all!" Ashley exclaimed.

"I'm turning over a new leaf, trying to lose some weight. I've been checking out information on the internet and it gave me some ideas. I have to change my eating habits," Mac confessed. "So, I guess the best place to start is with breakfast. No more coffee and doughnuts. I'll have to find something to stifle my hunger pangs."

"Mackie, I'm so glad," Ashley told her as she rushed to give her roommate a sincere hug. "I'll always love you, no matter what, but losing weight will be so good for your health. I've been praying for you."

"There's just one thing," Mac requested. "Let's keep this between us. It's an experiment and I don't want it to get all over campus that I'm on a diet."

"My lips are sealed," Ashley promised.

"Pinky swear?"

"Pinky swear," Ashley replied as they locked their pinky fingers, one of their long-time traditions since childhood days.

Almost before she knew it, Mac found herself sitting beside Ashley in the cafeteria, facing Mark and Bud on the other side of the table. Ashley had opted for a soft-boiled egg, whole wheat toast, and a glass of skim milk. Mac stared at her food, an entirely new choice of whole wheat cereal, skim milk, and a bowl of fresh fruit. It was going to take some getting used to.

Mark and Bud wasted no time digging into their heartier meals. Mark had no qualms about eating scrambled eggs, bacon, and biscuits dripping with butter and apple jelly. He would work off the extra calories during football practice. Bud, despite his slender frame, never had problems making a stack of waffles disappear in short order. Mac looked longingly at the waffles, watching the butter and syrup cascade down the sides as Bud expertly cut into the stack. She could almost taste the maple syrup. She licked her lips as Bud stuffed a large bite into his mouth. He seemed totally oblivious to her tortured state.

She snapped back to the present when she realized her name had been called. Mark was asking her a question, but what had he said? Her mind was a total blank.

"Would you mind repeating that, Mark?" she inquired, hoping she didn't appear as flustered as she felt.

"I said, 'What are you doing up this early? I've never seen you eat so early in the cafeteria before,'" he repeated.

"Well, I…um," she stammered, frantically bidding her brain to come up with some sort of intelligent reply.

"It's a roommate thing," Ashley interjected. "We decided to eat breakfast together. That's all. Nothing really exciting about that."

"Yes, it's an experiment. We're trying to see if eating breakfast improves our concentration," Mac added lamely, sincerely hoping the boys bought it. Having to eat cereal for breakfast was bad enough without being given the third degree.

"Must be all those pre-med courses you're taking," Mark observed.

"Yes, pre-med. Of course. Maybe I'll write a paper on it," Mac agreed as she gingerly started on her cereal, chewing slowly. It wasn't half-bad. Maybe she could get used to it, but she was going to have to find some other foods to add variety to her diet.

Mark and Ashley were soon engaged in conversation, leaving Mac to face Bud and his rapidly shrinking stack of waffles. She had to say something, but what? Bud was absolutely no help, staring at his plate the whole time. It wasn't like him not to even acknowledge her presence.

She cleared her throat. "Got any hard classes today?"

Bud looked up, meeting her eyes for the first time that morning.

"Not really. It's one of my easier days."

"Oh. Mine, too."

That went well. If I can't even talk to Bud, how will I ever be able to converse with a guy I've just barely met? I'll never make it in the dating game. I'm doomed, just doomed! she thought.

The boys finished their food quickly and excused themselves as they headed for class, rescuing her from what was quickly becoming an embarrassing situation. Mac and Ashley followed suit and headed back to their dorm to brush their teeth, freshen up their makeup, and grab their books before heading for class.

"How do you feel?" Ashley asked as she stood in front of the mirror, fluffing her hair as she spoke.

"Different," Mac replied. "My stomach misses the coffee and doughnuts."

"It will take some getting used to, but it'll be worth it in the long run. Trust me. I'm speaking from past experiences. I love junk food, too, but I try to limit myself to a healthy diet," Ashley told her.

"Breakfast was so exciting. I can't wait for lunch," Mac said, half-jokingly.

"You'll figure it out. Well, gotta go and face my favorite professor, Dr. Wilcox."

"Yuck, not a good way to start the day. Nothing more stimulating than a class in economics."

"It's better than dissecting those lab rats just before lunch in that anatomy class you're taking," Ashley shot back.

"You're right. Well, good luck and I guess I'll see you later," Mac responded as they walked into the hall, locking the door behind them.

Several hours later Mac found herself back in the line at the cafeteria, wondering what she would end up with on her lunch plate. She was accompanied by Sarah Thompson and Missy Callahan, two of her friends from other classes. They, too, were overweight and, although presentable, they were not particularly popular with the opposite sex. The usually spent a good deal of their time rating the boys who passed their table, scoring them on a scale of one to ten. Mac wasn't really into that game, but sometimes she found herself enjoying their antics.

Sarah and Missy were in front of her in the line and they went through it loading their plates, totally disregarding the consequences of poor food choices. Like Mac, they enjoyed food and enjoyed consuming it. Mac hesitated as she started down the line while trying to remember which foods were on her "safe" list. Determined not to call attention to herself by taking too long, she made her choices.

She finally reached the checkout register and swiped her food card, punching in her PIN number. She spotted her friends and headed towards their table, nervously anticipating their comments about her new eating habits. She placed her tray on the table and scooted into a seat as they, not unexpectedly, zeroed in on her food choices.

"Say, Mac, what's up with your appetite?" Sarah inquired.

"Yeah, it looks like you don't have enough food to keep a bird alive," Missy noted.

"Oh, I just decided to try something different," Mac replied.

"I'll say it's different. Since when have you liked grilled chicken, steamed vegetables, and fruit cup?" Sarah continued her inquisition.

Mac forced herself to smile. *Be polite. Be polite*, she kept telling herself mentally.

"It's an experiment. I might write a paper about people's eating habits, so I decided to try a different kind of diet for a while. That's all," she informed them.

If the little white lie had worked with the boys, maybe it would work with her two female friends, too.

They seemed to accept the explanation and wasted no time in turning their attention to their own food, commenting on how good everything was.

"I just love fried chicken," Sarah declared as she bit into a crunchy drumstick.

I hope this doesn't taste like cardboard. Maybe there's something to be said for lemon and pepper seasoning, Mac reflected as she averted her eyes from the fried chicken while cutting herself a bit of the grilled chicken breast.

Their chatter soon turned to other matters and Mac's eating habits were forgotten in the process. Soon they had finished everything except the dessert. Sarah had chosen coconut pie, while Missy had opted for a piece of double fudge chocolate cake. Mac ate her fruit cup slowly, watching as her friends attacked their desserts with relish.

More torture. Will this never end? she wondered. *How long can I sit by and watch my friends consume my favorite foods while eating only healthful stuff. One thing's for sure. I'm going to have to find somebody else to eat with unless they change their eating habits, too!*

She was finished with classes for the day, so she headed back to her dorm room after the meal. Following an impulse, she decided to check into the virtual weight-loss website. It would be interesting to read about other people's problems. Maybe one of them would have suggestions about how to handle food choices when dining with others.

After turning on the computer, she opened her desk drawer, looking for a notepad and pen just in case she wanted to take notes. She found herself staring at the contents of the drawer. Mixed in with the assortment of pens, paper clips, and Post-it notes were several candy bars, including Snickers, Butterfinger, and a package of M & M's. She had totally forgotten about her stash of junk food that was just waiting to tempt her to get off her new diet plan. She was going to have to do something about that later.

She jerked a pen out of the drawer and closed the drawer resolutely, spotting a small notebook at the edge of her desk at the same time. She logged onto the internet and typed in "Slimline Buddies," the name of the virtual weight-loss website.

Guess I might as well get started. Let's find out just how friendly these Buddies really are, she thought as she typed in her first question.

"Started my new diet today. Have managed to stick to it so far, but it hasn't been easy. People all around me are eating all my favorite foods, most of which are not taboo. How do I handle this? Patience."

She sat back and waited for the replies to come in. She didn't have to wait long. Evidently, there were a lot of overweight people eager to assist her.

"Hey, Patience. Welcome to the group. I had the same problem at first. You just have to get used to it. Sweet Pea"

"Look for new friends. Lotus Blossom"

"Some people don't have that many friends. Lonely Girl"

"Just ignore them. They're trying to be funny. Seriously, welcome to the group. Feel free to contact us whenever you feel like it yourself slipping. Hang tight and you will reap in the rewards from forming better eating habits. Check out our menu suggestions. Calendar Girl"

"Thanks, girls. I'm feeling better now. I made it through the first two meals, but still have supper to go. Any suggestions? Patience"

"Eat lightly but try to get some protein food. That will help stave off the hunger. Lotus Blossom"

"Get rid of any junk food you have stashed away. That's one of the first things that could cause you to crash and burn. Sweet Pea"

"Okay, thanks for the advice. Have to go now. Patience"

Just as she signed off, she heard Ashley's key in the door. Ashley bounded into the room with her usual pep and energy. She was hyped up after her cheerleader practice session.

"Hey, Ash. I was just checking into a virtual weight-loss website. I think I may have some new friends."

"Great. Anything to help with the diet. What's next?" Ashley asked.

"I have to get rid of my junk food," Mac admitted.

"Why don't you get it all together and I'll see what we can do with it," Ashley suggested.

Moments later they were staring at the pile of food accumulated on Mac's desk. Mac couldn't believe she had actually managed to stash so much away – several packages of cookies, chips, and an assortment of candy bars.

"You know, I think I have an idea," Ashley told her. "Give me a couple of minutes."

As Ashley headed out the door Mac reached for a plastic grocery bag and began placing the items in it, all except one Snickers bar. That she hid in her desk drawer, reasoning it might come in handy someday.

By the time she finished, Ashley was back with an important announcement.

"You remember Mildred, the maid for our dorm? She has four children and she said they would be thrilled to get all that food. So, problem solved."

"Yeah, problem solved," Mac repeated as she handed the bag to Ashley.

Great for Mildred, but not so great for me. Now what do I snack on? Mac wondered. *If I eat that Snickers bar, it will be like an alcoholic falling off the wagon. And this is just the first day of my diet. I can't let that happen. I won't let it happen!*

Her train of thought was interrupted as Ashley re-entered the room.

"Okay, Mildred's all taken care of. Now we have to get you some healthy snacks. What say we hit the grocery store before suppertime?" she inquired.

"I guess that would work. What should we buy?" Mac responded.

"Let's just go and see what they have and then we'll make up our minds," Ashley decided.

Grabbing their purses, they headed to a small, independent grocery store located several blocks from the campus. College students were the main patrons of the store, and the proprietor, Mr. McCobbie, had revamped his inventory to include their most requested items.

A short, rotund, and slightly balding man, he took a special interest in his customers and prided himself on knowing all their names. Mac had frequented the store ever since she enrolled in the college, stocking up on all her favorite junk foods. He knew her habits well. She sensed he was going to be surprised at her new food choices today. She just hoped he didn't comment on it too much, especially if there were other customers in the checkout line.

"Basket or buggy?" Ashley inquired as they walked through the store's automatic door.

"Uh, buggy, I guess. It will give us a place to put our purses," Mac replied.

"Okay, buggy it is," Ashley agreed as she pulled one out of the row lined up beside the door.

They made their way around the store discussing the pros and cons of their choices, giggling as they wheeled the buggy up and down the aisles. Suddenly, Ashley spotted a friend she wanted to talk to.

"Wait here. I'll be right back," she instructed, leaving Mac stranded by the produce section.

Mac picked up an apple and was about to bag it when she spotted a college boy approaching her, gathering speed as he moved.

She recognized him right away. It was a guy who had been pestering her for over a year. She didn't know his real name, but he had a distinctive facial tic that kicked in whenever he spoke. For that reason, she nicknamed him "Twitchy." She had to give him points for being consistent in his pursuit of her, but she wasn't about to go out with a boy who looked like he might bite her nose off any minute. Kissing him would be totally out of the question, as she might end up with no lips left intact. She had told Ashley about him and they had quite a laugh about it.

Thinking quickly, she wheeled her cart in the opposite direction and headed up the nearest aisle, paying little attention to what kinds of foods it contained until she stopped and noticed she was in the middle of the cookie and candy aisle.

Oh, great. Here I am, trying to find healthy snacks and I end up on the junk food aisle. Even worse, I'm being chased by Twitchy—again. Can my luck get any bleaker? Ashley, where are you?

Glancing back, she could see Twitchy was still following her. The guy was relentless! She maneuvered her cart around the end of the aisle and hurried to reach two aisles over, barely missing a collision with another cart.

"Sorry," she yelled as she rushed by, determined to shake Twitchy, for once and for all. Hopefully, reuniting with Ashley would stave him off. He seemed to be bashful, and approaching one of the most popular girls on campus just wasn't his style. She breathed a sigh of relief when she spotted Ashley near the dairy section talking to one of her fellow cheerleaders.

"Ash, it's getting late," she said as she wheeled her buggy up beside the two girls.

"Hi, Mac." Tiffany, the other cheerleader greeted her.

"Hi," Mac responded, offering no other comment. She knew she was out of her league and she wasn't about to try and start a conversation with one of the campus elite.

"Yeah, right. We've gotta go. See you later, Tiff," Ashley agreed, raising her eyebrows questioningly to Mac as she spoke.

Mac responded by tilting her head in the direction of Twitchy, who had managed to find her again. Spotting the other girls with Mac had slowed down his progress, and he had stopped at the end of an aisle and was looking intently at a stack of canned goods on display.

"Uh oh, not the Twitchster again?" Ashley joked.

"Afraid so," Mac lamented. "The guy never gives up."

"Let's get the rest of our stuff and get out of here. Like you said, it's getting late. It's almost suppertime."

They finished the shopping quickly and headed for the checkout counter. Fortunately, there was a long line and Mr. McCobbie had little time to chat with his customers, sparing Mac the ominous inquisition about her change in eating habits. She grabbed one bag while Ashley hefted the other as they headed back to their dorm.

Arriving back at their room, they entered quickly and placed their bags on Mac's desk. Mac flopped down on her bed, heaving a long sigh.

"Whew, that was a close one. Seems like every time I go to that store I run into Twitchy."

"You know, you ought to go out with the guy and put him out of his misery."

"Sez you," Mac exclaimed, rolling over and grabbing a throw pillow, tossing it squarely at her roommate.

"Hey, take it easy. I was just kidding," Ashley protested, tossing the pillow back.

Mac wasn't about to admit it, but her dream date had blond hair, blue eyes, a golden tan, and looked a lot like Mark. In fact, he *was* Mark, but she would never tell Ashley she had a crush on her boyfriend – a guy she had been dating ever since high school. No matter how hard she tried, she just couldn't get his image out of her head. Once, just once, she would like to have a date with a normal guy. *Why did she always attract weirdos?* she wondered.

She heaved herself off the bed, heading towards the desk and their stash of healthy snacks.

"Guess I'd better get this stuff put away before suppertime," she noted, unloading the sacks as she spoke.

It had been a tough decision, but they had settled on apples, bananas, and pears, all of which could be stored at room temperature. Refrigerated items included a couple of oranges and some fat-free yogurt. Then, at

Ashley's insistence, they had bought some regular popcorn and Molly McButter seasoning, over Mac's protests that she had no way to pop the corn.

"Don't worry. I'll take care of it," Ashley had assured her.

Mac worked quickly and had the items stored in short order. It was approaching five o'clock and her stomach was sending out signals that mealtime was at hand. She definitely didn't want to eat with Sarah and Missy again. Watching them down all her favorite foods would be too much to bear. Ditto for Mark and Bud. She could always eat by herself, but that was downright depressing.

The problem was solved when her train of thought was interrupted by Ashley.

"Mark's got football practice and won't be eating until later. Why don't we go to the cafeteria together?" she suggested.

"Oh, I didn't know you were free tonight. Yes, I'd like that," Mac agreed.

They walked the short distance to the cafeteria, greeting friends along the way. Ashley, being a cheerleader, knew practically everybody on campus, or at least everybody knew her. Being roommates with a popular girl had its advantages, Mac admitted to herself.

"I'm not very hungry tonight. Think I'll just go with a salad," Ashley announced as they walked into the cafeteria.

"Sounds good," Mac concurred.

The both settled on a tossed salad with Mediterranean chicken strips, dressing on the side, Melba toast, and iced tea. Ashley headed towards a small, secluded corner table with Mac following closely behind. They settled in and began tackling the salads. Mac was practically famished.

"Actually, this isn't bad. I just hope I don't get hungry later tonight," Mac commented.

"It's a whole different way of eating. You have to get used to it. Your stomach has to get used to it," Ashley informed her.

"Don't I know it!" Mac exclaimed.

They finished off the meal with soft-frozen yogurt, helping themselves at the self-serve machine.

Mark and Bud walked in just as they were leaving. Mac secretly relished the fact that she had already finished eating and wouldn't be subjected to watching both of them down another high calorie meal, totally oblivious to nutritional value.

"Are you girls leaving already?" Mark inquired.

"Yes, I've got some studying to do," Mac replied.

After Ashley made arrangements to meet Mark in the library later, the girls walked slowly back to their dorm room, breathing in the cooler air as dusk settled over the campus.

"Actually, Mac, if you really want to lose weight you should also try to get into some sort of exercise program," Ashley suggested.

"Yes, I've been thinking about that," Mac admitted. "But I just don't know what I can do. I don't want anything too strenuous. Remember, I've been a couch potato for most of my life."

"What about Pilates? I know a lot of people who've tried that and it's worked for them."

"I've heard of that, but how would I get started?"

"Well, there are DVD programs, or you could try to find a class on campus. I'm sure there are plenty of girls who are trying to keep in shape. I get enough exercise with my cheerleading activities, so I haven't checked it out."

"Like you would ever weigh a hundred pounds soaking wet," Mac lamented.

By that time, they had reached their room. They walked in and sat down on their beds simultaneously, propping themselves against the wall.

"What you have to realize is that everybody doesn't have the same body shape or type," Ashley informed her. "There are four basic body shapes for women, and you can't change the one you were born with, no matter what."

"Go on," Mac told her.

"Okay, take me, for example. I'm what is known as a 'P' type. I have a small frame and I will always be small and petite. That's why

I don't eat very much. It doesn't take much food to maintain such a small body."

"Makes sense. So, who else would be an example of a 'P' type?"

"Well, thinking of famous people, I would say Nicole Ritchie and maybe Mary Kate and Ashley Olsen."

"So, what's the second type?"

"There's the 'G' shape. She has a pear-shaped body with broad hips. No matter how much she exercises, she just can't make her hips smaller in comparison to the rest of her body. It's the most common body type for American women."

"Hmm…sounds like my friend Sarah. Reminds me of that old childhood song, 'She's got two hips just like battleships…'"

"Now you're getting the idea."

"Can you think of any famous people with that body type?"

"Even though she had a voluptuous figure, I'd say Marilyn Monroe would probably fit the bill."

"Marilyn! You've got to be kidding. She was gorgeous."

"Did you ever watch her last movie, *The Misfits*?"

"Sure. Who hasn't?"

"Remember the scene in the bar where she's hitting the paddle ball and the camera focuses right on her butt?"

"Hmm…I guess you're right. Her butt did look pretty big."

"I know my butts!"

They both had to laugh after that remark.

"I'm almost afraid to ask about the third type."

"That's the 'A' type. She has a larger bosom than hips and usually has a thick waist. She may not necessarily be overweight, but, once again, exercise won't change her basic body shape."

"That's definitely my friend Missy. I noticed that she and Sarah are different shapes, even though they're overweight."

"I would say that the most famous actress Rosalind Russell probably fits the 'A' category. And that leaves just one more shape, the 'T' type. Her hips and shoulders are the same size, no matter how much she weighs. It's actually considered the ideal shape. It's what most Miss

America contestants strive for. Plus, I've got some good news for you — I think that's the category you fit into."

"What? With these hips? No way!" Mac exclaimed.

Ashley jumped up off her bed and grabbed a hand mirror.

"Here, take this mirror and look at yourself backwards in the full-length mirror. You'll see what I mean. Go on, take it," she insisted.

"Oh, Ash, I don't know," Mac protested as Ashley pressed the mirror into her reluctant hand. She dragged herself off the bed and headed into the bathroom, stopping in front of the full-length mirror.

"Okay, turn around backwards and look at yourself. What do you see?" Ashley yelled through the door.

"Hmm…I think you're right. As big as my butt is, it seems to be the same size as my shoulders. I'm starting to feel better now."

"Now turn sideways," Ashley instructed.

"Do I have to?" Mac complained.

"Just do it. Look at your stomach. Does it poke out?"

"Is the sky blue?"

"The 'T' type gains a lot of weight in the stomach. Her waist gets thicker when she gains weight and then goes down again when she loses."

"Guess I fit the bill on both counts then. So, what you're saying is if I lose weight I might actually have a smaller waistline again?" Mac quizzed her.

"Yes."

"How do you know so much about all this stuff?" Mac asked as she re-entered the room, closing the bathroom door behind her.

"My mother was an image consultant for a major beauty company for years. She taught me all about body types and makeup, too."

"No wonder she always looked so gorgeous. I thought it was just good genes," Mac joked.

"Well," Ashley patted her hair. "That may be part of it, too."

"That deserves another pillow toss," Mac exclaimed, grabbing her throw pillow and tossing it at Ashley.

"Enough already! I have to meet Mark in the library. Look at the time. I'm late," Ashley retorted, tossing the pillow back as she jumped up off her bed.

"You've definitely given me a lot to think about. Plus, I've still got to study, too. Can't get behind in my classes if I want to get accepted into medical school."

"You study here and I'll study in the library with Mark. He needs all the help he can get!"

"Right," Mac replied, wishing she was the one tutoring Mark instead of Ashley. But that's how it had always been. She had been on the outside looking in where boys were concerned. *Well, there was always Twitchy,* she thought ruefully.

Mac spent the next few days adjusting to her diet. She was becoming more hardened to watching her friends down high-calorie foods while she opted for those that were less fattening. It wasn't easy to change what had become lifetime eating habits. Growing up in a Scottish family, she had been constantly exposed to what her mother referred to as stick-to-your ribs food. Her dad was a meat-and-potatoes guy, so that kind of cooking suited him just fine. Her mother was an excellent cook, and the entire family enjoyed sampling her dishes. Undoubtedly, Mac had done her fair share of sampling, as was evident in her big butt, she discerned.

She was surprised at how quickly a week had passed. She had made it through her classes each day, endured the hazards of the cafeteria line, and eventually ended up back at her dorm room, where she had logged onto Slimline Buddies. Somehow, having people to talk to who were in the same boat as she was held a certain kind of comfort. She began to actually look forward to messaging them every night.

Their personalities began to emerge, even though their identities remained anonymous. Lotus Blossom was the jokester of the bunch, always ready with a punch line. Lonely Girl, like her name, was definitely a lost soul who was searching for companionship. Sweet Pea and Calendar Girl were the practical ones, offering diet tips and boosting the others' spirits whenever they felt low.

There were others in the group, but somehow Mac felt closer to the four girls who had responded the first time she logged onto the Slimline Buddies website. Of course, they couldn't discriminate, so guys were also allowed to join, but members could indicate whether or not they preferred to receive messages from their gender only, and Mac had taken advantage of that feature, feeling she was not ready to discuss her weight problems with the opposite sex. Funny, but she had never thought of boys having weight problems. She had been too wrapped up in her own persona to even notice guys who were overweight. As far as she was concerned, Mark and Bud were the only two males in her life, and she liked it that way. At least most of the time, she did. Maybe if she lost enough weight she might actually attract some other male besides Twitchy. It was something to shoot for, even though none of them could compare to Mark, she pondered.

When she logged on the seventh night, she was bombarded with the same question, *"Have you weighed yet?"*

"Not yet." was her response.

"U need to weigh in to find out if your diet plan is working. Sweet Pea."

"I just haven't had time yet. Patience."

"Ah, yes, the formidable weigh-in. I hate that moment. Lonely Girl."

"The best thing to do is to weigh at the same time every week, preferably in the morning before you've eaten anything. Calendar Girl."

"And do it while wearing as few clothes as possible. Just underwear would be best. Sweet Pea."

"Even better, do it stark naked. Lotus Blossom."

"Okay, I get the picture. I'll weigh in tomorrow morning. I promise. Patience."

She logged off the website and turned off her laptop in preparation for a night of studying. As much as she tried to keep her mind on the subject matter, a picture of the bathroom scales kept popping into her mind. Well, it looked as though she would have to face the ominous scales the first thing tomorrow morning. She could almost swear the thing was laughing at her as it sat tucked securely in its own corner of the bathroom. Maybe she'd get lucky and the battery would be dead.

After several hours of studying, with images of bathroom scales keeping her company, she decided to call it a night. A quick shower and brushing her teeth were all the preparation she needed for bed and moments later she crawled between the sheets, looking forward to getting a good night's sleep. It was not meant to be, and she tossed restlessly as she dreamed she was being chased by gigantic bathroom scales, two enormous chocolate-glazed doughnuts, and a Big Mac the size of the New Orleans Superdome.

She awakened feeling ravenously hungry. A quick survey of the room showed that Ashley had already dressed and left, apparently without rousing her. If her suitemates were also gone, it would be the perfect time to weigh in. There was no tell-tale sign of light creeping underneath the bathroom door, so they, too, were probably already up-and-at-'em.

She flipped on the light, located some underwear, and slipped out of her pajamas, replacing them with the underwear. After knocking on the bathroom door and getting no response, she walked in, hit the light switch, and then locked both doors. This was it. Time for the big weigh-in. She glared at the scales before pulling them out of the corner.

"Okay, if you give me any trouble, I swear you'll end up in the recycling bin," she threatened, stepping on the corner of the scales to activate them.

She drew a deep breath and then exhaled, as if ridding herself of any extra air would help the situation, she thought ruefully. She stepped on the scales and waited for the reading to come up. The number flickered on clearly – 198. She had lost two pounds. But was that all she had managed to lose after torturing herself for an entire week? Was it really worth the effort? She would have to check with her online Buddies. No time for that now. She had to finish getting dressed and get down to the cafeteria for breakfast. Dreaming about food all night had whetted her appetite. It would be hard to stick to a diet this morning!

###

This was one morning she was going to eat something besides cereal, she vowed, as she walked into the cafeteria moments later. She spotted Ashley sitting with Mark and Bud. They were just finishing their meal. At least she wouldn't have to watch Bud down another stack of waffles dripping with butter and maple syrup.

That gave her an idea. Who said she couldn't have waffles? The cafeteria was now offering more foods for people who were watching their weight. The had low-fat waffles and she could top them with fresh strawberries. That would make up somewhat for dreaming about chocolate-glazed doughnuts half the night.

She had just finished loading her tray with the waffles and a glass of skim milk when her friends Sarah and Missy walked in. They waved and she returned the gesture, pointing to a table she had already picked out. They still hadn't changed their eating habits, so it would be interesting to see what they dredged up for breakfast this morning. She didn't care what they ate because she was having waffles! Plus, she had lost two pounds. It was going to be a good day.

Her mood was spoiled moments later as the two girls made a beeline for her table, toting their laden trays. She wondered what kinds of foods would be staring her this time.

"Seeing you with waffles gave me an idea," Missy announced as she set down her tray directly opposite Mac. It contained a stack of waffles accompanied by several packets of butter and maple syrup. Two links of sausage rolled around on the edge of the plate almost as an afterthought.

Mac sighed silently. It looked as if she would have to watch another round of cascading butter and syrup. Could things get any more irritating?

They could, she decided, as Sarah sat down beside Missy. She had chosen two jelly-filled doughnuts, bacon strips, and a latte topped with whipped cream. Neither girl appeared to be worried about the number of calories she was about to consume.

"Say, why are you eating waffles? I thought you were cutting back on food," Sarah commented as she bit into one of the doughnuts and the filling dribbled out onto her chin. She grabbed a napkin and began dabbing quickly at the mess, catching it just before it fell onto her shirt.

"They're low-fat waffles and I'm topping them with fresh fruit, not butter and syrup," Mac replied.

"Now there's something I never thought of," Missy exclaimed as she buttered her waffles and poured the syrup over them. "Waffles just aren't waffles without butter and syrup."

"I thought so, too, a week ago. But these are actually pretty tasty – if you like strawberries, that is."

"Well, it's something to think about," Sarah noted.

"Say, Mac. What's really going on? We know you have entirely changed your eating habits over the past few days. It's just not like you to skip desserts and eat only grilled chicken and such," Missy quizzed her.

"Yeah, what happened to the Mac we all know and love?" Sarah continued the questioning.

"Okay, I guess I'll have to admit it, but don't spread it all over the campus. I'm trying to lose weight. I read up on the different kinds of food plans and sort of came up with one I devised for myself," Mac informed them.

"Diet? Is it working?" Missy asked incredulously.

"I think so. I lost two pounds this week."

"Two pounds. That's not much. You ate all those salads and just lots two pounds," Sarah complained.

"That's considered a safe amount to lose. If you lose weight too fast, it will just come back, or else you will reach a plateau and not lose any more for a long time," Mac explained.

"When did you become such an expert on dieting?" Missy wondered.

"I found a virtual weight loss website. They have a lot of good information on there."

Both girls stared at her as if she had lost her mind. But they also stopped eating, Mac noticed. Missy's stack of waffles was only half finished, while Sarah had consumed only one of her jelly-filled doughnuts. She had their full attention.

"Virtual weight -loss website…can anybody join?" Missy inquired.

"Sure. It's called Slimline Buddies. Just log on and sign up. That's all you have to do."

"Hmm…I guess I could give it a try," Missy mused.

"Well, don't leave me out. If you're going to try it, so am I," Sarah declared.

"Great. Let me know how it turns out. I have to go to class now," Mac informed them as she rose from the table, picking up her tray.

They watched silently as she deposited her tray on the conveyer belt and headed out the door.

Missy was the first to speak. "Can you believe it? She's actually dieting!"

"If it works for her, it might work for us. Looks like losing weight is the only way we'll nab one of those 'tens' we're always joking about," Sarah told her.

"Okay, I'm going to check out that website as soon as I get through with classes today," Missy decided.

"Ditto for me," Sarah added.

Somehow, both girls had lost their appetites. They carried their trays with the half-eaten food over the conveyer belt and headed back to their dorm to pick up their books for class. It was the first time either one had ever left a bite of food on her plate.

###

After finishing her afternoon classes Mac headed to Walmart to look for a DVD on Pilates. The store was located within walking distance of the campus, so she decided to hoof it, thinking that walking might burn some extra calories. Getting some regular exercise might help to speed up her weight loss and tone her muscles, as well, she reasoned. Besides, she preferred exercising in the privacy of her own dorm room, not out in public.

The walk proved to be less strenuous than she had thought it would be. Walmart's DVD's offered quite a variety of exercise programs, and she finally settled on one called "Pilates for Dummies" plus a second one that featured ten-minute sessions on toning different parts of the body. She paid for the purchases quickly and headed back to the campus, eager to see just what kind of exercise Pilates required.

Upon reaching her dorm room, she discovered Ashley had already come and gone. She was evidently at cheerleader practice. That gave Mac an entire hour to herself. *Guess I'll start with the "Pilates for Dummies."* She thought. She plopped the DVD into their player and turned on the small flat screen TV, settling herself onto her bed as she listened intently to the instructor.

Thirty minutes later she was sure she understood it all. The whole thing was about muscle control, stretching, and breathing. She could do all those things, so Pilates seemed to be the way to go. She knew she couldn't jog and she wasn't about to tackle aerobics. Pilates seemed like the ideal compromise. She would start the program tonight after supper.

And speaking of supper, it was almost time to eat again, she realized. No matter how hard she tried, she just couldn't get rid of that appetite of hers. Her train of thought was interrupted by her cell phone ringing. She looked at the Caller I. D. and saw it was Missy. She rolled her eyes and sighed loudly before answering.

"Hello," she said, trying to sound upbeat.

"Mac, it's Missy. Sarah and I were wondering if you wanted to meet us in the cafeteria for supper."

"Um…sure. I guess I could do that," Mac replied.

"Great! See you in about ten."

Mac punched the phone to disconnect, slightly put out at being trapped into eating again with two prime candidates for Overeaters Anonymous.

"Why do I do this to myself? Why? Why?" she complained aloud, grabbing her dining card as she spoke.

Missy and Sarah were already standing in the foyer of the cafeteria waiting for her when she arrived. Both of them were smiling.

"We've got something to tell you," Missy announced.

"Yes, we've decided to go on a diet, too. We checked out that Slimline Buddies website and we both signed up this afternoon," Sarah added.

"You'll never guess what we picked out for our names," Missy told her.

"No, stop. Don't tell me! The website is supposed to be anonymous," Mac held up her hand, interrupting Missy before she could go any further.

"But they are so funny!" Sarah exclaimed.

"Still, I don't want to know. It's more fun when you check into the website if you don't know who anybody is."

"I guess you're right – for now anyhow," Missy admitted.

"So, what are you eating for supper tonight?" Mac inquired.

"We thought we would have one of those salads you're always talking about," said Sarah.

"Sounds good to me. It's a start on changing over to new eating habits," Mac informed her.

"What if we get hungry later on tonight?" Missy wondered."

"Then you will just have to do what I did and buy some healthy snacks. Check the website and they will tell you what to get," Mac replied.

The three girls went through the line and made their selections. They ended up sitting at a table close to the entrance, which provided them with a clear view of anyone who happened to come into the cafeteria. Sarah and Missy were up to their usual antics, rating every boy who walked by their table.

"Now that's definitely a ten," Missy commented, giggling as she spoke.

Mac looked up just in time to spot one of the star football players, Chad Jennings, who strutted in like he owned the world.

"What I wouldn't give to have a date with him," Sarah sighed as she spoke.

"Like that's ever going to happen," Missy enlightened her.

Mac echoed the thought silently but was too polite to repeat it aloud. Being overweight had taught her to be sensitive to other people's feelings.

"Bet you I can. If I stick to my diet, I'll bet I can get a date with him before school is out this spring," Sarah challenged.

"Girl, you're on, but it has to be something big – like the Spring Fling dance."

"Spring Fling it is. Now I'm doubly, no make that triply, inspired to lose weight." Sarah raised her forkful of salad as she spoke.

"Maybe we should all pick somebody we want to go to Spring Fling with," Mac joked.

"Okay, I dare you two girls to pick out a guy for that dance. In fact,

I dare you to choose the next available guy who walks through the door. Missy, you go first." Sarah was unstoppable when she was on a roll.

Mac almost choked behind her napkin when none other than her nemesis, Twitchy, sauntered in. All three girls burst out laughing.

"Give me a break," Missy pleaded.

"Nothing doing. A bet's a bet. Besides, the poor guy *really* needs a girlfriend," Sarah insisted.

Missy waved her fork. "He, I never agreed…oh, what the heck. Twitchy it is, but he'll be heartbroken because I'm not Mac."

The girls had long ago heard about Twitchy's relentless pursuit of Mac and her antics in avoiding him. Listening to her descriptions of the episodes had provided them with quite a few laughs.

"Oh, I think he'll survive. In fact, I think he will be so happy he'll probably forget all about me," Mac declared.

"You hope," Missy retorted.

"And that leaves Mac," Sarah reminded them.

"Oh, no. I'm not going that route. I have a guy picked out already," Mac defended herself.

"And just who might he be?" Sarah asked.

"Yes, tell us, please," Missy added.

Mac hesitated. She couldn't reveal her true feelings. Ashley would be absolutely horrified to learn that her roommate had a crush on her longstanding boyfriend. No, Ashley had to be protected, no matter what happened. *Think, girl, think,* she chided herself, willing a boy's name to come to mind.

"Bud Bishop. I'll go to the dance with Bud Bishop," she said.

There, it was out. She had finally thought of someone other than Mark, but at what cost? she wondered.

"Hey, that's not fair. You hang out with him all the time," Sarah protested.

"Besides, he's just too skinny, definitely not a jock," Missy pointed out.

"Maybe, but we've never been on an official date. Besides, we're just friends. He doesn't think of me *that way.* At least, I think he doesn't, but he's been acting very strange lately," Mac mused.

"Okay, okay, let her go with Bud. After all, you got to pick your date. I'm the one who's stuck with Twitchy," Missy chimed in.

"I suppose getting one guy to ask you out is as much work as getting any other one to. So, if you want to date Bud, that your choice," Sarah relented.

"Here's to Spring Fling and our dates-to-be," Mac said, as she raised her glass of lemon-flavored water.

"To Spring Fling," the other two girls agreed as their three glasses clicked together.

Mac walked back to her dorm, changed into comfortable clothes, and loaded the Pilates DVD into the machine. She knew that balancing her classes, studying, and following a workout routine wasn't going to be easy, but she resolved to do it. Watching attentively, she began the exercise routine, following it to the best of her ability. It wasn't as easy as she had thought, but she should master it in a few more sessions. At least she hoped she would. It was definitely easier than jogging!

After the session was completed she sank down onto her bed exhausted, but happy. Resting gave her time to think. Now she had not one, but two goals in mind. First and foremost, she wanted to lose weight. Second, she had to get Bud to ask her out to the Spring Fling. The two goals went hand-in-hand. If she failed the first one, she was bound to fail the second one, too. Never mind that Mark was the one she really wanted to go out with. She had committed herself to dating Bud, she hoped, and that was who she had to stick with.

###

The next few months became a blur as one day blended into another and then another. She was determined to maintain her grade point average in order to increase her chances of getting admitted to medical school. Finding time to exercise was a major chore, but she managed it somehow and was rewarded each time she stepped on the scales. A ten-pound loss soon became a twenty-pound loss, and before she knew it, she had lost a total of twenty-five pounds.

Her clothes were practically hanging off her, prompting her to buy several new outfits. She didn't want to spend a lot of money on clothes, though, because she was planning on losing even more weight and then the new clothes would be too big.

Her schedule was so crowded she hardly ever saw Ashley and Mark. Ashley was now coming in late almost every night, usually after Mac had gone to bed. Bud seemed to be avoiding her at every turn, which puzzled her to no end. No matter what had happened in the past, she and Bud had always stuck together, especially after Mark and Ashley paired off. How was she going to get the guy to ask her out if she never saw him?

Her one salvation was her connection with Slimline Buddies. Every night, without fail, she checked into the website, often munching on her newest favorite snack, unbuttered, air-popped popcorn. Ashley had presented her with a brand-new air popper in celebration of the loss of her first ten pounds and she was now putting it to good use. Her lone Snickers bar was still in her desk drawer, untouched. She prided herself on the fact that she had resisted the temptation to eat it so far. Somehow, staring at it every time she opened the drawer seemed to give her more willpower to stick to her diet.

As she became better acquainted with the group, she began to reveal more and more about herself and her personality. That was the one place where she could confide her true feelings about Mark and her dilemma in being torn between her feelings for him and her love for her roommate. Her online friends had plenty to say about the situation.

"Wow, that guy sounds like a cutie. Any more like him on your campus? Lonely Girl."

"Hunks and jocks are too self-centered. Look for a man who's not into sports. Lotus Blossom."

"Guys come and go, but friends are friends for life. Forget the guys and protect your roommate at all costs. Calendar Girl."

"What you need to concentrate on is getting that date for Spring Fling. Sweet Pea."

"Once again, thanks for all the advice. I'll keep you posted. Patience."

She logged off and pulled out her books in preparation for a nightly study session. But studying was the furthest thing from her mind. She just couldn't concentrate. Images of Mark and Bud kept creeping into her thoughts, drifting in and out among the pages of her notes.

Her online friends were right, she realized. Since her chances of getting a date with Mark were almost nil, what she needed to do was find Bud and through some conniving method get him to ask her to Spring Fling. What the guy was doing was a mystery. Where could he be?

She still saw Missy and Sarah and often met them for lunch. Since they had changed their eating habits, mealtime with them had become more pleasant. No longer was she staring at foods that were taboo on her diet. In fact, the two girls almost seemed to be in a competition to see who could lose the most weight.

They also kept her up to date on their progress in getting dates for Spring Fling, sometimes with surprising results.

"So, how are you making out with getting closer to your dream date with Chad Jennings?" Mac inquired one day as they sat down at their usual table.

"Yeah, Chad the Cad." Missy snickered knowingly behind her napkin.

Sarah tossed a frown her way. "Not too bad," she replied. "I signed up for tutoring and got assigned to help Chad with his math classes."

"Really?" Mac asked doubtfully.

"Seriously. I'm not joking. Remember, I'm an accounting major, so math is one of my best subjects."

"Yes, I had almost forgotten about that. So, how is that working out for you?"

"It's coming along. Chad isn't as conceited as he appears to be. Actually, he's pretty down-to-earth and easy to talk to."

"Well, that's one point in your favor," Missy noted.

"And you, Miss Giggles, how's it going with Twitchy?" Mac addressed Missy.

"I'm making headway. I saw him in the library, so I 'accidentally' dropped one of my books right by the table where he was sitting. The guy almost fell out of his chair as he rushed to retrieve it for me."

"And then?" Mac inquired.

"Well, naturally, we just had to talk," Missy replied in her best imitation of a Southern accent.

Mac rolled her eyes. "Talking to him doesn't count. Besides, how could you even get close to him with that twitch of his?"

Missy placed her hands on her hips and drew herself up to her most defensive position. "Don't talk about him like that! He's really a very sensitive guy. For your information, we've been meeting at the library ever since then."

"Easy, girl, she's just asking," Sarah interceded.

"Well he *is*. He's a psychology major. He says he wants to help others because of people being so mean to him because of his facial tic."

"What do you know about that? I never would have guessed it," Mac pondered.

"And by the way, his real name is Dennis Ouchley, not Twitchy."

"Got it. I'll never call him Twitchy again. I promise."

"And that leaves you and Bud," Sarah reminded her.

"I never see the guy anymore. He's just disappeared," Mac complained.

"I know where he is," Missy and Sarah spoke in unison.

"Really? Then clue me in. I never see him, Mark, or Ashley, for that matter, except when she comes back to our dorm room."

"He's in the gym," Sarah informed her.

"Working out," Missy added.

"With Mark," said Sarah.

Mac digested the information and then repeated what she'd just heard. "In the gym...working out..."

"With Mark," the girls recited again in unison.

"And just how do you two know that?" Mac continued her inquisition.

"We've taken up water aerobics," Sarah told her.

"Yes, it burns up a lot more calories than Pilates," said Missy.

"Water aerobics? Do you mean you actually appear in a swimsuit in front of all those people at the gym? What about the guys?" Mac asked skeptically.

"They have a special class for girls only. No guys allowed," Sarah explained.

"Yeah, why don't you come along and try it? See for yourself that Bud really is working out with Mark," Missy suggested.

"I don't know…I would have to buy a swimsuit." Mac considered the offer.

"Then get one. Don't be bashful. It's fun." Sarah encouraged her.

"It would give you a chance to talk to Bud." Missy sweetened the pot, using her most enticing voice.

"Okay, okay, I guess I'll do it, but I'm not buying a bikini!" Mac exclaimed.

"Don't worry, babe. None of us in that class have bikinis. Trust me," Missy assured her.

Less than a week later Mac exited her dorm room wearing a new navy-blue swimsuit underneath her sweats. She headed for the gym, hoping she wouldn't meet anybody she knew along the way. She also had a tote bag filled with gym essentials, things she would need, according to Sarah and Missy. The gym would supply towels and a locker with a key. Getting everything else was up to her.

She walked into the gym, not knowing what to expect. She hadn't been in the place since her disastrous attempt at basketball last fall. Staying in her room and doing Pilates had been enough exercise for her. She began to question her motives. What was she really doing here? She almost turned and walked out the door when she spotted Bud and Mark through the door of the weight room, working out just like Sarah and Missy had reported.

She paused. It was true then. Bud hadn't really been avoiding her altogether. He had been otherwise occupied. At least he wasn't with another girl. That was some consolation. But what had gotten into him? Bud had never been athletic and, furthermore, he had never shown the slightest interest in working out. What had inspired him? And why was Mark taking such an interest in Bud's progress – Mark, who never seemed to have time for anybody but himself and maybe Ashley on the side? There had to be more than met the eye. It was going to take some digging, but she would find out the truth. Bud had never lied to her. Bud would tell her what was going on – eventually.

She walked through the door of the weight room, unable to stop herself. It was almost as if she were watching the scene from above with somebody else in her body.

"Hi, guys. What's up?" she inquired as she approached the pair.

Bud looked flustered, she noticed. Mark, well, he was just Mark, cool as ever. Nothing ever seemed to bother the guy. And as good-looking as ever, too! Did any other guy fill out a muscleman tee shirt quite as well?

"Oh, nothing. Just a little workout session. Trying to tone up the old muscles," Bud half-joked.

"Ah and are those actually biceps I see?" Mac joked back as Bud lowered the weight he had been lifting.

"Well, yes, maybe a little." Bud flexed his muscles, unable to keep himself from grinning.

"We're going to whip this little wimp into shape yet," Mark announced, draping his arm around Bud's shoulders as he spoke.

Bud blushed and lowered his head slightly, embarrassed by all the attention.

"What are you doing here?" Mark inquired, shifting the focus from Bud to Mac, much to her consternation.

"Oh, I'm just meeting some friends," she responded lamely. "I'm late now, so I'd better go. Talk to you guys later."

"Right, later," Bud echoed as the two boys watched her walk back through the door.

"You know, Mac has lost a lot of weight. She's turning out to be a nice little piece of ..."

"Shut up, Mark," Bud interrupted before Mark could finish the sentence.

"Man, you're always telling me to shut up! It's a good thing I like you. Little buddy. A real good thing!"

"If you would stop thinking about every girl as a sex object, I wouldn't have to tell you to shut up."

"Yeah? Well, let's not forget how this whole thing started. You wanted to make yourself into more of a man so Mac would like you. Isn't that so?" Mark demanded an answer.

"You're the one who brought up the subject of Mac, not me," Bud reminded him.

"Maybe so, but I know you, little buddy. I know you like a brother."

"It seems like the only time we're fighting is whenever Mac is around, so let's just forget about her."

"You're right. I don't know what I'm thinking. Between classes, sports, and helping you work out, I hardly have time for Ashley anymore. She's getting antsy about it, too. We've been arguing a lot. She thinks I have another girl on the side."

"You have lots of girls on the side, Mark."

"None seriously. I told you before, I've never cheated on Ashley."

"Some people might find that hard to believe."

"Ashley is my woman, my one true love. I don't know what I would do if I ever lost her. I can't even think about it."

"Then don't."

"Don't what? Don't think about it or don't lose her?

"Both."

"Sometimes, little buddy, you actually offer some good advice."

"Yeah, I just can't help myself. Sometimes, that is."

"I'd say this workout session is about over. I'm supposed to meet Ashley for supper, so I guess I'll take off and get cleaned up. See you back at the dorm."

"Sure. See you," Bud agreed as he watched Mark pack his gear.

He leaned back against the weight bench, wiping his face with a towel. Why did he have to be best friends with a jock? There were plenty of nerds on campus, and he'd fit right in with them. Jocks and nerds didn't mix, but he had been friends with Mark since elementary school. Old habits were hard to break, he decided. Real hard. Just like his feelings for Mac.

They, too, had been friends since elementary days, but his feelings for her had changed over the years. She was a warm and caring person with a quick wit and a brain capacity that matched his, brain cell for brain cell. He didn't care if she was thin or stout. What he cared about was the woman within. But Mac would never notice him. Not as long as Mark was around.

He had seen the way she looked at Mark when she thought nobody was watching. Mark was too blind to realize it, and Ashley trusted her completely. That put Mac in a really bad place. He knew her well, and she would never do anything to hurt Ashley. Heck, *nobody* would do anything to hurt Ashley Angel Gordon. Not on their lives!

That brought another situation to mind – Spring Fling. Mark would be escorting Ashley, an undisputable fact that was already set in stone. That left both him and Mac at loose ends. Would she possibly consider going with him? They had never been on a formal date. Oh, they had been together at basketball games and movies, but they usually tagged along with Mark and Ashley, almost as an afterthought. He was tired of it! It was time for him to get a girl of his own, and the girl he wanted was Mac.

Mac had been warmly welcomed into the water aerobics class. Not all the girls were overweight, she noticed. In fact, some of them had gorgeous figures, something she envied immensely. Well, maybe in time she would look like they did. She wasn't giving up just yet. She had worked too hard and come too far. The goal line was in sight, just in time for the Spring Fling.

The pool emptied quickly after the session as the girls headed for the locker room. Mac rubbed herself briskly with a towel, standing by her locker as she conversed with Missy and Sarah.

"Okay, you two were right. I saw Bud and Mark in the weight room. I guess they have been working out together," she admitted.

"Told you so. Why did you ever doubt us?" Missy asked flippantly.

"I really didn't doubt you. I just had to see for myself. Bud has never been much of an athlete, you know. I wonder what made him change his mind."

"Who knows? Does any woman understand how a man's mind really works?" Sarah contemplated.

"Well, I know Bud, and he doesn't do anything without a good reason."

"Never mind that. What about getting him to ask you to Spring Fling?" Missy reminded her.

"It didn't come up. I barely spoke to him."

"But you did – speak to him, I mean?" Sarah asked.

"Yes, yes. We spoke. I actually walked into the weight room and talked to both of them in the smelly weight room with all those sweaty male bodies."

"Those gorgeous, sweaty male bodies." Missy sighed.

"That, too, but I wasn't really paying attention to anybody besides Mark and Bud."

"Well, at least you made contact. That's the important thing," Sarah observed.

"What we need now is a game plan," Missy announced.

"Make that three game plans. Remember, we all must get the guys to ask us to the dance. You two seem to be making more progress than I am," Mac lamented.

"The main thing is to stay in contact. If the guy keeps running into you, there's more of a chance he will think about you. And if he's thinking about you, maybe he'll ask you out," said Sarah.

"Since when did you become such an expert on dating?" Mac asked.

Oh, I have my ways. Tutoring a jock is definitely an eye-opening experience."

"In what way?"

"They start revealing little facts about themselves and other members of the teams. You'd be surprised at what I know now."

"Such as?" Now Mac's curiosity was getting the best of her.

"Sorry, but I'm sworn to secrecy. I really shouldn't have said anything."

"Okay, okay, point taken. Back to the original thought – we need a game plan. So, everybody go home tonight and think, really think about what to do," Mac instructed.

###

Several days passed before Mac had time to confer with her two friends about their ideas. They met for lunch, as usual, in the cafeteria. Choosing healthy foods had become second nature to them. None of them even thought about what they were consuming as they became engrossed in conversation. For once, Missy and Sarah were totally unaware of any attractive male who happened to pass by their table.

"What did you two decide?" Mac introduced the topic as she dug into a baked potato topped with low-fat sour cream and chives. She had discovered that particular food would fill her up until suppertime.

"I don't think *Dennis* will need much persuasion." Missy emphasized his name. "He's ripe and ready for picking. All I have to do is hint about Spring Fling and I'm sure he'll ask me to go with him."

"Well, Chad will require a subtler approach. I'm working on the psyche," said Sarah.

"Good luck with that. I think Ashley's friend Tiffany has staked her claim on him. I see them together all the time around the campus," Mac informed her.

"Maybe so, but I'm still betting I can get him to ask *me* to Spring Fling."

"I guess you know him better than we do. Keep us posted."

"And what about you and Bud?" Missy asked.

"I've been thinking and thinking. As I told you, I hardly ever see the guy anymore. I think I'm going to have to call on Ashley for help. If I can get her to have Mark and Bud meet us for supper one night, maybe she can get Mark to leave with her and then Bud and I will be alone – finally."

"Do you think she'll go for it?" Sarah wondered.

"Of course, she'll 'go for it.' She's my roommate. We've been friends since kindergarten."

Mac shook her head in disbelief. People who didn't know Ashley thought she was conceited like most of the other cheerleaders. Somehow, Ashley's beauty had never gone to her head. *Maybe being friends with an ugly duckling has helped with that*, she thought ruefully.

"It might work — if he doesn't take off like a scared rabbit," said Missy.

"Oh, he won't run. Bud's too polite for that," Mac assured them.

Later that night she broached the subject to Ashley. Her roommate was excited and almost enthralled with the idea.

"Mac, I had no idea you even thought of Bud in *that* way!" she exclaimed.

"Well…" Mack sputtered, unable to come up with a reply.

"Don't worry. I've got it covered. We'll meet for supper tomorrow night, and I'll make sure Mark brings Bud along."

"Great," Mac responded half-heartedly, wondering what she had gotten herself into this time. Dating wasn't her thing. She had been content to stay in her room and daydream about the perfect date — with Mark. Now she was trying to get Bud to ask her out. *Oh, what a tangled web we weave…,* she contemplated. Whoever thought that one up must have been the master of deceit. She had always prided herself on being honest and now she would be deceiving Bud by going out with him. Why, oh, why, had she ever let herself get talked into this silly bet?

The following night Ashley ran into their dorm room, yelling as she flung the door open.

"Mac, it's all set. Mark is bringing Bud along to the cafeteria. They're on their way right now. Hurry up and get dressed!"

"I am dressed, Mac replied, rising from her desk chair as she swung around to face her roommate.

"No, you're not! You have to wear something better than jeans and an oversized shirt!"

Ashley began to look through Mac's closet, pulling out garments as she spoke.

"Here's something…no, this one's better…no, I think this will do. Here, try this on," she instructed as she held out one of Mac's new outfits.

"I just bought that. I was saving it for a special occasion," Mac protested.

"Girl, if this isn't a special occasion, I don't know what is. You have to look good if you want a guy to ask you out. If only we had time to do something about your hair," Ashley mused.

"Bud knows what I look like. He's been looking at me for sixteen years," Mac reminded her.

"Hmm…I suppose you're right. But if you do get a date for Spring Fling, we've definitely got some work ahead of us."

Twenty minutes later they walked into the cafeteria and spotted Mark and Bud waiting for them in the foyer. Mac felt all sparkly from the bronzer Ashley had insisted on brushing over her face. She wasn't in the habit of wearing much makeup and was feeling a bit conspicuous. Besides that, her eyelashes were sticking together every time she blinked, due to several applications of Ashley's mascara. She just hoped her glasses didn't spot from rubbing the lashes against them. They had given up on her hair, though. That was too much of an undertaking, Ashley had decided, and they would tackle it another time.

"Hey, girls, let's eat. I'm starved. Mac, long time, no see," Mark greeted them.

"Hi, Ashley. Hi, Mac," Bud added.

"Hello, guys," Mac and Ashley responded together, laughing at the stereo effect.

"Ladies first," Bud insisted, gesturing towards the line as he spoke.

"Thank you, kind sir," Ashley joked, as she fell in behind the last person in the line.

Mac followed her and Bud stepped in next, with Mark bringing up the rear.

Moments later, they were seated at their favorite table. Mark dug into his food with relish and Bud followed suit. Mac smiled to herself. Her mother had always appreciated men who savored their food and she had also enjoyed preparing the food for them. Somehow, watching them eat no longer bothered Mac.

Ashley and Mac approached their food more subtly, taking their time in order to stretch the food out until the boys had finished eating. That was one trick Mac had learned since she had cut back on her portions, thanks to her online sessions with her Slimline Buddies.

It didn't take long for the meal to end, as the boys appeared to be ravenously hungry. Mac was getting nervous. She and Ashley exchanged glances before Ashley began to speak.

"It's almost time for Spring Fling. Can you believe it? Our junior year is drawing to a close."

"Yeah, it seems like we just got here as freshman and now we're almost seniors," Mac observed.

"Spring Fling…I guess Ashley and I will be going together, right Ash?" Mark asked.

"Well, if that's the best invitation I'm going to get, I suppose so," Ashley conceded.

"Oh, babe, you know I didn't mean it that way. It's just that we've been going together so long everybody just takes it for granted that we'll go to the dance together. You haven't had any other offers, have you?" he inquired anxiously.

"Of course not, silly. Everybody knows I'm your girl. And yes, I will go to the dance with you," Ashley assured him.

"Great. Well, I've got some studying to do. Let's meet at the library in a few minutes. I have to go back to the dorm and get my books and notes," Mark informed them.

"Sure, I'll meet you there. I'll see you two later," Ashley addressed the last remark to Mac and Bud, who were listening in somewhat uncomfortably during the entire exchange.

"Right, see you later," Mac agreed.

"Bye," Bud added.

"Well, alone at last. It's been a long time since it was just the two of us," Mac began the conversation again.

"Yea, yeah, a long time," Bud agreed as he shifted uncomfortable in his chair.

"So, how about that Spring Fling? It's supposed to be quite an event this year," she hinted.

"So I heard," Bud agreed again as he swallowed hard before venturing another remark. "Mac, I have something to ask you."

"Oh?"

"Would you do me the honor of accompanying me to Spring Fling?"

Mac looked down at her plate and then back up at Bud, looking him straight in the eyes. This was it, the big moment she'd been waiting for – her first official date ever. She took a deep breath before replying.

"Yes, Bud. I'd be happy to go with you."

Well, it was just a little white lie, she told herself. She really wanted to go with Mark but would have to settle for Bud. Anyhow, just being at the dance would make her happy, no matter who she was with. At least that part wasn't a lie.

"Great. We'll work out the details later. May I walk you back to your dorm?" he asked as they rose and carried their trays to the conveyer belt.

"That would be gentlemanly of you."

It was the only remark she could dredge up. She had to play her hand carefully if she was going to keep Bud hanging on until after the dance. For the time being, she had accomplished her goal. She had to get back to the dorm and report the results to Missy and Sarah. Sometimes she didn't like herself very much.

Mac moved through the next few weeks of school in a daze. Bud and Mark had all but disappeared as they were caught up in the hectic round of late spring activities. Her schedule was filled with studying as she finished her semester projects and crammed for finals. Then there was her exercise program of Pilates and water aerobics. She was rewarded with happy results at each weekly weigh-in as the pounds continued to melt away.

It was almost time to pick out a dress for Spring Fling, and her life-long dream of actually finding one to fit right off the rack now seemed to be a realistic goal.

She brought up the subject to Ashley one night as they were both heading to bed after a long study session.

"Looks like it's about time to pick out our dresses for Spring Fling. I have no idea of how to start."

Ashley responded quickly. "Why don't you get your friends Missy and Sarah to meet us one afternoon this week and we'll go shopping?"

"You'd do that for me? *For us?*" Mac asked, thinking it was almost too good to be true.

She had intentionally avoided shopping for clothes with girls her own age up to this point. Nothing ever seemed to fit, and when it did, the garment usually hung off her like a sack. Shopping with friends would be a totally new experience, maybe one she could actually look forward to.

"You did say they both have dates for the dance, didn't you?" Ashley inquired.

"Yes, I got a report from both of them. Missy is going with Twitchy…I mean Dennis, and Sarah managed to finagle a date with Chad Jennings."

"Oh, brother, I heard about Chad. Tiffany was all set to go with him when she found out he was taking somebody else. You'd better tell Sarah to watch it. She doesn't want to end up like the girl in that movie *Carrie*!"

"You don't think Tiffany would actually try something like that, do you?"

"Probably nothing that drastic but tell Sarah to watch out for water balloons on her way up the dorm stairs."

They both giggled, remembering their antics of past years when they had dropped water balloons onto unsuspecting dorm mates who were ascending the stairs late at night. They never actually got caught, but someone had left a threatening note under their door after the last incident, prompting them to retire from that pastime.

Several days later, Mac found herself standing beside Ashley in front of Angelina's Boutique and Dress Shop, a place she had never had the nerve to enter before. Missy and Sarah had agreed to meet them there at 3:00 p.m., but they were running late.

"I wish they would hurry up," Ashley complained. "It's too hot to stand out here. Let's go inside."

"Okay, I guess you're right," Mac agreed, peering anxiously down the street as she spoke.

A blast of cool air swept over them as they entered the brightly lit and equally brightly colored store. Soft music played in the background as patrons made their way around strategically placed racks of clothing and artistically displayed tables of accessories. The place was packed with college girls who evidently had the same idea of getting ready for Spring Fling.

Mac almost turned around and walked out, but she was detained by Ashley, who gently took her arm and began leading her towards a display of prom and dance dresses.

"Come on, roomie. Let's find the right dress for you."

Before Mac could respond, Missy and Sarah rushed through the door.

"Sorry we're late," Sarah apologized breathlessly.

"Yes, we ran into Tiffany at the Student Center. She was pretty mad about Sarah snagging Chad as an escort for Spring Fling," Missy added.

"Oh, juicy gossip," Mac exclaimed, clasping her hands together in anticipation.

"Save it for later. We've got work to do," Ashley instructed.

The three girls stopped short, exchanged glances, and nodded before they all headed towards the racks of dance dresses, giggling as they each grabbed an armful of dresses and headed towards the dressing rooms.

An hour later, they converged in front of a full-length mirror, turning this way and that as they admired their final selections. They formed a rainbow of colors as they lined up. Ashley had chosen a sky-blue dress that matched her eyes. Missy was decked out in hot pink, while Sarah's dress was sea green. Mac, at their insistence, had settled for a maize-colored dress that fell softly over her newly formed curves.

"Mac, you're the only one who can get away with wearing yellow. It makes the rest of us look washed out, but with that red hair of yours, it's striking," Ashley informed her.

"I never thought of yellow as my color, but I must admit, it looks pretty good on me."

Mac was totally amazed at the transformation as she peered into the mirror.

"The dress looks great, but what about the rest of me?" she wondered out loud.

Their conversation was interrupted by Madame Angelina, who took an interest in her clients. Something told her that these four girls were special, and she was ready to give them her full attention.

"My darlings, just look at you. You look like a flower garden with so many colors! You have made excellent choices." She almost purred as she spoke with a heavy French accent.

"Now, come, we must choose the right accessories for you," she continued, leading them back out into the store.

Less than thirty minutes later, the girls found themselves standing at the checkout counter, their arms laden with their selections of dresses, shoes, dainty evening bags, and jewelry. Closing time was rapidly approaching, and the store had all but cleared out.

Mac's head was spinning as she tried to mentally calculate just how much this little jaunt was going to cost her. She had been saving her allowance for months in anticipation of the occasion, but would she have enough money? Nothing would be more embarrassing than having to put an item back at the last minute.

She was the last one to be checked out, and she held her breath as the final total appeared. She exhaled as she dug the money out of her purse, relieved that she would have enough with exactly two dollars to spare.

Madame Angelina approached the group again as they were about to head for the door, waving slips of paper in her hands. The girls stood mesmerized as her diamond rings, gold bracelets, and red fingernail polish blended together under the bright lights in a sparkling display of color.

"Mademoiselles, I almost forgot. I have something very important to tell you. Since it is now prom season, I am running a special where I am giving coupons for a spa treatment to all my clients. Here are your coupons."

Ashley was the first to speak. "Madame, thank you so much. We will put them to good use."

"Yes, yes, we will," the other girls echoed in chorus.

"Use them wisely, my darlings," she said as she reached over and gently touched Mac's wiry hair, her diamond rings glistening with each movement. "So much promise." She shook her head slightly as she spoke. "So much promise. The beauty is there, my precious. You just have to find it.

Back at the dorm, Mac and Ashley sat down on their beds, backs propped up against the wall as they viewed their purchases. Their dresses were hung on the closet doors, while the shoes and other accessories were lined up on top of the dresser.

"I can't believe I spent all that money," Mac exclaimed. "What was I thinking?"

"You were thinking that you are going to have a wonderful time going out with Bud," Ashley replied.

"What do you suppose Madame Angelina meant with that remark about 'the beauty is there' but I just have to find it?" Mac pondered.

"Mac, you've always been beautiful to me, but I know a few tricks that will make you beautiful to everyone."

"Then share them with me. Please do.

"Okay, for starters, let's take your glasses. I know a place where you can get a prescription for contacts and have them by the next day."

"Wow, that is fast. But it's only two more weeks until Spring Fling. Would I have time to get used to wearing them by then?"

"Oh, sure. These new contacts don't take any time to get used to. Besides, do you think all the girls on campus have perfect vision? I'd say probably at least half of them wear contacts."

"Well, I guess I could try, but I would have to ask my parents for the money, as I used up all my allowance."

"Okay, let's call tomorrow and get an appointment for you. Now, the next thing we need to tackle is your hair. Of course, we could iron it, but the curls would just come back the next time you washed it. My suggestion is to visit a beauty salon. They can style it and put a relaxer on it to take those kinks out."

"I guess I'm game for that, too. If I'm going to have a makeover, I might as well go all the way."

"I'll handle your makeup. All those years of helping my mom with her cosmetic sales taught me a few tricks."

"You're a good person," Mac mumbled sleepily. "I think I'm going to head to bed. It's been a long day."

"Wish I could do the same, but I have to meet Mark for a little while. I haven't talked to him all day. So, I'll be back by curfew."

"Bye and try not to trip over anything when you come in," Mac joked as her roommate exited the room.

Mac rolled off the bed and walked over to the dresser, pulling out a pair of pajamas and a bath towel. She headed for the shower in a giddy mood, thinking that for the first time she might actually fit in with the crowd.

The bathroom scales still sat in the corner. She stuck out her tongue at them as she stepped into the shower.

"There's nothing you can do to put me in a bad mood tonight," she declared. "In fact, I'm going to pretend you're not even there, smirking at me, as usual."

Making the appointments the next day was surprisingly easy. Mac found she could get in to see the optometrist in two days, while the beauty salon Ashley suggested took clients on a walk-in basis. She worked the appointments around her class schedule and soon found herself walking around campus with a new look. Never mind that it had taken hours of what she considered torture in the beauty salon to achieve that status. All she cared about was the end result. At long last she looked like an average college co-ed, and that had been her goal all along. She just wanted to look normal and fit in with normal-sized people.

Everyone she met did a double take, as they almost didn't recognize her. She did her best to avoid Bud and Mark because she wanted to surprise Bud on the night of Spring Fling. Seeing either one of them would foil her plans.

Getting her parents to agree to pay for the contacts and beauty salon treatment had not been an easy task. Her father was tight-fisted with money, and he put up his usual fight, but her mom had won out in the end. She could still almost hear their argument.

"Sean McGregor, you will not deny our daughter this chance for happiness. She has never asked for anything extra from you. This dance is something that will come about just once in her life, and I'm going to see that she looks beautiful for it. If you don't give her the money, so help me, I will," her mother had declared.

"Now, Maggie, don't be gettin' your dander up. I'll pay for the contacts and the beauty shop. You're right. She's the only daughter we've got, and I'm so proud of her," he had responded.

Mac had thanked them both profusely. She hated to grovel, but this was an emergency situation and there wasn't much time left. Her parents were the best, just a little old-fashioned at times, she thought. She had smoothed things over by promising to send them a picture of her and her date all decked out in their finery.

Sarah and Missy were understandably impressed. Seeing Mac's new hairdo had given them both the inspiration to go for makeovers, also. All three girls could hardly wait for Spring Fling to arrive. Ashley wasn't quite as excited, as she had attended the event every year since she came to the college. Besides, she was already beautiful, and beautiful people didn't have a lot to worry about, Mac decided.

That reasoning came to a screeching halt four days before the dance when Ashley burst into their room, sobbing uncontrollably as she threw herself down onto her bed.

Mac jumped up from her desk, where she had been studying, and rushed over to Ashley's side.

"Ashley, what's the matter? What happened?" she inquired anxiously.

"It's Mark. We broke up." Ashley was sobbing so hard she could barely get the words out.

"Broke up…but how…why?" Mac asked incredulously.

"He was in the library, up in the stacks. I went to look for him and found him kissing Tiffany."

"Kissing Tiffany? I thought he couldn't stand the girl."

"Oh, who cares? If I can't trust him to be faithful to me, it's all over as far as I'm concerned. He can go out with whomever he wants to."

"What about your date for Spring Fling?"

"I don't care if I go or not now. Let him find somebody else. In fact, I dare him to find another date."

Ashley rolled over on the bed and covered her head with her pillow, leaving Mac feeling helplessly incompetent. Ashley, the popular one, always so poised and sure of herself, was now the picture of despair.

What's a roommate to do? Mac wondered. She cleared her throat nervously.

"Um, Ash, I'm supposed to meet Sarah and Missy in the cafeteria for supper. Can I bring you anything?"

"No, I'm not hungry. I may never eat again." The response came through the pillow, so muffled it was barely discernable.

"I'm going now. I'll be back in a little while."

Mac grabbed her purse and meal card, heading out the door as she spoke. Giving Ashley some time to herself was the best thing to do, she decided.

She relayed the news about the breakup to Sarah and Missy over supper. They both sat with jaws practically sagging. Mark and Ashley had been a couple ever since they had known them. The idea of them going their separate ways was almost too much to comprehend.

"Now don't go spreading it around campus. I'm sure everybody will know soon enough," Mac cautioned.

"What kind of friends do you think we are?" Missy retorted.

"Yeah, we've stuck together through thick and thin," Sarah added.

"Mostly thick," Missy observed.

"Well, we're all a lot thinner now," Mac noted.

"Amen, sister," Sarah joked, and they all giggled in response.

"On a serious note, I need to get back to the dorm. I don't want to leave Ashley alone too long," Mac informed them.

They rose and carried their trays to the conveyer belt just as Mark and Bud walked through the door. Both boys were staring at the girls as if they had never seen them before.

"Speaking of the devil," Missy commented.

"Oh, no, I was trying to lie low and avoid both of them until Spring Fling and now here we are, practically face-to-face," Mac worried.

"Just keep walking, girl. Keep your chin up," Sarah advised as they headed toward the exit.

Mac couldn't resist sneaking a glance at the boys, who were talking animatedly, shaking their heads as they spoke. Both of them had their eyes practically glued to her. Feeling a flush creeping up her neck, she quickly averted her eyes as she stepped through the door.

She was grateful for the cover of darkness as she headed back to the dorm, wondering just how she could minister to her distressed roommate.

###

"My God, was that really Mac? Our Mac?" Mark exclaimed as he watched the three girls walk out the door.

"Yes, it was Mac, for sure and for certain," Bud replied.

"I knew she was losing weight, but I never knew there was such a beautiful girl inside, just waiting to be discovered."

"I knew," Bud spoke softly. "I always knew."

"Yeah, right, little buddy. And you *are* taking her to the Spring Fling. Lucky you."

"That's right. I am, and don't you be getting any ideas. Breaking up with Ashley doesn't give you the right to horn in on anybody else's girl."

"Oh, so now she's your girl? Just because she's going to the dance with you doesn't mean you're going steady."

"Maybe not, but consider yourself warned, just the same."

"Okay, duly noted. I have to find a date, though. How would it look for me, Mark Guillory, to be dateless for the biggest social event of the year?" Mark thumped his chest with his fist as he spoke.

"Oh, you'll find somebody who'll go out with you. I have no doubt about that. You should have had better sense than to break up with Ashley."

"I didn't break up with Ashley. She broke up with me."

"Right. Now what was the reason for that? Let me think…could it have been because you were *kissing another girl?*"

"Actually, I wasn't kissing Tiffany. She was kissing me. She took me by surprise when I went up in the stacks to look for a book."

"Ha!" Bud guffawed as he helped himself to a roll. The boys had been working their way down the serving line during the conversation. "Like any girl ever took you by surprise!"

Mark paused by the iced tea dispenser as he filled his glass. "Well, if you think I'm asking Tiffany out, you're sadly mistaken. I know what kind of girl she is."

"Seems to me that's the kind you'd want to go out with," Bud half-muttered under his breath as he reached the cashier.

The conversation paused until the boys reached a table where they had more privacy.

"Seriously, I have to find a date before Saturday night. Got any suggestions?" Mark asked after they were seated.

"You're asking me, the Clark Kent of the campus, for suggestions on dating?"

"Okay, I can see you'll be no help. Guess I'm on my own. Maybe I'll surprise you."

"Just don't make it too much of a surprise…and stay away from Mac!" Bud reminded him.

Mac had been unable to relieve her roommate's justifiably gloomy mood. Ashley was in a funk and there appeared to be little anyone could do to bring her out of it. Mac decided to make one last effort the next afternoon by suggesting they make use of Madame Angelina's offer.

"Ash, I know it's hard, but why don't we just forget about the world for a little while and go for a spa treatment? Remember, we have the free coupons."

Ashley was lying on her bed. She hadn't left the room all day, declaring she couldn't face anybody just yet. Her eyes were red and swollen, and what was left of her makeup was streaked from all the crying jags. Her hair, usually picture-perfect, lay flat against her head in long, greasy streaks, somewhat matted from all her tossing and turning.

She sat up and blew her nose before responding, throwing the used tissue into a nearby wastebasket.

"What's the point?" she asked dejectedly.

"The point is you're you, Ashley Angel Gordon. You're your own person, not an extension of Mark Guillory. I know you've been going with him like *forever*, but do you want to know how many other guys on campus would give up a semester's tuition to date you?"

"Really? It never occurred to me. Mark's always been the guy for me. He's the only one I've thought about since junior high."

Mac stifled a sigh. She supposed it was one of the perks of being born beautiful. Ashley didn't realize how good-looking she was, with or without makeup. Guys just naturally flocked to Ashley, or at least they would have, had it not been for her involvement with Mark. She could get a date with almost any guy on campus, whereas Mac had never been on a real date in her entire life.

"You never know what will happen. I'm sure there's some guy out there still looking for a date for Spring Fling. Why don't you go anyhow and show Mark he's not the only guy in your life?"

There, she had said it, even though she felt somewhat disloyal to Mark. Being torn between her roommate and Mark, the guy she wanted to date more than anything else, was definitely not a good place to be. Conniving to get a date with Bud had been bad enough, but this was even worse. Now Mark was available for Spring Fling and she wasn't. What an ironic situation!

"Maybe I will. Maybe I'll just do that very thing," Ashley declared as she jumped off her bed and headed for her closet. "I'm going to shower and change clothes. Then I'll be ready to use that spa pass."

"Great. I'll call Sarah and Missy and see if they want to meet us there. No sense in letting all those coupons go to waste!"

Mac rubbed her forehead as she spoke. All this tension was giving her a headache. She opened her desk drawer and pulled out a bottle of Tylenol, noticing her Snickers bar was still in there. How much longer would she be able to resist the temptation to go off her diet? she wondered. If this kept up, she might have to eat everything on the cafeteria's menu.

She popped a couple of pills into her mouth and washed them down with some bottled water as she brought up Missy's number on her cell phone. Missy and Sarah agreed to meet her and Ashley in the dorm foyer before they all headed to the spa.

Two hours later the four girls leaned back in lounge chairs, encased in fluffy white robes and completely relaxed after a sauna treatment and massages. They were all getting facials. Mac's headache was starting to fade away as she inhaled the scent of the cucumber and melon facial mask. She hoped Ashley was feeling better, also. Missy and Sarah seemed totally oblivious to their friends' situations, giggling their way through the entire spa routine. Mac managed to restrain herself, but she could barely keep from chastising them for their flighty attitude. Her roommate was in trouble, and this was no time for tomfoolery.

"How are you doing, Ash?" she called out softly, her view of her roommate blocked by the cucumber slices that covered her eyes.

"I never thought I would say this, but I'm actually feeling a lot better," Ashley replied.

"Good. Very good," Mac responded, glad her plan had at least partially worked.

Their conversation was interrupted by an attendant who inquired if they wanted manicures or pedicures.

"It's all included in the coupons," the attendant assured them.

"Well, if it's free, I say, let's go for it," Mac exclaimed.

Minutes later, with facial masks removed and skin glowing, the four girls set about selecting just the right shade of nail polish to match each of their dancing dresses.

"I wish we had brought our dresses," Mac spoke worriedly.

"Don't worry. I'm an expert at matching colors," Ashley assured the group.

After what seemed like an endless debate, each girl finally settled on a color, and they went through the process of having it applied to both fingernails and toenails. It was the first time Mac had gotten a pedicure, so she found the procedure completely baffling.

"You want me to do what with my feet?" she inquired, as the nail specialist instructed her to soak both feet in a water solution that was specially treated to soften the calluses and corns.

Thirty minutes later she had to admit it was worth it all when she looked down at her matching toenails and fingernails. She and Ashley had taken turns painting each other's nails when they were growing up, but it was nothing compared to this.

"I'm speechless," she announced to the group.

"Since it's still two days before Spring Fling, we should all buy some bottles of touch-up polish," Ashley told them.

The attendant suggested matching shades of lipstick, and no one turned her down. The walked out of the spa moments later in a giddy mood. Mac was so relieved to see the dark circles gone from under Ashley's eyes, which were no longer red and swollen. Ashley looked more like herself, the Ashley Mac had always loved and admired.

"Now all I need to do is find another date for the Spring Fling," Ashley declared.

"As soon as word gets out, guys will be lined up," Mac promised.

###

Back at the dorm, Mac and Ashley plotted their strategies. Somehow, they had to get Ashley back into the public eye and let it be known she was available for Spring Fling. All this had to be done, of course, without any damage to Ashley's reputation or ego.

"First things first: we have to eat," Mac decided, as her stomach began to, once again, remind her it was getting close to mealtime.

They changed clothes and headed for the cafeteria. They had just gone through the line and settled at a table when Mark and Bud walked in. Ashley's mood changed quickly when she saw Mark looking in her direction.

"I don't know if I can do this," she whispered.

"You can do it. Remember what I said. Just keep smiling," Mac instructed, determined to be the strong one for Ashley's sake.

"If he comes over, I swear, I may slap him," Ashley replied through clenched teeth, smiling as she spoke.

"If he comes over, I may slap him, too," Mac seconded the idea.

They both burst out laughing as the picture of two girls simultaneously attacking a star football player came to mind.

"We have to stop," Mac declared as she grabbed a napkin and wiped her eyes.

"Yes, otherwise Mr. B.M.O.C. will think we're laughing at him," Ashley agreed.

"Well, we are, but don't let him know it!"

"Uh, oh, he's about to head over here," Ashley observed as Mark turned to walk in their direction.

His progress was halted as Bud grabbed his arm. The boys appeared to be in a heated argument as they stepped out of the line, both of them gesturing vigorously. Bud evidently won, as they moved to the back of the crowd and continued their journey down the serving line. Mark looked as if he had lost his last friend, and Bud didn't look much happier.

Mac and Ashley turned their attention to their food and were finished eating by the time the boys made it through the cashier's stand. They picked up their trays and prepared to leave as the boys headed for a table on the other side of the cafeteria. Ashley sashayed up to the tray depository with her usual graceful gait. Mac followed closely, feeling all eyes on her and Ashley as they set down their trays and exited. Evidently, it hadn't taken very long for the news of the breakup to make it around the campus gossip circuit.

"Looks like the word is out. All you have to do is make yourself available and you should have a date for Spring Fling by the end of the night," Mac observed as they headed back to the dorm.

"So, what should I do?" Ashley wondered.

"Girl, get out in the public eye. The best place to go is the library or the student center. Everybody ends up there sooner or later."

"I guess you're right, but I don't feel like going out alone. Would you come to the library with me for a study session?"

"Aw, Ash, you know I can't concentrate in the library," Mac complained. She was sorry as soon as she said it. She was supposed to be supporting her roommate, not arguing with her.

"Maybe there's a solution for both of us. I'll stay downstairs where most of the students congregate, and you can go upstairs to a study cubicle."

"That might work if I can find a cubicle that's not occupied," Mac agreed, feeling better about the situation.

After brushing their teeth, applying lip gloss, and combing their hair, the girls headed for the library, ready to put their plan into action. Finals were scheduled for the following week, so studying was the sensible thing to do. Mac just hoped she could concentrate after all that had transpired during the last twenty-four hours.

They glanced around as they walked through the library entrance, judging what available males might be hanging around in hopes of starting a conversation with an attractive co-ed. There was usually an assortment to choose from, as the library was a popular meeting place.

Mac spotted a couple of football players sitting at one of the tables. Catching Ashley's eye, she cocked her head in their direction.

"Umm…no. They're already taken," Ashley whispered, shaking her head as she spoke.

"Are you sure?"

"I'm positive. They're dating other cheerleaders."

"I guess you would know about that. Okay, you scout around down here while I go upstairs to study. I've got to review my chemistry notes if I want to pass that final," Mac told her.

She headed up the stairs, hoping she would find an empty cubicle. They were coveted sites just before finals. Lighting in the stacks was a lot dimmer than on the main floor, so it was easy to get lost if one did not pay close attention to where one was going. Mac didn't spend much time in the library, so it was unfamiliar territory to her. She spotted an empty cubicle and plopped her books down quickly before somebody beat her to it.

She flipped on the study light and spread out her materials, grabbing a pen and a highlighter from her purse. Soon she was totally engrossed in her notes, paying little attention to anyone who happened to pass by. She lost track of time as she tried to cram as much information as possible into her brain before the study session ended.

Sometime later, the study session was interrupted by the sound of someone clearing their throat. She looked up to find Mark standing beside her, displaying his most charming smile. She was quite familiar with all his expressions. After all, she still had a major crush on the guy. She had no doubt this smile was meant to totally disarm her and wear down whatever resistance she might have of his inquires. He wanted Ashley back. She was sure of it. Furthermore, he planned to use Mac to achieve his goal.

"Hi, Mac. What's up?" he asked, white teeth flashing in his deeply tanned face.

"Oh, nothing much. I'm studying for a chem. final."

"Chem final, huh? I'm glad I didn't have to take that course."

"Yeah, well, it's a requirement for pre-med, you know."

"Say, Mac…" He cleared his throat nervously again. "I was wondering if you would like to go to the Spring Fling with me."

Mac stared at him, almost glaring. At least she hoped she was glaring. She took her time in answering, watching him shift from one foot to another.

"I already have a date with Bud. I think you know *that*," she responded coolly.

She actually surprised herself with that answer. Here she was, turning down a date with a guy she had envisioned herself in love with for eight years.

What to do; what to do, she pondered, wondering what his next move would be.

"Dates can be broken."

"Like Ashley broke her date with you?"

"Not exactly…" His words trailed off under her scrutinizing gaze.

"Then what exactly do you want, Mark? You could get a date with almost any girl on campus, yet you pick me when I already have a date with Bud. If I go out with you, we'll be double-crossing our two best friends. Do you want that on your conscience?"

"I don't have a conscience anymore. It went out the door with Ashley."

"That figures."

His demeanor changed after that remark. Mac could see it in his eyes. Suddenly, the old Mark was back – charming and as self-assured as always.

He flashed another smile. God, he was one good-looking guy!

"Mac, Mac, Mac. You want to go out with me. You know you do. Why are you turning me down?" He leaned in closer as he spoke, his voice growing huskier by the minute.

Her resistance began to weaken. She was trying, really trying for Ashley and Bud's sakes, but she could feel herself slipping. She felt almost faint as she envisioned herself twirling around the dance floor in Mark's arms. She took a deep breath to steady her nerves.

Mark seemed to sense he was winning as he made his final plea.

"So, what'll it be? Do we have a date for Spring Fling?" His face was almost even with hers now. The scent of his after-shave infiltrated her nostrils, making her almost giddy. She breathed deeply, savoring the aroma, totally aware of his masculinity.

She paused and then relented, giving in against her better judgment. "All right, I'll go with you. I just have to figure out how to break the news to Ashley and Bud."

"Great. It'll be fun. I'll pick you up about 8:00 p.m."

She nodded, unable to speak as the realization of her betrayal hit her full force. Mark spun sharply on his heels and exited quickly, mission accomplished. She had made a pact with the Devil, and the Devil had won.

What was I thinking? I'm no better than he is. We deserve each other. Bud and Ashley are both going to hate me now.

Well, that was the end of her study session. There was no way she could concentrate anymore tonight, she decided. She might as well head downstairs and see if Ashley had any luck with snagging a date for tomorrow night.

Try to act normal, she told herself as she descended the stairs, searching the main room of the library for Ashley. She spotted her roommate sitting at a table with several other cheerleaders. Funny, cheerleaders weren't exactly known for being studious. More than likely, they had ulterior motives for coming the library.

She approached the table cautiously, hoping she appeared normal to Ashley and everyone with her. Was she a marked woman? She felt as if there should be an enormous "B" for "Betrayer" stamped on her forehead.

"Hi, Ash. Are you ready to go? I've finished my study session," she managed to announce in an almost-normal tone.

"Oh, hi, Mac. Yes, I'm ready to leave. See you guys later," Ashley agreed as she rose, gathered up her books, and pushed the chair under the table.

"Any luck with the date?" Mac asked as they began the long trek back to their dorm.

"No, I had no luck at all. Everybody seems to be hooked up for the dance. I think I'm the only girl on campus without a date."

"I still say there's got to be a guy out there somewhere for you."

"If there is, I wish he would make himself known. After all, the dance is tomorrow night. I'll look like a dunce accepting a date at the last minute."

"I didn't think you worried about things like that."

"I never had to because I always had a date with Mark. Ever since junior high, it was always Mark," Ashley lamented.

Mac was glad for the cover of darkness to hide the sudden blush in her cheeks. She still had to break the news about her date with Mark to Ashley and Bud. It wasn't going to go over well. She would bet on that!

"Um…Ash, I have something to tell you," she began.

"Oh?"

"Something happened while I was up in the stacks. Mark came by my cubicle and…" Her voice failed as her courage waned.

"Mark! So, what did he say?"

"He asked me to go to Spring Fling with him." Mac's voice cracked on the last syllable, despite her efforts to remain calm.

"What?" Ashley stopped so suddenly Mac was caught off guard.

Mac whirled around to face her roommate, grabbing her books to keep them from falling.

"You turned him down, of course." Ashley's observation was a statement, not a question. She trusted her roommate to do the right thing.

"No," Mac whispered.

Her answer was met with a long silence. It was a warm night, but Mac sensed a sudden chill creeping over her entire body. She felt like someone on the guillotine about to be beheaded.

"So, let me get this straight – you have a date with Bud for the dance, and now you have a date with Mark, too?"

"That about sums it up."

"You do know you can't go with two guys to the same function?"

"Yes, I know; I know. I'm going to break my date with Bud."

Ashley shook her head and blinked hard as a lone tear snaked its way down her cheek. "This is all too much for me. First, I was betrayed by Mark, and now my own roommate, my friend of sixteen years. I have to get away. I have to think."

She turned and began walking in the other direction, away from the dorm and off campus. The library was closing and other students were coming up the walk, headed to their respective dorms. Mac craned her neck as she watched Ashley merge into the crowd.

"What about curfew?" she yelled after her departing roommate.

Ashley never looked back.

Mac walked slowly to the dorm, hating herself more with every step. Tomorrow was supposed to be the happiest day of her life – her first real date to a dance with the guy she had always wanted to be with. Now the whole thing had turned into one big catastrophe. That was the only word to describe it – a catastrophe!

She unlocked her door and slammed her books onto the desk. Then she opened the desk drawer and took out the Snickers bar that had been tempting her for months. She unwrapped the candy slowly and deliberately, scrunching the wrapper into a little wad, then tossing it and hitting the wastebasket dead center. She bit into the bar and began chewing slowly, savoring the sweet-and-salty taste she had denied herself for so long.

###

Mac awoke the next morning to find Ashley's bed had not been slept in. Where had her roommate been all night? She hoped Ashley wouldn't get into any trouble for not reporting back to the dorm. If necessary, she would cover for Ashley, she decided, hoping it wouldn't come to that.

It was Saturday, so nobody had classes. Everybody on campus was getting ready for Spring Fling. The few girls who didn't have dates had left last night in order to avoid embarrassment. Mac was well-aware of that routine, having gone through it a few times. This time she had two dates. She had to break one of them and in the process maybe break somebody's heart. She just hoped that heart wouldn't be hers.

She glanced at the clock, which read 10:00 a.m. It was too late to go to breakfast in the cafeteria. She would have to settle for a Pop-Tart and some juice from their dorm fridge. Not the healthiest breakfast in the world, but she had already gone off her diet with the Snickers bar last night, so what did it matter?

Moments later, hyped up by the sugar rush from her hasty meal, she felt ready to tackle the chore she most dreaded – breaking her date with Bud. She pulled up his number on her cell phone. It had been so long since she called him she was surprised it was still there. It seemed as if they had both been doing their best to avoid each other for the past few months. Why had it gone wrong?

Bud answered on the first ring.

"Hi, Mac."

"Bud…" her voice faltered, despite her best efforts. "About tonight…I won't be able to attend the dance with you."

She waited for his response, wondering who she despised more – Mark for asking her out, or herself for accepting his invitation.

"I know, Mac. I know all about it. I've been waiting for your call."

"How…"

"Ashley told me. We were together last night, all night. She told me everything."

"You were together all night? You didn't…"

"Of course not. What kind of guy do you think I am? We spent the whole night talking, out by the lake."

"Then you know why I'm breaking the date?"

"It's no surprise to me. I've always known you had a thing for Mark. I just didn't say anything about it because he was so wrapped up with Ashley."

"Oh, my God! If you knew, do you suppose Ashley knew?"

"No, she still has no idea you had a major crush on her boyfriend all these years. Don't worry. Your secret is safe with me."

"Then I guess there's nothing left to say except goodbye."

"Right. Goodbye," Bud said.

She punched the phone to disconnect, staring at it as Bud's number disappeared from the screen. Should she keep his number or delete it? Chances were he might never speak to her again.

###

She decided to skip lunch. Her appetite had all but disappeared. Somehow, she didn't feel like facing anybody out on campus. She texted Sarah and Missy, asking them to come over to her room. The original plan had been for them to all congregate in her and Ashley's room to do their hair and makeup. She didn't know what would happen now that she was going out with Ashley's former boyfriend. She just hoped wherever Ashley was, she was safe.

Two hours later, Missy and Sarah arrived with all their finery, in a giddy mood and eager to get ready for the dance. They were both giggling when Mac opened the door. They stopped short when they saw the expression on her face.

"What's up, girlfriend?" Missy asked.

"I suppose I might as well tell you the whole sordid tale," Mac informed them. They all sat down on Mac's bed as she proceeded to fill them in with all the details of what had happened that night. When she had finished, her two friends, for once, were speechless.

Missy found her voice first. "Let me get this straight. You were going out with Bud, but now you're not going out with Bud. You're going out with Mark, who's not going out with Ashley."

"Right."

"So, who's Ashley going out with?" Sarah inquired, a puzzled look on her face.

"I have no idea. I haven't seen her all day. For all I know, she went home."

Mac had no sooner spoken than they heard the sound of a key opening the door. Ashley walked in, wearing the same clothes she had on last night, hair askew, and her face streaked with smudges.

She surveyed the crowd calmly before she spoke.

"I see you girls made it over here on time. We have a dance to go to, so let's start getting ready."

"You're going, too?" Mac posed the question that was on all their minds.

"Yes. *Surprise, surprise* – I'm going with Bud. He asked me last night."

"So, he asked you before I even broke my date with him?" Mac could hardly believe it, even as she heard herself speaking.

"No sense in postponing the inevitable. He knew what was coming."

"Does he hate me? Do *you* hate me?" Mac had to know.

"No, we don't hate you, or Mark, either, for that matter. I guess you could say we're both hurt, but we don't hate you. It took the whole night, but I got it out of my system."

Well, then, let's get started. I've got a long way to go to make myself beautiful," Missy chirped brightly.

"Ditto for me," Sarah echoed the thought.

"All right, girls, let's make Madame Angelina proud," Ashley exclaimed, managing a half-cheerful reply despite last night's events.

###

They spent the rest of the afternoon performing various beauty rituals in hopes of making themselves irresistible to their respective dates. Hair and makeup were of utmost importance since they had already gotten manicures and pedicures.

"The right makeup worn in the correct way can make you look like Miss America. The wrong makeup can have the opposite effect. It's all about finding the right colors for your skin type," Ashley informed them.

"It's too late to go out and buy more makeup if we don't have the right kind. What can we do?" Mac asked worriedly.

"Remember, I was trained to assist my mother in her cosmetics sales. I have lots of free samples she sent me a few weeks ago. I'm sure we can find something for all of you," Ashley assured her.

It was almost like old times as they laughed and joked their way through the afternoon, trying out different shades of eye shadow and blush and different hairstyles. Ashley was cheerful, almost too cheerful, Mac thought.

They settled on PB&J sandwiches, which they washed down with some cold milk from the dorm canteen.

"This should stave off hunger until we make it to the dance. They're sure to have a refreshment table there," Ashley noted.

"I'll probably be too nervous to eat," said Mac.

"I'll probably be too scared to eat," Missy added.

"Scared? Scared of what?" Sarah asked.

"Scared I'll get food on my dress, silly."

"I never thought of that," Sarah admitted.

"You probably won't have much time to eat. Everybody is usually so busy dancing they forget about the food," Ashley enlightened them.

As the afternoon wore on, they got serious and got down to the business of making themselves look as good as possible. Each girl selected what she felt was the best makeup and hairdo to go with her dress. As eight o'clock approached, their task was almost finished. They took turns standing in front of the full-length mirror to get the full effect of their efforts.

"I'd say we've done an outstanding job," Ashley declared as she made one last turn by the mirror.

"It's mostly thanks to you," Mac said. *And the ugly duckling has now truly turned into a swan. Is that really me I see in the mirror? The problem is, I fixed myself on the outside, but now I'm broken on the inside. Life will never be the same again between us four friends, thanks to Mark and me. I should have left well-enough alone, but, no, I had to go and screw everything up. If I get through this date tonight, I may never date again. In fact, I may swear off men for life!*

They began to hear the names of various girls being called out over the intercom, summoning them to the lobby for their respective dates. The dance was being held off-campus, so it was up to each guy to find transportation for him and his date.

Missy and Sarah were riding together with their dates in Chad's SUV, thanks to Sarah's persistence in snagging them both a ride. Mark would be driving his Corvette, while Bud could always be depended on to show up in his rattletrap Jeep. Mac had never ridden in Mark's fancy car, as it had only two seats. She hoped she could get in and out of the low-slung vehicle without looking like a klutz. She felt a little guilty, knowing Ashley would be bouncing around in that old Jeep, but there was nothing she could do about it. It would be nice to ride in an expensive car for once in her life, so she might as well make the most of it, she reasoned.

They didn't have to wait long before their names were called, beginning with Missy and Sarah, who were paged in quick succession. They had barely exited the room when Mac heard her name, followed by Ashley's.

The two girls looked at each other as they gathered their purses. Ashley walked over to Mac and held out her arms for a hug.

"Good luck, roomie," she told Mac.

"I love you, Ash," Mac responded, blinking back tears as she gently hugged her roommate, careful not to muss their dresses.

They descended the stairs together, scanning the lobby for their dates. Mac spotted them first. Mark wasn't hard to find. He was by far the handsomest guy in the room. It was little wonder she had maintained a crush on him for eight years. Bud was standing over to one side. She was surprised to see their eyes focused on her rather than Ashley.

What a strange turn of events, Mac thought. Mark was supposed to be looking at her, but Bud should be watching his own date. At least she thought he should. After all, that was the gentlemanly thing to do, and Bud was always a gentleman.

"Looks like all eyes are on you. Told you that you look good," Ashley whispered.

"Stop it! I could never outshine you," Mac protested as they reached the bottom of the stairs.

The boys stepped forward to meet them, corsages in hand. Mark appeared a little unsteady on his feet.

"I got you flowers," he said, holding out a box that contained a mixed corsage featuring a yellow orchid.

Great, now I have a date with Forrest Gump. Is that all he can say? Mac wondered.

"It's beautiful. How did you know what color to get?" she asked.

"Ashley told Bud, and Bud told me," he admitted, almost shamefacedly.

"Let's pin them on," Ashley suggested as she accepted her flowers from Bud.

The boys stepped back by the wall as the girls occupied themselves with getting their corsages on just right. They began to converse in low tones, their voices somewhat deadened by the noise of the crowd in the room.

"I don't think I've ever seen two such beautiful girls," Mark exclaimed.

"They've always been beautiful to me," Bud reminded him.

"It's going to be *some* night," Mark observed.

"So help me, if you do anything to hurt Mac..." Bud threatened.

"Hurt her? Whatever gave you that idea? I love the girl."

"Like you loved Ashley?"

"Let's not go there."

"You've been drinking, haven't you? You don't need to be driving, especially with Mac in the car."

"I can handle it, little buddy."

"See that you do. Remember, I'm going to be watching you," Bud warned him.

Their conversation was interrupted as the girls walked over, their corsage problems solved.

"Looks like we're ready to go," Ashley told them.

"Right. Guess we'll see you at the dance. Ready, Mac?" Mark inquired, offering his arm as he spoke.

Mac tucked her hand over his arm, feeling all tingly as they walked outside and headed towards his car.

She managed to squeeze herself and her dress into the passenger seat without looking too clumsy. The faint scent of her corsage wafted its way upward, tickling her nose after Mark closed her door and walked around to the driver's side of the car. He climbed in, started the engine, and put the car into gear without saying a word. Mac felt herself pinned to the back of the seat as he floored it unnecessarily, accelerating as the car headed for the main road.

"Whoa, Mark, do you want to slow it down a little?" she protested.

"This baby's made for speed," he replied, apparently unconcerned for any oncoming traffic.

He reached into his pocket and pulled out a flask. He managed to take a swig from the flask as he continued driving. The smell of the liquor permeated the vehicle. Mac knew what was in the flask without asking. A slow chill began to creep up her spine, wrapping itself around her shoulders and squeezing her chest like icy fingers, making it hard to breathe. This was a side of Mark she had never seen, and she didn't like it.

"That's some good stuff! Want to try it?" he asked.

"No! No, thank you," she managed to reply, barely able to restrain herself from chastising her date. *What was he thinking, drinking and driving, especially with a girl in his car?*

"Okay, suit yourself. More for me."

Does that mean he's going to down the whole flask before we even get to the dance? So much for my dream date. I should have stuck with Bud.

Somehow, they managed to make it to the parking lot of the city's Convention Center, where the dance was being held. Mac's nerves were totally on edge by the time they got there. She just hoped they didn't get evicted from the event before they had even one dance together.

She spotted Chad's SUV when they pulled into the parking lot. At least Missy and Sarah had made it safely with their dates. Bud and Ashley rolled in behind them, the Jeep engine sputtering as Bud brought the vehicle to a stop. She began to feel guilty all over again, seeing her classy roommate rattling around in that old jalopy.

Mark remembered his manners and walked around to open the car door for her. offering his hand to help her exit. It was the first time she could remember actually holding hands with him. That little tingle she had felt back at the dorm returned. Maybe everything would work out for this date after all.

They walked into the dance, which was already underway, passing the chaperones without incident. Mark could put on a good act when he wanted to, and at the moment he wanted to act like he was totally sober. Mac could sense that. There was no way the star football captain was going to be embarrassed by being ejected from a dance. She began to breathe a little easier.

Mac spotted Missy and Sarah on the dance floor with their respective dates. Both girls looked blissfully happy. She was glad of that. At least things were going right for somebody. Dieting had paid off, as both girls looked stunning. *Who would have thought months ago three overweight girls would even have had a chance of being asked to Spring Fling?*

The song ended and the girls headed in her direction, their dates tagging along behind. Chad was his usual handsome, virile self. *No surprise there,* Mac deduced. Then her eyes turned to Dennis. At least she thought it was Dennis. He had undergone a complete transformation. He had apparently discovered hair gel and succumbed to a punk rock hairstyle, losing his glasses in the process. His former facial tic appeared to be nonexistent. She had to find out what had happened to the guy.

"I think I need to go to the powder room," she announced.

"Already?" Mark asked, apparently surprised his date had a weak bladder.

The four girls entered the lounge area, where they simultaneously collapsed on a large leather sofa. Missy removed her shoes and began massaging her feet gingerly.

"These shoes are killing me! I knew I should have broken them in," she moaned as she spoke."

"Never mind about the shoes. What's up with Dennis? Is it really Dennis out there dancing with you?" Mac inquired.

"One and the same, Missy replied.

"The hairstyle I can understand, but where are his glasses?"

"Contacts, like you," Missy reminded her.

"Plus, he's not twitching anymore. How is that possible?" Mac continued her inquisition.

"Botox."

"B…Botox?" Mac couldn't get the word out for stuttering.

"Yes, he found a doctor who suggested he try Botox treatments to control the tic, and it worked," Missy announced proudly.

"I'll say it worked! He's actually a good-looking guy," Ashley exclaimed.

"Thanks, I totally agree," Missy concurred.

"Hey, what about my date?" Sarah interjected.

"Oh, girl, you already know Chad. He's always been good-looking," Mac told her.

"Well, don't dare offer an opinion on Bud," Ashley teased.

"He's not too shabby, either, especially after all those workout sessions at the gym," Missy contemplated.

Everyone carefully avoided mentioning Mark, and Mac wasn't about to bring his name up. Nobody had to tell her how fine-looking he was. She had been aware of his looks ever since that first football game in junior high. *And that was the beginning of my downfall*, she lamented.

"We'd better get back out to the dance floor," Ashley decided.

"Yeah, we don't want to keep the guys waiting too long," Missy agreed.

Mac spent the next few hours dancing, first with Mark, and then with her friends' dates as everybody exchanged partners. She was starting to feel warm and a little dizzy from all that swirling around the room. Mark had brought her several glasses of punch, which didn't taste right, but she drank them anyhow. Refusing would be impolite.

Dancing with Mark was all she had envisioned. He moved about the floor with the grace and coordination of a true athlete with no hint of intoxication. However, Mac could smell the liquor on his breath every time they danced. She just hoped nobody else could, but she doubted it. Using alcohol was strictly against school policy, especially for athletes. Mark would pay dearly for his transgressions, should anyone besides her find out.

She found herself back in his arms for a slow dance. He was holding her tightly, so tightly it drew frowns from the chaperones on the sidelines. She should be happy, but somehow it just didn't feel right. She noticed Bud and Ashley staring at them from the other side of the dance floor. *Were they both wishing they had switched partners?*

She didn't have time to think about that, as her attention turned back to Mark, who was asking her a question.

"What? What did you say?" she inquired.

"I said, 'Why don't we get out of here? This place is starting to bore me.'" he repeated.

"Okay, but where can we go?"

"Let's go out by the lake. I know just the spot," he informed her, as he guided her toward the edge of the dance floor.

"I need to let Ashley and the others know we're leaving," she told him.

"Forget them. You're with me," he insisted as he began leading her out the door and towards his Corvette.

Moments later, they were parked in front of the lake in a secluded spot. Mac began to feel a little calmer as she gazed out over the water. It was a picture-perfect night, with a full moon complemented by a host of stars, all of which were reflected in the placid, mirror-like surface of the lake.

Her serenity was short-lived, as Mark began to make his move. It started when he shut off the engine and took her hand, bringing it slowly to his lips, the lips she had often dreamed about.

"Mac, you're so beautiful," he whispered, kissing her hand softly.

He leaned towards her, pulling her closer to his side of the car. She instinctively followed his lead. For a moment, she surrendered to her feelings as their lips met, letting loose all the pent-up emotions of the past eight years. Then the realization of what she was doing hit her with full force. She was betraying her roommate! She pulled away just as Mark let out a yelp of pain when he accidentally hit the gearshift.

"This blasted gearshift gets in the way every time," he complained.

Mac saw her chance to escape and she took it, grabbing the door handle and tumbling out of the car as soon as the door opened. She lost her balance and halfway stumbled but managed to right herself just in time.

"I can't do this," she yelled as she took off running, her progress hindered as her spiked heels dug into the soft dirt.

She glanced back, and to her horror, she saw Mark climbing out of the car and heading in her direction. There was no way she could outrun an athlete, especially in heels. Her only hope was to lose him in the cover of the nearby woods.

She hit the edge of the woods at full speed, paying little heed to the briars and brambles that tore at her clothes and left bloody slashes on her skin. Her dress was of little consequence now, and the shoes were already ruined. One of the heels broke off, causing her to run with an uneven gait and slowing her progress. Had she gone far enough to escape Mark's advances? She was almost out of breath, but she pressed on, clawing her way through the relentless underbrush. She could hear Mark closing in as twigs crackled in the distance. Or was it a bear? She couldn't be sure. She glanced back just as her foot hit a root, causing her to lurch forward, hitting her head on a low-hanging limb. She ended up in a heap, dazed from the blow and still trying to catch her breath.

Before she could move, Mark was standing over her. He looked a lot bigger from that angle.

"Why are you running?" he asked, panting as he bent over her.

"I…I…" was all Mac could muster as she gasped for air.

He knelt beside her, grasping both her hands as she tried to fend him off. She began to twist this way and that, trying to break his hold, but he was too strong.

"Mac, Mac, don't fight it," he said.'

"No, let me go," she screamed, but there was no one to hear her. She was in trouble, and she was on her own.

He pushed her backwards, all semblance of gentleness gone, covering her body with his as she continued to scream. Her screams ceased when he covered her mouth with his in a kiss that threatened to suck the very life out of her. She couldn't breathe, and she felt herself slipping into a dark hole as everything began to swirl around her.

Suddenly, Mark's weight was lifted off her, and she was drawn back to her surroundings. Two pairs of legs in matching tuxedos wove back and forth by her head as she became aware of the sound of fists making contact with their target. Still in a daze, she looked to the other side and saw a pair of shapely legs belonging to someone wearing heels.

Ashley! She'd recognize her roommate's legs anywhere.

"Ashley," she repeated the name aloud, speaking weakly.

"Mac, are you all right?" Her concerned roommate knelt beside her, smoothing Mac's hair back from her face as she spoke.

"I think so."

"Let me help you up," Ashley suggested, offering her a hand.

Mac sat up and looked over to a clearing where two males were still struggling.

"Who's that with you?" she asked.

"Bud. We were worried about you, so we followed you out to the lake. When we saw Mark's car sitting there with both doors open, we started looking for you. Then we heard you screaming." Ashley explained.

Mark went down hard as Bud landed one final blow. The football captain had been defeated by a nerd. There was no way Mark would ever live that one down if word got out around campus. Mac almost felt sorry for him.

"Get Mac out of here," Bud ordered, tossing his keys to Ashley.

"But…what about Mark?" Ashley asked hesitantly.

"I'll take care of this. In fact, it will be my pleasure," Bud replied.

He walked over to where Mac was sitting, and, without speaking, offered her his hand. She latched onto it like a drowning person reaching for a life preserver as he pulled her upwards with an unexpected show of strength. She was feeling somewhat dizzy and a little unsteady on her feet.

"What's wrong with me? I can't seem to walk straight," she wondered, thinking maybe her missing shoe heel was the cause of the problem.

"Mark was spiking your punch," Ashley informed her.

"What? That's why it didn't taste right. How much of that stuff did I drink?"

"I counted three cups," said Bud.

"Three cups? Were you watching me that closely?"

"Never took my eyes off you," he teased.

Their conversation was interrupted by a loud moan as Mark began to regain consciousness.

"You girls clear out of here now," Bud ordered.

They began to slowly pick their way back through the woods, once again encountering all the briars and brambles that had hindered Mac's flight.

"This isn't doing my dress any good," Ashley complained.

"Mine is already ruined, and I lost a shoe heel, too," Mac observed.

Just when Mac thought she couldn't walk any further, they reached the edge of the woods. Bud's Jeep parked next to the Corvette was a welcome sight. Mac never thought she would be so glad to see a beat-up jalopy.

"Let's get going before the boys catch up with us," Ashley exclaimed.

They scrambled across the remaining ground and climbed into the Jeep. Ashley put the key into the ignition and turned it on. The Jeep responded with a whimper and the motor finally turned over and then started with a roar, emitting a black cloud of smoke as Ashley gave it more gas.

"Are you sure you can drive this thing?" Mac asked.

"We're about to find out," Ashley responded as she put it into gear and headed towards the main road.

The following morning Mac awoke at 9:00 a.m. She had set her alarm with the intention of attending church. She sat up in the bed and then fell back down again, clutching her head as a dull pain encased her brain.

Opening one eye again slowly, she observed her roommate sitting on her own bed, calmly taking in the situation.

"Oh, God, my head is killing me. What's wrong with me?" she whimpered.

"I think you might have a slight hangover," Ashley told her.

"A hangover? From just three spiked drinks?"

"You aren't used to alcohol, so it probably had more of an effect on your system than on someone who drinks frequently." Ashley rose as she was speaking and walked into the bathroom, returning with a cool cloth, which she laid across Mac's forehead.

"How's that?" she inquired as she stepped back from the bed after fluffing Mac's pillow and adjusting the covers.

"A little better, thanks. There's no way I'm going to make it to church today. You'll just have to go without me."

Ashley sighed. "To tell you the truth, I'm not feeling too well myself. That trek through the woods didn't do me any good, either. Besides that, you're all covered with scratches. I still think you should have gone to the school nurse last night after we got back on campus."

"No, I told you, I couldn't do that. It would just mean trouble for Mark. Despite everything, I still don't hold it against him. I mean, with the drinking and all, he just wasn't himself."

"You're right. I've never known Mark to take a drink, not a single drink in all the years we dated."

"Well, he picked a lousy time to start."

"I'm going to find out what really happened. Maybe Bud can talk to him. We have to get to the bottom of this, one way or another," Ashley declared.

"In the meantime, do we have anything for a headache? I could sure use some extra-strength Tylenol or aspirin, or *anything* for pain," Mac could barely get the words out without moaning.

"I think I remember seeing some Tylenol in your desk drawer," said Ashley. She opened the drawer and rummaged through it, triumphantly bringing out a bottle of the medicine.

"Gimme! And could I please have some water, too?"

"I think we have a couple of bottles of water left in our fridge. Yes, here they are," Ashley reported, handing her roommate a bottle as she spoke.

"You're a Godsend! You're the best roomie ever," Mac declared as she popped two pills in her mouth and washed them down.

"And *you* are in no condition to go anywhere. You stay in, and I'll bring you some food," Ashley decided.

"I don't know if I can keep anything down."

"You have to try. Remember – finals start in three days. You have to keep up your strength."

"*Finals* –did you have to mention that word?" Mac almost moaned again just thinking about it.

"At least we have two 'dead days' to study with no classes on Monday and Tuesday."

"God is good."

Ashley grabbed her purse and sunglasses off the dresser. "I'm going now. I'll be back later with some food. Try to rest."

Mac lounged on the bed in the darkened room, welcoming the silence, but rest was the furthest thing from her mind. It seemed she had come almost full circle since that day of her disastrous fall in the gym. Just what had she accomplished since then? she wondered.

I lost weight and gave myself a makeover. That part was good. I had a real date to a formal dance, something I've never done. That was good. Well, sort of good and bad, all at the same time. I betrayed Bud by breaking my date with him and Ashley by going out with Mark, who turned out to be a real heel. So much for dating. Looks like I wasn't cut out for that. Now I have to get over the hangover, or whatever it is, and study for my finals. That's the important thing. Guys are secondary. If I manage to figure out what_went wrong with Bud and Mark and Ashley, then I'll try to repair our relationships if it's not too late.

Having made that decision, Mac turned over on her side. Her headache was beginning to let up. Hopefully, by tomorrow things would be back to normal. She dozed off again, smiling faintly as she settled into a more restful slumber.

###

Six days later, with finals over and the spring semester finished, the campus bustled with activity as students were either packing to leave or getting ready for summer school. Mac and Bud had opted for summer school. They were both moving off campus. Mac had plans to rent an apartment with her friends Missy and Sarah. Bud and several of his friends had found an older house a landlord was willing to rent in exchange for their doing some minor renovations. They all had just one more day to vacate their dorm rooms.

The four friends hadn't been together since Spring Fling. Mac still felt guilty about how she had double-crossed Bud. Mark had done a complete about-face, but it was too late to repair the damage as far as the school administration was concerned. Word of his drinking bout had reached the ears of the higher-ups on campus, and they gave him the choice of either transferring to another school or being expelled. Mark chose the transfer without giving it a second thought. He and Ashley had several serious talks about their relationship and decided to give it one more try. Ashley could see no point in remaining on a campus where her boyfriend was not welcome, so she decided to leave with him. She explained it to Mac late one night.

"Mac, you know I love you like a sister, don't you?" she asked as they shared a bowl of unbuttered popcorn.

Mac tossed a kernel of popcorn in the air, catching it in her mouth before she responded.

"And I feel the same way about you, roomie."

"Mark and I have made up and we're back together now. He's going to transfer to a lower-level college so he will still be able to play football his senior year."

"I'm glad for him."

"I'm transferring to that same college. I'll have to change my major from theater and drama to secondary education, but it will work out. I already have all my background courses. All I need to take are the education courses and do my student teaching."

"Ash, you'll be great at anything you do. The kids will love you. Who knows, you might even end up being a cheerleader sponsor," Mac told her.

"I want you to be the first to know – Mark and I are getting married right after we graduate. I'm counting on you being my maid of honor."

"I wouldn't miss it."

"Pinky swear?"

"Pinky swear," Mac repeated as the two friends sealed the promise in their long-observed tradition, both girls blinking back tears in spite of themselves.

"There's one more thing – Mark is really sorry about what happened on the night of Spring Fling. He wants to tell you himself."

"I've already forgiven him. It was as much my fault as his. I should have never broken my date with Bud…" Mac's voice trailed off as the memory of the tragic night came to mind.

"Make that two more things we need to talk about. You do know Bud is in love with you, don't you?"

"What? No, we're just friends," Mac protested.

"Maybe in your eyes, but Bud told me all about his feelings the night of Spring Fling."

"So, we were friends when I was a plain Jane, but now that I've changed my looks, he's in love with me?"

"Actually, I think he's been in love with you ever since junior high."

Mac slowly mulled over the information. The last thing she needed right now was a steady boyfriend. She had med school to think of, along with the applications she had already filled out.

"I'll have to give that some thought. I've sworn off dating for the time being. I really need to concentrate on my studies during my senior year. Getting into med school these days is harder than ever, and my grades and test scores have to be top-notch."

"That's for you and Bud to work out. I've delivered the message, and that's all I'm going to say about the subject."

Mac peered at the bottom of the popcorn bowl, which had only a few unpopped kernels remaining. She walked over to the wastebasket and dumped them, wiping out the bowl with a paper towel.

"What are you going to do without me and my air popper next year?" she joked.

"I don't know. I'm going to miss you like crazy, but we'll keep in touch," Ashley promised.

"You'd better," Mac threatened.

"Tomorrow's going to be a long day. We have a lot of stuff to move if we're going to get out of this room on time," Ashley noted.

"Right, let's call it a night," Mac agreed.

###

The following morning, Mac and Ashley were scheduled to meet Mark and Bud in the cafeteria for their final breakfast of the semester. Mac was a little nervous about seeing both of them for the first time since the dreadful Spring Fling outing.

"What will I say to them?" she wondered, as she and Ashley headed out of the dorm.

"Just act natural. I'm sure everything will be fine," Ashley assured her.

The boys were waiting for them when they walked into the cafeteria. After an awkward moment, everyone exchanged "hellos" and they headed down the line. It was almost like old times, Mac thought.

Mark and Bud made short work of their meal, as usual. *Was there ever a time when males weren't hungry? Probably not,* Mac speculated. The girls managed to finish as the same time as the boys, eager to get back to their dorm and empty out their room. It would be the first time they were heading in different directions since they started rooming together. Mac felt a little sad about that.

"I hope you don't have too much stuff to move," Mark told Ashley.

"No more than usual," Ashley informed him. She had borrowed her parents' SUV because Mark's Corvette was too small to hold all her belongings.

"I'll bring my vehicle around to the front of the dorm and then you guys can come up to our room and help us haul everything down," she told them.

"Sounds like a plan," Mark agreed.

They walked back to the dorm, which was practically a madhouse with everyone moving their belongings out and new tenants moving in. The boys waited in the foyer for Ashley to fetch her vehicle while Mac went upstairs to their room. She took one last look around, partly to make sure everything was packed and all the drawers were empty, but mostly to store up the memories of the past three years. Living in the dorm had been fun, but she was looking forward to living in an apartment. She knew she would never have another roommate like Ashley, so it was best to move on.

Her reminiscing was interrupted as Ashley and the boys entered the room. They began gathering up Ashley's belongings and soon had them all packed into the SUV with no room to spare.

"How can girls accumulate so much junk?" Mark grumbled as he shut one of the SUV doors on the last of the lot.

"It may look like junk to you, but it's all important to me," Ashley insisted.

"I can see it all now. I'm going to have about a foot of closet space when we get married, while Ashley gets all the rest," he declared.

"Sez you," Ashley countered, punching him in the shoulder as she spoke.

"Ha! For your information, I got all my stuff into the Corvette."

"So, guys travel light. Girls need more stuff. Speaking of which, it's about time for this girl to get her belongings on the road," Ashley announced.

"Okay, and I guess we're about ready, but first I need to talk to Mac," said Mark.

Ashley and Bud exchanged glances, a move that did not escape Mac's attention. They walked back to the front of the dorm to give Mac and Mark some privacy. Mark cleared his throat before he began a speech he had evidently rehearsed.

"Mac, I want to apologize for the way I treated you during Spring Fling. It was totally wrong of me. The only excuse I can offer is that I was just about out of my mind after Ashley broke up with me. She wouldn't ever take my phone calls. I didn't know what I would do without her. She's the love of my life, and I intend to never lose her again."

"Mark, I accept the apology. I've already forgiven you because I know it wasn't really all your fault. The alcohol was partly to blame. You and Ashley belong together. I think deep down I've always known it. I was just following a young girl's silly dream by going out with you, and I wronged Bud in the process, so I'm partly responsible for what happened."

"Thank you for that. I hope we can still be friends."

"Of course, we'll be friends. I'm going to be in your wedding," Mac declared as she held out her arms for a hug.

To her relief, he reciprocated and they hugged each other tightly.

"I'm not going to kiss you goodbye because Bud might take a notion to knock me out again," he whispered in ear.

"Oh, you big oaf! Go on and get out of here," she exclaimed, glancing in Ashley and Bud's direction. They were both grinning as they headed back towards the SUV.

"Well, I guess this is it," Ashley said when she reached the vehicle.

"Roomie, I'm going to miss you," Mac told her.

"Not as much as I'll miss you."

The girls hugged each other as they spoke, tears welling up in their eyes.

"Now don't you two start blubbering," Mark ordered.

"Oh, who's blubbering?" asked Mac.

"Not me!" said Ashley as she climbed into the driver's seat of the SUV. She started the engine and was rewarded when it began humming softly, unlike the rough experience she had with Bud's Jeep.

"Ha! No black smoke," Mac joked.

"Somehow, I feel like that's an insult to my Jeep," Bud complained.

"I love your Jeep," said Mac.

"Hey, you two, we're leaving now. Babe, meet you at your house," Mark yelled just before he lowered his hulky frame into the Corvette.

"Bye everybody," Ashley called out, waving as she shifted into "Drive" and headed towards the main road.

"Goodbye," Mac and Bud shouted in unison, waving vigorously as Mark pulled in behind her. They continued waving until both vehicles drove out of sight.

They turned and began walking back to the dorm. Bud glanced at Mac and posed a question.

"Do you really?"

"Do I really what?" She gave him a puzzled look, squinting in the bright sunlight.

"Love my Jeep!"

"Of course, I love your Jeep. It rescued me in my time of distress. It's a wonderful Jeep."

"Don't lay it on too thick, now," he warned.

"And just why would I be doing that?"

"Maybe because Mark and Ashley left and all your stuff is still in the dorm and you have no way to get it home?"

"Ah, you know me so well!"

Bud stopped in his tracks, grabbing her arm and whirling her around in the process. "Not as well as I'd like to know you," he said in a serious tone.

"Bud, I'm going to devote myself to my studies my senior year so I can get into med school. I won't be having a lot of time for dating or anything like that," she explained, placing her free hand over his as she spoke.

"So, we can still be friends, can't we?"

"Friends…sure, I can do friends," Mac agreed.

"Great!" He bent down and gave her a peck on the cheek. "Now I'm going to get my Jeep and pull around to the front of the dorm so we can get your stuff loaded."

Mac rubbed her cheek gently, contemplating what had just happened. He had evidently forgiven her transgressions on the night of the dance, even though she still owed him a formal apology. And he would get it, she vowed.

She watched as he reached the edge of the sidewalk and headed around the corner to the parking lot in the back. He had certainly filled out after all those workouts. Plus, he had held his own the night of Spring Fling.

So, I'm not the only one who made a transformation this year. The ugly duckling and the nerd are gone for good.

She smiled slightly as she hugged herself, totally satisfied with the situation.

Yes, I can do friends —for the time being, that is. But just you wait a couple of years, Bud Bishop. Just you wait!

Lagniappe
Mama Rosa's Recipes

Mama Rosa's Sicilian Marinara Sauce (100 to 150-year-old recipe)

Sauce:

2 cups onions, chopped	red pepper to taste
1 cup celery, chopped	black pepper to taste
1 lg. whole bud garlic	salt to taste
1 (12 oz.) can tomato paste	1 t. celery seeds
Olive oil to cover bottom of lg.	1-2 T. parsley
heavy pan or deep skillet	1-2 T. basil
2 lg. bay leaves	1-2 T. oregano
Water	3-4 T. Parmesan cheese

Combine veggies and spices in pan with olive oil. Sauté until veggies are clear – do not burn, makes sauce bitter. Add tomato paste and continue to sauté for about 30 to 50 minutes. IMPORTANT!! If tomato paste starts to stick, you need more olive oil. Sauté over a medium to low heat, stirring frequently, and keeping the mixture bubbling. Do not add water. The sauce will turn a dark color. At the end of the cooking time, add enough water to fill the deep pot to about ¾ full. Sauce will then require cooking at a slow rolling boil for about 2 and ½ to 3 hours.

Meatballs:

2 lb. ground meat	2-3 slices of day-to week-old bread, grated
Olive oil (to fry meatballs)	(old French bread or hamburger buns work)
Garlic granules to taste	Parmesan cheese to taste
Black pepper to taste	2 T. parsley
Salt to taste	1 T. fennel seeds
Red pepper to taste	1 t. celery seeds
1 egg	

Combine all ingredients in a large mixing bowl, using your hands to mix. Form meatballs and fry in olive oil until all sides are brown. DO

NOT FRY TOO LONG, AS THIS WILL MAKE THEM HARD. The centers will finish cooking in the sauce. About 1 to 1 and ½ hours before the sauce is done, add the meatballs to the sauce. Cook until sauce is thick.

Completing the recipe:
 4 c. uncooked pasta   Water to fill 3/4 of cooking pot
 Splash of olive oil   Salt to taste

Add olive oil and salt to water and bring water to a boil. Place a wooden spoon across the pot to prevent water from boiling over. Cook the pasta for 8 minutes. Remove the meatballs from the pot and set aside. Drain the pasta and place in the sauce 2-3 minutes before serving. Sprinkle Parmesan cheese and mix well in the entire pot. This procedure will keep the noodles from having water in the bottom of the plate when you serve it. It takes a few tries at this recipe to get it right. After that, it becomes a base recipe for a lot of Italian dishes. You can add new spices, make pizzas, serve with veggies, use as a dip, and use it many other ways.

Mama Rosa's Drop Dumplings
2 c. plain water
1 heaping T. shortening
1 egg, slightly beaten
Enough water to make a stiff dough

Mix all ingredients and drop by spoonfuls into simmering chicken broth. Add small amount of onion and celery to chicken while boiling and season to taste.

Mama Rosa's Corn Casserole
 1 can cream style corn   1 med. Bell pepper, chopped
 1 can whole kernel corn (undrained)   2 eggs, beaten
 1-8 oz. carton sour cream   1 pkg. cornbread mix
 1 med. Onion, chopped   salt and pepper to taste.

Mix all ingredients well. Bake at 350 degrees for 45 minutes in a rectangular baking pan.

Mama Rosa's Carrot Cake

2 c. flour	2 jars Jr. baby food carrots (7 ½ oz.)
1 t. baking powder	2 c. nuts, chopped
1 t. baking soda	½ c. butter
1 t. cinnamon	8 oz. cream cheese
¼ t. salt	1 t. vanilla
½ c. oil	
2 c. sugar	
4 eggs	

Mix first 5 ingredients together. In a separate bowl combine oil and sugar. Then alternately add 1 egg at a time with dry ingredients until all 4 eggs and dry ingredients are combined. Then add the two jars of baby food carrots and the 1 cup of chopped nuts.

Bake at 350 degrees for 40-50 minutes in loaf pans or 4 round layer pans.

Icing
Beat softened cream cheese and butter until light and fluffy. Gradually add 1 lb. powdered sugar. Then add vanilla and 1 cup chopped nuts. Mix well.

Let cake cool before icing.

Mama Rosa's Red Punch
Boil together: 1 cup sugar and 1quart water. Dissolve in water: 2 pkg. cherry Kool-Aid.

Chill and then pour into punch bowl. Add one 46 oz. can of pineapple juice and 2 quarts of ginger ale. Add crushed ice, if desired, just before serving.

Mama Rosa's Shrimp Dip
5 oz. can of shrimp, drained
3 oz. softened cream cheese
¼ c. sour cream
1 T. lemon juice
¼ t. Worcestershire sauce
1 T. catsup
1/8 t. onion powder
Dash of hot sauce such as Tabasco
Mix and chill. Serve with crackers, chips, or vegetables as a dip. Makes one cup.

Mama Rosa's Homemade French Bread
2 T. cooking oil
2 T. sugar
1 T. salt
1 pkg. dry yeast
6 c. all-purpose flour
1 c. very warm water
1 c. cold water

Mix oil, sugar, salt, and cold water in a very large bowl. Dissolve yeast in 1 c. very warm (not hot) water, and then add to bowl. Add flour. Mix and turn out onto floured board and knead until smooth. Place in greased bowl. Cover and let rise until doubled in size. Punch down. Shape into rolls or loaves of bread and place on greased baking sheets. Let rise again. If desired, brush with unbeaten egg white and sprinkle with sesame seeds just before baking. Bake at 350 degrees for 30 minutes for loaves or about 10 to 15 minutes for rolls. Remove from oven and let loaves cool slightly before slicing.

###